Five interesting things about A. M. Goldsher:

1. If you laid all of A. M. Goldsher's CDs on the ground in one single row, it would run from the Tower of London to somewhere around Windsor Castle.

2. Favourite food: sushi. Favourite dessert: sushi. Favourite snack: sushi. Favourite position: sushi.

3. According to the author's mother, A. M. began reading aloud at the age of two. First book? *Valley of the Dolls*.

4. Goldsher hasn't paid for a haircut since 1995.

5. A former sportswriter, the author has seen far too many professional basketball players wearing not nearly enough clothes.

By A. M. Goldsher

Reality Check
The True Naomi Story
Today's Special

No Ordinary Girl

A.M. Goldsher

little
black
dress

First published in Great Britain in 2010 by
LITTLE BLACK DRESS
An imprint of HEADLINE PUBLISHING GROUP

A LITTLE BLACK DRESS paperback

1

Cataloguing in Publication Data is available from the British Library

ISBN 978 0 7553 5858 8

Typeset in Transit511BT by Avon DataSet Ltd,
Bidford-on-Avon, Warwickshire

Printed and bound in Great Britain by
Clays Ltd, St Ives plc

Headline's policy is to use papers that are natural, renewable and
recyclable products and made from wood grown in sustainable forests.
The logging   to the
e

For Natalie, my superheroine.

Acknowledgements

This is my fourth book with Little Black Dress, and, as was the case with the previous three, my U.K. friends were lovely in the creation and production of this book. Editrix extraordinaire Claire Baldwin, thank you for your patience, support and enthusiasm in the face of several missed deadlines. A massive shout-out goes to the entire LBD team: Siobhan Hooper, Jo Gledhill, Sarah Badhan, Maura Brickell. And finally, a special thanks to my former editor Cat Cobain, who took a chance on this project based on a four-page outline and a long and chatty (and thus probably quite expensive) international phone call.

Part One

It's after midnight and autumn is open for business: the skies are clear, the stars are twinkling, the Illinois air is cool, and the fingernail moon is as fingernaily as can be. We see Abbey Bynum staring at the top of the ancient oak tree in front of her bland suburban Chicago condo building, an oak tree that's too big and dignified for her cookie-cutter, pre-fab neighborhood. The light from the twinkly stars, the fingernaily moon, and the seven too-bright streetlights that dot Abbey's block bring the oak's leaves to life: yellows and reds, browns and oranges. The tree looks crisp and pretty, and from Abbey's angle, those leaves – which are further changing colors as we speak – look as if they were painted on by Monet. Or maybe Manet. No, Monet. Or maybe Manet. Even though she takes a pass through the Art Institute of Chicago at least once a month, Abbey always forgets which is which. All she knows – and cares about – is that it's pretty.

The breeze blows a chunk of her barely tamed curly brown ringlets into her eyes. She tries to flick them off her forehead, but the wind in her face is too strong, so they just flop right on back. Abbey again kicks herself for not grabbing a hair tie or a scrunchy, and again wonders why she never properly prepares for her silly late-night jaunts. But she realises that that's a ridiculous thought, because the fact of the matter is, she knows *exactly* why she never properly prepares for these silly late-night jaunts: you see, for Abbey, these silly late-night jaunts aren't a choice. They're a compulsion. When she has to do it, she *has* to do it, and when Abbey Bynum *has* to do something, she goes and does it *immediately*. She can't help it; it's always been that way and she's certain it always *will* be that way.

Planning isn't in the equation, and unfortunately, without planning, there are consequences. In this case, the consequence is a small one, a mere case of hair-in-the-eyes. It's not a complete buzzkill, like, say, a bird pooping on her shoulder, or a low-flying private airplane (both of which happened in the not-too-distant past), but it's annoying, nonetheless. *Way* worse things could happen, though. Way worse things *have* happened. One night, for instance, the compulsion to leave her apartment was so intense that she forgot to put on her pants, and zipped through the neighborhood wearing only a strappy tank top with a teddy bear on the front and an ancient pair of light-blue panties.

Using her left hand, Abbey again pushes her hair out of her face and holds it flat against the top of her head. The problem with this tactic is that now Abbey relies

solely on her right hand for balance. Using one hand to
navigate isn't an issue when she's in motion, but when
she's trying to stay somewhat still, when she's trying
to hover in a single area, as is the case right now, two
hands are *way* better than one. She's wobbling, and
even though she knows she's in no danger of falling, it
diminishes the experience, nonetheless.

She's well aware that if she practiced her one-handed
balancing on a regular basis – scratch that, if she
practiced her one-handed balancing *at all* – this would
cease to be an issue. Thing is, she hates practicing it.
Thing is, she hates doing it at all. But when this compulsion rears its head – when she *has* to breathe the
night air at its cleanest, when she *has* to see the trees
from above, when she *has* to go where nobody can find
her – her body goes up to the roof of her apartment
building and jumps right on off, despite her brain's and
heart's numerous protests.

She wants to stop it. Badly. But, goddamnit, she can't.
She just can't.

If you saw Abbey Bynum on the Illinois Metra train –
which, if you're so inclined, is something you can do each
weekday morning at precisely 8.14 a.m. – you'd check
out her smart business outfit, and the oversized aviator
sunglasses that she's had since her freshman year at
Northwestern University, and that shaggy mop of hair,
and think, 'Now that's an attractive, well-put-together
girl. Looks like she doesn't have much money for the

latest outfits or fancy jewelry, or whatnot, but she sure makes what she has work.' When she takes off her huge shades and fumbles with her iPod, you might smile at how intently and intensely she scrolls through the menu, trying to figure out the perfect mix for her train ride to the office, trying to decide whether Miles Davis, or Arcade Fire, or A Tribe Called Quest will get her jazzed for the workday.

You'd also notice one thing that Abbey Bynum doesn't: at least once a ride, Abbey Bynum gets checked out. Big time.

If she happened to catch the young gentleman leaning on the train door giving her a well-justified once-over – the young gentleman wearing the vintage blue Pulp T-shirt and the baggy khaki shorts, the young gentleman whom Abbey would unfairly dismiss as potential boyfriend material because she used to date a guy who looked almost exactly like that, and he was a massive jerk – she'd probably turn away, blush, and forget about it several seconds later. See, Abbey doesn't like being checked out. Not because she's self-conscious about her looks (she knows her place in the beauty pantheon; a couple dozen miles South of Angelina Jolie, and a few hundred miles North of Betty White), but because there's the chance that somebody will see her for who she is, that they'll notice the Weird Stuff.

This, of course, is a ridiculous thought – nobody could see Weird Stuff, unless she showed them the Weird Stuff – but it's a thought she can't help but think.

*

Abbey Bynum's parents didn't come down to earth from the third moon of Neptune – Gary and Carin Bynum are from a middle-class section of Buffalo, New York – and she never fell into a vat of nuclear waste, nor was she hit by a meteorite, nor was she kidnapped by the FBI and injected with an experimental drug. It just happened. It just was.

Whenever Carin recalls the first appearance of what Abbey calls her 'Weird Stuff', she's instantly transported back to the bedroom of the Bynums' first condo in the less-than-middle-class section of Buffalo, back to the far left-hand corner of her and Gary's bedroom, back to Abbey's crib.

It was just after 2 a.m., and Abbey, then six months old, was loudly mewling for a snack, or a change, or a burp, or whatever it is that babies mewl for at 2 a.m. The Bynums both sat up, then Gary grunted, 'Your turn', and promptly fell back asleep.

Carin grunted, 'It is *so* not my turn. I was up at midnight. Remember? *Remember?*' She shook her husband. '*Hello?* Remember? *Gary?*'

Gary's response was a snore, then a snuffle, then a louder snore.

Carin mumbled, 'Jerk', then got out of bed and padded over to Abbey's crib.

At first, Carin thought it was the remnants of a dream, or a trick of the light. After all, there was no way her daughter could have been hovering three feet above her mattress, moving to and fro like a pendulum. Carin tried to rub the sleep from her eyes, then clicked on the bedside lamp. Abbey looked at her mommy, then promptly crashed down on to the crib *fast*. It wasn't a long fall, and she had a soft landing, but wouldn't you freak out if, one minute, you were fast asleep, dreaming about whatever babies dream about at 2 a.m., then, the next minute, you were floating in the air, then, the next minute, you were tumbling on to your bed?

Understandably, Abbey let out an ungodly scream that even Gary couldn't snore his way through. Carin reached into the crib to pick up her daughter, but the freaked-out little girl rolled away from her, then bounced off the side of the crib, then shot up towards the ceiling as if she had a jet engine in her diaper.

The poor baby zipped uncontrollably around Carin and Gary's bedroom for a good three minutes; every time she crashed against the wall and let out a pained wail, the Bynums' hearts shattered a little bit more. Finally, for no apparent reason, her ride in the sky came to a crashing halt; fortunately, the crash was on Mommy and Daddy's bed. Abbey promptly fell back asleep, contentedly snuffling and snoring.

The Bynums, however, were awake. *Wide* awake. And they stayed that way for the remainder of the night.

Gary Bynum was a pragmatic man. In his mind, a flying daughter was a big problem, and if there's a big problem, you figure out how to fix it, and if you can't figure out how to fix it yourself, you find somebody who can, so at precisely 9 a.m., Gary called his general practitioner, Dr Stu Jorgenson – he'd been seeing the guy since he was a teenager, so it was like he was part of the family, and they trusted him implicitly – and told him the score.

Unfazed, Dr Jorgenson asked, 'She seem okay now?'

Abbey was sitting in her little swing, swatting the plastic fish thingie that hung from the top bar and giggling. Gary ruffled her hair – it was a curly mess, even then – then rubbed her chubby tummy. She batted her father's hand, and giggled louder. Gary said, 'She's fine.'

'Has she eaten?' the doctor asked.

'Plenty.'

'Has she peed or pooped?'

'Yes, and yes.'

'She look okay?'

To Gary, his daughter was one of the two most beautiful things in the world – the other, of course, being Carin – and Abbey appeared to be as lovely as ever. He said, 'She looks great.'

After several beats, Jorgenson said, 'I've got nothin'. Leave her be. Wait and see. See what happens. But I've got one piece of advice: don't tell a soul. Keep it quiet as hell.'

Gary, almost in tears, said, 'But what if it happens again? What if she hurts herself? What if—'

The doctor interrupted. 'What if, what if, what if. I'll tell you *what if*. If you blab about this to anybody, Gary, *anybody*, some busybody from some government agency is going to hear about it, and they're going to come to your house in the middle of the night, and they're going to take your little girl away from you, and they might disappear you and Carin for good measure. Before you reach out to anybody else about this – *anybody* else – try and figure out what you can do by yourself.'

And that's exactly what the Bynums did.

Abbey isn't wearing a watch – remember: late-night jaunt, undeniable compulsion, leaving the house without a scrunchie, et cetera – so she doesn't realise she's been out and about (and above) for three hours. It's almost 3.30 a.m., and if she knew the time, she'd zip back home and crawl into bed immediately, because it's Thursday. The Thursday-morning staff meetings require everybody's full attention, and it's hard enough for Abbey to give her full attention to the partners' endless yammering about legal gobbledygook on seven hours of sleep, let alone three or four. (Suffice it to say that Abbey Bynum isn't the most motivated person that the legal profession has ever seen.)

She peers down at the ground to get a gauge of her location, and all she sees is water. Abbey, who doesn't have the best sense of direction when she's in the air – probably because she never practices – curses aloud; she thought she was heading south, towards downtown Chicago, but it appears that she's gone north-east, towards Michigan. She slows down and does a sexy little mid-air pirouette – think Tinkerbell, only without the wings, the wand and the shiny leotard. Now she sees the downtown lights of the John Hancock Building and the Willis Tower, and now she knows where she's at, and now she turns in the opposite direction, south, towards home. She puts it into overdrive, and is back at her building just like that. Thirty-seven miles in eight minutes. And she wasn't even trying that hard.

Whether she's on the ground or in the air, when Abbey Bynum wants to move, she can *move*.

Despite the fact that, not more than two seconds ago, she was zipping through the sky at the speed of a commercial airliner, Abbey brakes to a halt above her apartment building without even having to slow down. She lands on her roof as lightly as a hummingbird, making certain that nobody in her condo building hears; no one in her place has any clue or knows about the Weird Stuff, and Abbey wants to keep it that way. (Mrs Vance, the octogenarian on the fifth floor, thinks something ain't right with her young, curly topped neighbor, but Mrs Vance stopped trusting her eyes and ears several years back, so she chooses not to dwell on it.)

Back in her small, tidy living room, Abbey peers at the glow-in-the-dark Mickey Mouse clock on her living-room wall: 4.27. *Where the hell did the time go?* she thinks . . . which is exactly the same thought she has whenever she gets home from one of her jaunts, jaunts during which time always seems to evaporate.

Abbey wants to curl up under the covers, but she

knows it'll take thirty or forty minutes for her to calm down and fall back asleep – flying gets her all revved up, natch – and her alarm is set to go off at 5.47, so what's the point? She decides to treat herself to a long bubble bath. Sure, it'll throw off her schedule, but it'll be a great way to relax, kill time, and – thanks to her coconut-lime shower gel – smell yummy for the entire day.

Oh, about that schedule.

Right about now, you may be thinking, *Why does Abbey set her alarm for 5.47? Why not a more symmetrical time like 5.45 or 6.00?* Why? Well, because Abbey Bynum's mornings are planned to the minute. Almost to the second, even. To wit:

- 5.47 – Abbey awakens to the sound of News-Radio 78. Their slogan: 'You give us twenty-two minutes, we'll give you the world.' Abbey wishes she had twenty-two minutes to spare, but that would require waking up at 5.25, and our girl needs all the sleep she can get.
- 5.48 – Abbey listens to NewsRadio 78's 'Weather and Traffic on the Eights.' And that's 'eights' as in 5.48, 5.58, 6.08, et cetera. For somebody as time-conscious and – let's just go ahead and say it – anal retentive as Abbey, that's greatly comforting.
- 5.50 – Abbey pees.
- 5.51 – Abbey showers.
- 6.03 – Abbey puts on her make-up. This is the

only part of her morning where the time can get away from her. She's far from an expert make-up-applier, and if she's off her game, she'll be saddled with an eyeful of lumpy mascara, a faceful of lumpy powder, or a lipful of askew lipstick, which means grabbing a cotton ball, dipping it in her vat of make-up remover, and starting from scratch. On average, she ends up leaving the bathroom at 6.20.

- 6.21 – Abbey gets dressed. Aside from peeing, this is the easiest part of her morning, because unless Murphy stayed the night – which won't be happening anytime in the near future, believe you me – she'll pull out tomorrow's outfit before she goes to bed. It's not like that's a particularly difficult task, as Abbey's work wardrobe is simple and interchangeable. Monday through Thursday, we're looking at a solid-colored button-down cotton shirt, black or gray slacks, and one of her three pairs of black pumps. (Abbey is the only woman she knows who owns less than fifteen pairs of shoes.) Friday is Casual Day at the office, so we're talking a solid-colored T-shirt, blue jeans, and one of her four pairs of Puma trainers. Nobody would argue that Abbey Bynum's wardrobe could use some sprucing up, Abbey Bynum included.

- 6.34 – Abbey goes down to the lobby of her building, grabs the newspaper, then heads back up to her apartment.
- 6.37 – Abbey makes her breakfast smoothie, which consists of fruit, oatmeal, skimmed milk, orange juice and protein powder. This is the only part of her morning ritual that allows for variables, specifically, her choice of fruit. You see, each Saturday morning, there's a wonderful farmers' market in Evanston – Evanston being the first town south of Wilmette – where the local Illinois and Wisconsin growers sell their wares. Every week, Abbey loads up on whatever fruits look and smell the best. If it's spring or summer, she might grab a bag of juicy, sun-kissed peaches, or big, bright strawberries. In the fall, we're talking apples as big as your head, or blueberries as sweet and tart as the finest aged balsamic vinegar. The farmers' market is one of Abbey's favorite parts of the week.
- 6.41 – Abbey simultaneously sips her smoothie and reads the newspaper from cover to cover. Easily the best twenty-ish minutes of the workday.
- 7.03 – Abbey makes an espresso with the fancy espresso maker that her little brother Dave bought her for her twenty-fifth birthday. At first she thought it was a lame gift, because a)

she was not an espresso drinker by any stretch of the imagination, and b) Dave was a big-time espresso drinker, and, at that time, had gotten into the habit of crashing at Abbey's place after one of his many nights of boozing it up. But Abbey was too polite to complain about the gift. She was also too polite to not use it, and it wasn't long before she was addicted to the stuff.

- 7.06 – Abbey throws down two shots of espresso, *boom, boom*.
- 7.08 – Abbey does her tooth ritual: floss, water-pik, brush with Colgate Total Mint Stripe Gel, swish with Arctic Mint Listerine. The whole process takes twelve minutes. Abbey has beautiful teeth, and she wants to keep it that way, so she knows she'll be doing the ritual twice a day, every day for the rest of her life. She once calculated that if she lives to be ninety, she will have spent eight full months of her time on this planet cleaning her choppers.
- 7.21 – Abbey attempts to make her hair presentable. Her mop is a disaster – always was, always will be – and she could spend several fruitless hours trying to shape it into some semblance of coolness, but she only allows herself ten minutes. Honestly, there's only so much you can do with a mop.
- 7.31 – Abbey sits down on her sofa and reads.

She's an obsessive reader – more often than not, her nose will be buried in a high-minded science fiction book, but she also loves American Literature, and she'll also never say no to a good memoir – and as her job requires very little creative brainpower, she feels that if she doesn't take some time to exercise the vital parts of her cerebral cortex, she'll lose IQ points.

- 7.42 – Abbey grabs her purse, her cellphone and her iPod, takes leave of her apartment, then makes the sixteen-minute walk to the train station. It doesn't matter what the weather is doing, rain, snow, hurricane, whatever, Abbey's walking. It's a point of pride, her way of telling the extreme Chicago weather to piss off.

- 7.59 – Abbey buys her train ticket, then walks over to the third-car-from-the-last, sits in the first seat behind the door on the left side, pulls her iPod from her pocket, picks some music – this morning, she's listening to the new Belle and Sebastian album for the eighth day in a row, and it still sounds damn good – and stares out the window until the train pulls into Union Station at . . .

- 8.49 – Abbey jog-walks the six blocks to the offices of Roscoe, Belmont, Paulina & Addison, the law firm where she's been paralegal-ing since she moved back to the Chicago area the year after she graduated from Northwestern.

- 8.59 – Abbey sits down at her desk in her cubicle, one minute early.
- 9.00 – Abbey turns off her brain, and gets to work.

Some might say that the fact that Abbey keeps to this schedule day in and day out is a superpower in and of itself.

Considering nobody's ever written a book called *What to Expect When You're Expecting a Superheroine*, Gary and Carin did a wonderful job of teaching Abbey how to keep her flying under control. Thanks to her parents' patient cajoling; by the time her third birthday rolled around, Abbey only left the ground when she wanted to, which, fortunately for everybody's sanity, wasn't all that often.

Abbey was ten when she started calling it the Weird Stuff; Gary, Carin and her then-seven-year-old brother David, quickly followed suit, because the moniker was so damn *apt*. Her powers – which, at that point, consisted of flying, insanely fast running, and ungodly strength – were neither good, nor were they bad; they were just weird. Since she never used them, they didn't help her, nor did they hurt her. They were simply *there*, an annoying part of her, slightly more annoying than the yucky mole on the inside of her left thigh, or her pigeon toes, or that damned untamable hair. She did her best not to think about the Weird Stuff, and for the most part, she succeeded.

At the first class of Abbey's first day of high school – a high school for super smart kids, none of whom she went to elementary school with – she found herself sitting next to a girl with purple hair, a nose stud and clunky glasses. The girl pointed at Abbey's Talking Heads T-shirt and said, 'Cool top. You like Black Flag?'

Abbey shrugged. 'I don't know. Who's Black Flag?'

The girl said, 'They're this eighties punk band that made a lot of noise. Like Nirvana, except without intonation or hooks.'

Abbey, who didn't know intonation from hooks, gave a noncommittal nod and grunt.

The girl continued, 'So yeah, if you're into eighties music, you should totally check 'em out.'

'I'm not really into eighties music,' Abbey said. 'I just think the shirt is cool. It used to be my dad's.'

'It's pretty tight. It makes your boobs look good.'

'Um, thanks, I suppose.'

'Your dad must be a small dude.'

Abbey smiled. 'Well, I guess he was small in the eighties.'

The girl chuckled, then stuck out her hand. 'I'm Cheryl Sheldon.' Abbey shook her hand, then introduced herself. Cheryl half bowed. 'It is lovely to meet you, Abbey.' She said it quite formally, in a faux-hoity-toity accent, as if Abbey was a visiting dignitary.

Abbey giggled. 'It is also lovely to meet you, Cheryl.'

In her normal voice, Cheryl asked, 'So do you know anybody who goes to this dump?'

20

'No. Do you?'

'Nope.' She leaned toward Abbey and whispered, 'They all look like a bunch of tools. We should hang out.'

Abbey, who thought that her new classmates looked perfectly swell, and not in the least bit toolish, said, 'Cool.'

'You could come over to my house after school, if you want. My parents are divorced. I live with my mom. She's pretty cool. She lets me do what I want.'

'Like what?'

'Like whatever I want.'

'Like what do you want to do?'

Cheryl slumped in her chair. 'Weird stuff.' Abbey sat bolt upright, and coughed, and coughed, and coughed. Cheryl whacked her on the back and said, 'You okay?'

Once she got her hacking under control, Abbey asked, 'What do you mean, weird stuff?'

Cheryl shrugged. 'It's not that weird, I guess. Play music loud. Practice my guitar. Eat vegan food. Fart around on Facebook. Smoke a fattie once in a while. That sort of thing.'

Abbey said, 'Um, yeah, that's not weird. That's normal. Me, I know weird.'

Cheryl sat up and grinned. 'Yeah? You know weird? Hunh. Talk to me about weird, Abbey. I'm intrigued.'

The teacher then strode into the room and said, 'Okay, kids, put a sock in it, and let's try to enjoy the first day of the rest of our lives.'

Cheryl smiled. 'The first day of the rest of our lives. I like that.'

Abbey whispered to Cheryl, 'I'll never talk to you about weird. *Never*.'

Cheryl said, 'Oh, you'll talk, my new friend. You'll *totally* talk.'

The purple-haired girl was right. Three months later, Abbey talked.

Considering how little she tries, Abbey Bynum is an excellent paralegal. If she bothered to put forth any significant effort – if she amped up her brain to a ten, or even an eight (and if she smartened-up her wardrobe) – she'd probably become the firm's Chief Para. But she doesn't care. Researching arcane Illinois laws about copyrights and intellectual properties isn't her life's dream.

And therein lies the problem: Abbey doesn't have a life's dream.

Oh, she's done her fair share of dabbling, but none of the dabbling panned out. Even though she's pretty good at it, writing bores her to tears; she'd rather read. Painting was nothing but frustrating. She doesn't think she has the intestinal fortitude to teach continuing adult education. And she gave up on the Big Sister program when her Little Sister snatched her purse off her shoulder and took off down the street. (Abbey has the ability to run forty-seven m.p.h. on land, and she would've gone after the bitch, but this went down in the middle of Michigan Avenue, and it was a beautiful Saturday summer afternoon, and the streets were clogged with tourists and shoppers, and going into gazelle mode would've caused nothing but trouble. Yeah, it would've been nice to teach that obnoxious little girl a lesson, but there's a time and a place for everything.)

So Abbey goes to work, and comes home, and does it again. She isn't unhappy, but she isn't happy. She just is. For Abbey Bynum, at this point in her life, *just being* is just fine: as far as she's concerned, the less excitement, the better.

Cheryl Sheldon turned out to be the coolest person whom Abbey had ever met. By far.

Abbey was a casual music fan – British Invasion-era rock was her first choice, and she gravitated to the Beatles, the Stones, Led Zep, and the like – but Cheryl was a music obsessive, and happy to share both her knowledge and her CD collection. Thanks to Cheryl, Abbey grew to love eighties punk (e.g., Black Flag and the Minutemen), nineties riot grrrl bands (e.g., Bikini Kill and Bratmobile) and contemporary chick singer/ songwriters (e.g., Shawn Colvin and the Indigo Girls).

Her new friend was also a demon in the kitchen, and Abbey loved it when Cheryl invited her to dinner, especially when Cheryl quit being a vegan. For the first time, Abbey had fish that wasn't cooked all the way through, and risotto with truffle oil and mixed mushrooms, and tenderloin whose insides were as pink as a sunset.

And this isn't even taking into consideration that sometimes hanging out with Cheryl meant getting a free concert. You could even call it a command performance.

Cheryl was a prolific songwriter, and whenever the girls got together, she would regale Abbey with her latest tune. Some of them were good, and some of them not so good, and it got to the point where Abbey could discern what songs were worthy, and Cheryl trusted her enough to take her opinion to heart. Cheryl once told Abbey, 'When I get my record deal, you'll be my producer.'

Abbey said, 'No way.' She pointed to her ears. 'See these? They're made of tin. I'll stick to listening and applauding, thank you very much.'

'Okay,' Cheryl said, 'fine. Let's try this: When I get my record deal, you'll fly all over the country wearing a neon T-shirt with my face on it, carrying a gigantic bullhorn, which you'll use to extol my many, many virtues. And just for you, I'll call my first album *Weird Stuff*.'

Abbey smacked Cheryl on the noggin with a pillow. 'In your *dreams*!'

'Listen, babe, if you want to ride on the Cheryl Sheldon train, you're either going to produce me or promote me. That's your choice.'

'What if I just keep being your bestie?'

Cheryl shrugged. 'I guess that's okay. But if some other superhero starts promoting some other chick singer/songwriter, and that chick singer/songwriter sells more records than me, I'm never speaking to you again.'

Abbey nodded. 'I'm willing to take that chance.'

*

'Sweetie, you look exhausted.'

This is Suzanne Addison, Abbey's boss. If you were to say to somebody, 'Hey, show me what a successful female lawyer should look like', they'd pull out a picture of Suzanne. Short black hair with a few strands of gray, done up just-so. A large collection of smart power suits, one for almost every day of the month, perfectly tailored, perfectly pressed. Small, hip, expensive designer glasses that spend more time in her hand than on her face. Thin lips, severe eyes, a gym-toned body, and an unmistakable air of competence and confidence. A force to be reckoned with in the office and the courtroom.

Abbey kind of wants to be Suzanne when she grows up. Except for that whole lawyer thing, of course.

As long as you do your job competently – which Abbey does – Suzanne is a wonderful boss, always ready to buy her staffers a nice lunch, always happy to grant an extra personal day, always comfortable sending an employee home if they have the sniffles. But Suzanne does have one annoying habit: she likes to point out your physical flaws, especially perceived tiredness.

Abbey gives Suzanne a weak smile. 'Don't worry. I'm not exhausted. I'm fine.' Lies, lies, lies: she *was* exhausted; she *wasn't* fine.

'I hope so,' Suzanne says. 'Staff meeting today.'

Abbey nods. 'Yep. Staff meeting today.'

Suzanne gestures to the pile of books and legal pads on Abbey's desk. 'Are you okay with everything? Are you overwhelmed?' Then, without waiting for an answer, she continues, 'Where're you at with the Landmark case briefs?'

The Landmark case involves a young, small-time self-help guru who stole the intellectual property from a shady self-help conglomerate, then tried to enlist his followers to recruit other followers, and so on, and so on. It was a pyramid scheme, and the young guru is gross, and Abbey is certain they'll win the case, and guru boy will justifiably be forced to pay the firm's client a whole lot of dineros. But even when it comes to a seeming slam-dunk of a case, the lawyers of Roscoe, Belmont, Paulina & Addison like to be *prepared*. This is where Abbey and her paralegal brethren come in.

Abbey says, 'I'm almost there, Suzanne. It's looking good. Next week at the latest.' And then, as if to prove Suzanne right about the whole you-look-exhausted deal, Abbey lets out a lion-sized yawn.

Suzanne smiles triumphantly. 'I *thought* you looked tired.'

'I guess I was up pretty late last night,' she admits.

'Murphy problems?'

'No. No Murphy problems. Murphy is never a problem.'

Lies, lies, lies.

If you were measuring his level of nerdiness on a scale of one-to-ten, Murphy Napier would be a nine. Once or twice a month, he'd hit a nine-point-five (some of those haircuts ... oy), and a few times a year – specifically when he pulled out one of his three outdated, mismatched, ill-fitting suits – he'd be right up at a ten. Or even an eleven.

You would never have guessed it from her general cuteness, but Abbey Bynum used to be quite the nerd herself – actually, truth be told, she's still pretty nerdy; she just hides it well – and nerds easily recognise their own, so when Abbey and Murphy's eyes met on the first day of the first semester of her senior year at Northwestern University in Evanston, Illinois during an African History class, it was curiosity at first sight.

Murphy may have been a nerd, but he wasn't a shy one, so he marched right on over to Abbey after the class, pointed at her chest, and said, 'I like your shirt.'

Abbey was astounded. She'd had the T-shirt since high school – Cheryl had begged her on numerous instances to burn the damn thing – and had worn it several zillion times, and nobody had ever said anything nice about it. She said, 'You like *Dr Who*?'

Murphy shook his head. 'I don't like *Dr Who*.'

Abbey said, 'You don't?'

'No. No. No, I don't like *Dr Who*, Abbey. I *love Dr Who*!'

The two of them went to a local ice cream parlor, and, over drippy banana splits, geeked out on *Star Trek* and *Star Wars* and Arthur C. Clarke. Once Murphy started lecturing her about superhero comics, Abbey abruptly changed the subject.

The college version of Abbey was less severe than the paralegal version of Abbey, thus she was even cuter, thus she was – at least on paper – out of Murphy Napier's league. But that was only on paper. The reality was that thanks to their overlapping interests (e.g., sci-fi TV shows, war documentaries, David Foster Wallace novels, dweeby emo rockers like Weezer and Promise Ring), similar IQs, and mutual disdain for people they considered to be less than serious, they were relatively compatible.

As Murphy walked over to the cash register to pay their check, Abbey gave him a serious once over, and thought, *He can be fixed*. She intuited (correctly, as it turned out) that his bowl-cut was an act of defiance, a *screw you* to the cool kids, Murphy's way of saying, *I don't want to be like you. As a matter of fact, I want to be the* opposite *of you*. His clothes weren't too bad, but the way he wore them ... *very* bad. Buttoning the top button of a short-sleeved shirt went out in 1984, and everybody knows that you don't tuck a tight shirt into a pair of loose-fitting flared jeans.

Abbey again thought, *Yep, he can be fixed.* So she went about fixing him.

She started from scratch. Neither the Bynums or the Napiers had much money, but fortunately for Murphy, Abbey knew where all the best thrift stores in Chicago were located, so over the course of three months, she replaced his entire wardrobe with ringer T-shirts, well-worn jeans, and retro Doc Martens, without putting a significant dent in either of their budgets. She dragged him kicking and screaming to a funky barbershop, where he got his first (and only) buzz cut. For a while, Murphy Napier looked pretty good.

But that was only for a while.

One night near the end of the school year, Murphy invited Abbey over to his apartment for a home-cooked meal. She was touched at the effort, but the lemon chicken was too lemony, the roasted asparagus was overcooked to the point of solidity, and the baked potato was burnt on the outside and hard on the inside. After she choked down what she could, she cleared the table; as she washed the dishes, Murphy talked.

'Ab,' – he called her 'Ab', which she didn't care for, but she never told him to stop, because she didn't want to hurt his tender feelings – 'I appreciate what you are trying to do for me here, but I need hair on my head, and I want to tuck my shirt in, and I do not care what you or anybody else says, that is the way it is going to be, and that is the deal, and now I would like to kiss you.'

Abbey dropped a plate on the floor, sending shards all over the kitchen, and scaring the hell out of Murphy's skittish Yorkshire terrier. 'Jeez, Murphy,' she said, 'don't hold anything back. Tell me what you really think.' Then she forced out a laugh.

'Please do not turn this into a joke, Ab,' Murphy said. 'This is really hard for me.'

Abbey kneeled down and wordlessly cleaned up the shards of broken plate.

After a silent minute, Murphy walked over to her and said, 'Helloooo. Anybody home? Care to chime in on the topic?'

Not wanting to draw this scene out any longer than was necessary, Abbey closed her eyes and steeled herself, then said, 'I'm sorry, Murphy. I don't feel the same way about you.'

Murphy chuckled. 'Sure you do. You just do not realise it yet.'

Oh, she realised, all right. She wasn't attracted to him in the least, but even if she was, Abbey wasn't interested in helping Murphy Napier lose his virginity – for that matter, she didn't want to help *any* boy lose his virginity; that would've been *way* too much pressure – but she didn't want to hurt the poor guy's feelings, because she did care for him an awful lot, so she went into avoidance mode. She stood up and said, 'I think I should go.' Then she zipped out the door.

And she zipped fast.

Like superpowers fast.

She hoped Murphy hadn't noticed, but he was a pretty aware guy. It concerned her, but not enough to ever ask him about it.

Murphy started pulling away: unreturned voicemails, and emails, and text messages; it was all quiet on the Napier front. Abbey understood. Back in high school, she was always the one who wanted to be more-than-friends, then would get rebuffed. (What made that situation more difficult for Abbey was that Cheryl was able to score any guy she wanted. It didn't make Abbey jealous, just depressed.) She knew what it was like, how painful it was to be the sister-figure when all you wanted to do was shove your tongue down that certain someone's throat. So she let Murphy have his space.

Three weeks before graduation, she was sitting on the lawn in the quad, leaning against a tree, poring through a John Irving book – Irving was her favorite author of the moment, and her snobby American Lit teacher, out of the goodness of his heart, let Abbey do her final paper about him, even though Irving had had books published in the (gasp!) Twenty-first Century – minding her own business, when she felt a tap on her shoulder. She jumped, and it took all of her strength not to give the tapper a backhand to the face that would've sent him flying twenty yards in the air, and permanently dislocating his nose in the process.

She turned around and snarled, 'What do you—' then before she could finish the thought, her mouth snapped shut. She found herself staring into the most gorgeous male face she'd ever been this close to.

He pointed to Abbey's book and said, '*The World According to Garp*. Love that one. You read *The Cider House Rules*?'

Abbey stammered, 'O-o-o-o-nly, like, t-t-t-en times.'

The gorgeous male face chuckled. 'You got me beat there. I've only read it twice.' He stuck out his hand and said, 'James Caraway. Mind if I join you?' They shook. He had awesome hands. Her whole body tingled.

And thus began the most torrid three weeks of her young life.

She couldn't get enough of James's body. He was a swimmer and a rower, and his arms were like pythons, and his legs were like tree trunks. He manscaped his entire body, and Abbey adored licking his smooth chest. James was only the third boy she'd slept with, and even though she didn't have much to compare it to, she thought he was astounding in bed. (If nothing else, he went down on her for long, long, *long* stretches, which is more than she could say for her other two lovers.) Abbey and James rarely went out; their usual date consisted of delivery sushi and lovemaking sessions that lasted hours. Abbey probably would've kept it going, but after two weeks of incessant fucking, the Weird Stuff started getting weirder.

The weirder Weirdness kicked in one afternoon during her American Lit class, when she made eye contact with her teacher, and all of a sudden, her world disappeared.

And she was in Dr Maxwell Paulson's brain.

She knew that he wanted to 'stick it to her'.

She knew that he'd been suspended from teaching seven years previously, when he was at Northern Illinois University, for sticking it to another student, a willing freshman with a daddy complex.

She knew that, given the opportunity, he'd have smacked his ex-wife into the next universe.

She knew that he hadn't spoken to his sister in three years, because he'd grown tired of his fruitless efforts to get her off of meth and coke.

And she knew that she didn't want to know anything else about Dr Paulson, so she leapt up from her chair and left the classroom. (The following week, she mailed in her John Irving paper, for which she received an A-, and a note saying, 'Good luck with all your future endeavors. I wish I could have told you that in person.')

On her way back to her dorm room, Abbey rubbed her scalp almost to the point of opening a wound, hoping that she could somehow clear her head. She knew what had just happened was real. It wasn't a hallucination, or a brain-lucination, or a whatever-the-hell-it-was-lucination. She saw into the man's mind – into his soul, for that matter – and she didn't like it one bit.

After a quick shower, she texted James that she was on her way over. When he opened his apartment door, she ran into his arms and burst into tears. He ran his hand up and down her back and asked her repeatedly what was wrong. Even if she could speak, she wouldn't, no, *couldn't* tell him. He knew nothing of the Weird Stuff, and this was the weirdest stuff yet, so it was a bad place to start. When she got herself under some semblance of control, she pulled away, and caught James's eye, and it happened again.

She knew that James had once stolen $20 from his old roommate, and still felt guilty about it, but would do it again if necessary.

She knew that James sometimes cried at night for no apparent reason, and it scared the shit out of him, because his father suffered from clinical depression, and he was afraid that it ran in the family.

She knew that James had had sex with three boys, and wished that Abbey would enter into a threesome with Walt Shaver from his Poli-Sci class.

Worst of all, she knew that James was going to dump her after graduation, because he was going to propose to his girl back in Nebraska, an evil girl who was willing to do a threesome (or a foursome) whenever James wanted.

Abbey broke away from James, pulled his door off the hinges, and ran home at full speed – she didn't care who saw – and didn't leave her dorm room for three days. The only phone calls she made and took were to and from the four people who knew about the Weird Stuff: Mom, Dad, Dave, and Cheryl. She gave them all the scoop about the ESP, and they tried their best to talk her down, but they knew that whenever Abbey had Weird Stuff issues, there was little they could say or do to make her feel better. But they loved her, so that didn't stop them from trying.

She finally started getting stir crazy, plus she'd run out of food other than Ritz Crackers and popcorn, so she forced herself to leave her room. During her walk to the store, she avoided looking anybody in the eye, because the last place in the world she wanted to be was inside anybody's head.

Her grocery trip was okay. No mind-reading. No revelations. Just food.

After she dropped her bags back at her room, she went for a stroll around Evanston. Cautiously, she began to make the tiniest bit of eye contact with every other person she walked by, and it was all good. No Weirdness. She was cured, hopefully forever.

Abbey's working theory about the ESP was that the non-stop sex with James got her blood, and/or her hormones, and/or her adrenaline boiling at a jillion degrees, and some of the Weird Stuff oozed, and/or shifted, and/or started bubbling into her brain, causing some sort of *something*, and that *something* caused *something else*, and next thing you knew, she was inside everybody's damn head. But that was over now. She could move on.

And then she got her period.

*

Suzanne says, 'If it's not Murphy problems, then why do you look so *exhausted*?'

Abbey picks up one of the Landmark files and protests, 'I'm *not* exhausted.' Actually, she's quite exhausted, but she doesn't want to tell Suzanne, because Suzanne would probably send her home for a mental health day, and the last thing Abbey wants is a break in her routine. Yes, her routine is dullsville, but little in life comforted Abbey Bynum like boredom. The less excitement, the better. If you were saddled with Weird Stuff that you didn't want, you'd *totally* understand.

Suzanne gives Abbey a motherly pat on the shoulder and says, 'You can go home if you want, sweetie. I don't even mind if you skip the staff meeting. It's fine. I'll have Giselle cover for you.' Giselle Collins is Suzanne's other para, a sweet ditz who everybody at RBP&A loves having around, but hates working with. Abbey thinks that if Suzanne is ready to turn to Giselle for help, she must truly look horrible.

'I'm fine, boss lady. Don't stress.' For reasons beyond Abbey's understanding, Suzanne finds the phrase 'boss lady' hilarious, and Abbey uses it when she needs to change the subject or create a distraction.

Indeed, Suzanne laughs. 'Okay, fine. Ten o'clock, then.'

Abbey nods. 'Ten o'clock it is.' A cramp radiates through her entire midsection. As Suzanne walks away, Abbey thinks, *Wonderful, great timing*, then she opens her top desk drawer and pulls out a bottle of Advil, dry-swallows four of them, then, feeling that tell-tale tickle down in her nether regions, reaches into her bottom drawer, snatches a tampon from her emergency box of Kotex, then speed-walks to the ladies room.

Ladies, if you think your periods are bad, you ain't got nothin' on Abbey Bynum.

One of Abbey's least favorite books in the world is *Carrie* by Stephen King. It's not that she has issues with the book itself; King is a wonderfully scary storyteller, and being the nerdy reader that she is, Abbey is always up for some scary storytelling. No, her problem with *Carrie* is that one of the novel's central threads is the protagonist's connection between menstruation and telekinesis.

Here's the thing: this connection, this menstrual cycle/paranormal connection, as bizarre as it may sound, is real . . . if you have Weird Stuff, that is. Carrie's Weird Stuff was weirder (and *way* more messed-up) than Abbey Bynum's Weird Stuff, but the similarities were disconcerting as hell.

The irony is that when Abbey got her period after the James fiasco, it was a relief, because condom-wise, they'd slipped up a couple of times, which was her fault, and her fault alone. She knew it was moronic not to reach over to her nightstand and pull out a Trojan before James slipped inside of her – it would've taken all of thirty seconds, and James wasn't the type to lose his hard-on – but she was sooooo wet, and he was sooooo hard, and he felt sooooo good that she couldn't bring herself to stop. James always had the good grace to pull out before he came, but pulling out, as many of us know, is far from a foolproof birth-control method. Fortunately, in this instance, pulling out was enough. Abbey thanked whatever power it was that ran the universe for her good, non-pregnant fortune, because she wasn't even close to ready to care for a little Abbey.

In any event, at the beginning of that post-James period, her cramps were a little worse than usual, but otherwise, it was your run-of-the-mill monthly visit.

That was, until the last day, when Abbey Bynum had the ability to read *every* mind in sight, an ability that, she now realised, she was stuck with, for better or worse.

Abbey sits on the toilet in the far stall – her favorite stall during menstruation, because it's the farthest away from the entrance to the bathroom, and it's easier to deal with this crap without any prying ears – and tries to chill the hell out. Over the years, she's found that if she relaxes her breathing and lowers her heart rate, the side effects of her period are far less severe. On the other hand, if she freaks out, the Weird Stuff freaks out.

Did we mention the telekinesis?

Like if she remains calm of mind during that time of the month, there's a far lesser chance she'll trash her next-door neighbor's car just by looking at it. (That happened during her first visit home after graduation. She still doesn't know how Gary managed to keep that situation under wraps, and she doesn't want to ask. Some things are better left unknown.)

If she stays tranquil, odds are she won't break a cabinetful of glass plates with a mere glance. (Ever since that fiasco, all of Abbey's plates are plastic, save for the for-company-only four-piece set that she keeps down in the storage closet in the basement of her condo building.)

If she keeps her head, she probably won't blow her neighbor's new grill to bits with the shrug of a shoulder. (Thankfully, that particular boo-boo coincided with an astoundingly severe thunderstorm, so her neighbor – a lovely man with whom she would've hopped into bed in a heartbeat, if he weren't married to an equally lovely woman – blamed it on the eminently blameable Chicago weather.)

The problem is that ever since her thing with James – and her thing with James was years ago – her cramps are painful, sometimes unbearably so, and it's hard to get into a tranquil headspace when your entire midsection is on fire . . . which is the case today.

After she puts in her tampon and readjusts her outfit, Abbey closes the top of the toilet, sits down, rubs her temples, and thinks about the one thing that almost always chases her blues away.

I f it weren't for her family – the most supportive, caring, discreet family a girl with Weird Stuff could hope for – Abbey might well have turned herself over to a government agency that would have made the damn Stuff go away years ago. But her mom, dad and brother have managed to keep Abbey grounded and sane.

For example, when she was thirteen – an age when most girls are having awkward conversations with their mothers about the joys of sex – Abbey asked Carin if it might be a good idea for her to experiment with her powers. (She refused to call them *super*powers, because she didn't find them super in the least.) 'I mean, I don't think it's going anywhere, so I may as well see if I can, I dunno, *do something* with it.'

'We always knew this day would come,' Carin said as she took her daughter's hand. 'Honey, you can do whatever you want. All we ask is that you have one of us with you when you *do* do what you want. Every time.'

'*Every* time?' Abbey asked.

'Every time.'

'How can I have one of you with me if I'm way up in the air?'

Carin squeezed her daughter's slender bicep and smiled. 'What with those muscles of yours, I don't think you'll have any problem hauling one of us around.'

Abbey pulled her arm away, giggled, and said, 'Okay. Fine. Let's go now.'

Carin stood up, cleared her throat, and said, 'Actually, when I said *one of us*, I meant your father.'

So early the next morning – at 3.12 a.m., to be exact – when most of Buffalo, New York was curled up under their sheets, Gary and Abbey took to the sky.

Fearing thin air, airplanes and being spotted, Abbey flew high enough so that they weren't visible from the ground, but low enough so that they wouldn't slam into a Boeing 767. Considering the highest point she'd ever previously hit was the ceiling of her bedroom, Abbey did a fine job of navigating the skies. Even while holding Gary tightly to her chest, her balance was remarkable; never once did she or her father have the sense that they would fall. It was like she was a trained missile.

But the most remarkable thing was that flying was *fun*.

The breeze smelled better up in the sky – then again, that shouldn't have been a surprise, as Buffalo wasn't (and still isn't) known for its air quality – and Abbey's muscles felt tauter, and her head was clearer. She grinned during their entire fifty-two-minute jaunt, never saying a single word. When they landed softly in the backyard, Gary gave Abbey a hug, told her he loved her, then said, 'You're an expert, Sweet Pea, so I don't think I need to do that with you again.' (What Abbey never learned was that Gary then ran to the bathroom and threw up.)

Unlike Gary and Carin, Dave was *always* asking his sister for a pre-dawn ride. She took him up every so often, maybe once every other month, just to keep him off her back. But the rides stopped when she was eighteen.

A prototypical second-born child, the high school version of Dave was somewhat of a smartass. Unfortunately for him, he was a short and slight teenager, and if you're short and slight, it's generally prudent to keep your smartassy jibes to yourself, a lesson Dave refused to take to heart, no matter how many times he got his butt kicked.

Until The Event.

The Event, as it became known in Bynum family lore, lasted a grand total of one minute and twelve seconds, but it changed everything. Here's a breakdown:

- 0.01 – Freshman Dave Bynum – who, at the time, hated jocks on general principle – tells sophomore running back Jerry Feinberg (who, two days previously, had fumbled at the one-yard-line, thus booting away the homecoming game, and disappointing the entire school) that he couldn't hold on to a football even if it was covered with Krazy Glue.

- 0.07 – Jerry tells Dave to take it back.
- 0.11 – Dave tells Jerry to blow him.
- 0.20 – Jerry tells Dave that he's going to 'equalise him.'
- 0.25 – Dave grabs his crotch and says, 'Equalise this, dickweed!'
- 0.30 – Jerry shoves Dave to the concrete and yells, 'Take it back!'
- 0.32 – Dave yells, 'Never!'
- 0.41 – Jerry kicks Dave in the ribs.
- 0.45 – Senior Abbey Bynum drives by in her parents' Honda CRV, sees Dave writhing on the ground, screeches to a halt, opens the door, and jumps from the car.
- 0.46 – Abbey begins the fifty-yard run to the spot of the fight.
- 0.47 – Abbey ends the fifty-yard run to the spot of the fight.
- 0.50 – Abbey tells Jerry to lay off her brother.
- 0.55 – Jerry laughs and says, 'Awesome! This little bitch has to call in his sister bitch to fight his bitch battles. Jesus Christ, the Bynums are such . . . *bitches*!'
- 1.00 – Abbey picks up Jerry by his wrist, twirls him around her head three times as if he was a lasso, then slams him to the ground.
- 1.07 – Abbey kneels down and whispers to

Jerry, 'If you tell anybody about this, it'll happen again. Worse.'
- 1.09 – Jerry nods and moans.
- 1.11 – Abbey yanks Dave up and, as she drags him to the car by the scruff of his neck, says, 'You're a goddamn idiot, and you deserve everything you got.'

Back in the car, Dave thanked Abbey every which way he could think of, but she didn't say a word. When they pulled into the driveway, she turned off the engine and quietly said, 'I'll tell you the same thing I just told your pal Jerry: if you tell anybody about this other than Mom and Dad, it'll happen to you. Worse.'

Dave, who was near tears, said, 'I'm so sorry, Abbey. I'm so sorry. So, so, so sorry.'

She said, 'Don't apologise to me. Apologise to Jerry.'

'But he kicked the crap out of me.'

'But you insulted the crap out of him.'

'But he's a jock. He deserved it.'

'But you're an idiot. *You* deserved it.'

He wiped the tears from his eyes, opened the door, and said, 'Whatever, dude.'

Lightning quick, she grabbed him by his shoulder and pulled him back into the car. 'Don't you *Whatever, dude* me, kiddo. If I hadn't helped you just now, you'd be in the hospital.' She shook her head disgustedly and said, 'You know what? No more flying. I'm not taking you up any more. We're done with that. *Done.*'

Dave looked like he'd been punched in the gut. 'Awwww, come onnnnnn, Abbey. Don't roll like that.'

'Oh, I'm rolling like that. It's over. Finito. You're earthbound, little boy. And your next punishment is going to hurt. Bad.' Right then, it took all her strength to keep from laughing. What was funny? Well, in order to teach her brother a lesson, she wasn't going to take him flying any more, and that was just about the stupidest thing she'd ever heard.

Dave said, 'Quit laughing at me.'

'I'm not laughing.'

'Yes, you are.' (Yes, she was.) 'I so hate you.'

Abbey said, 'You so love me. Now get out of my sight.' And then the laughter floodgates opened.

Dave whined, 'What's so funny?' And then, after a few seconds, he realised *exactly* what was so funny, and joined Abbey's gigglefest. They laughed for a good ten minutes, then went inside the house, Abbey's arm draped around Dave's shoulders.

They were all good, but Abbey kept her promise, and never took Dave flying again.

The lesson here, of course, is don't cross Abbey Bynum, because if she punishes you, you're going to stay punished.

Either the Advil has kicked in, or the reminiscing about her family has chilled her out, so Abbey feels better, and is ready to go back to her cubicle. On the way, she tries to avoid looking anybody in the eye, for fear that she'll accidentally get a peek of what's inside their brain. (Over the past five years, she's learned how to control that whole mind-reading thing, but when the cramps are particularly bad, her brain has been known to do its own thing.) Unfortunately for Abbey, most everybody at Roscoe, Belmont, Paulina & Addison is either legitimately friendly or exceedingly polite, so it's impossible for her to get to her desk without saying hello to whomever crosses her path. And saying hello means making eye contact. And making eye contact means . . .

. . . that Abbey learns William Roscoe is cheating on his wife.

. . . that Abbey learns Jerrell Washburne lost his wallet, which happened to be filled with hundred-dollar bills that he'd been planning to use at his weekly poker game, and man, he's pissed, pissed enough to punch a hole in his cubicle.

. . . that Abbey learns Carla Belmont's mother is sick, and she's afraid to tell her mommy exactly how sick she is, because if Mommy knows she only has eight, maybe ten weeks to live, she'll probably ask Carla to euthanise her.

. . . that once again, Abbey is reminded she doesn't like learning these sorts of things.

She plops down into her cushy, black leather office chair – good boss that she is, Suzanne wants her staff to be as comfortable as possible, thus the expensive ergonomic seat – grabs a random file, and leafs through it unseeingly. She glances at the clock on her laptop:

9.45. Fifteen minutes until the staff meeting but, more importantly, it's 10.45 on the East Coast, which means that Cheryl is awake, and possibly even coherent.

Cheryl picks up her phone on the fifth ring and grunts, 'Shit. Bynum. Time z'it?'

Abbey says, 'Almost eleven by you.'

'Hold on.' Cheryl clears her throat, graces Abbey with a phlegmmy cough, then says, 'I was at the studio last night. We didn't get out of there until eight . . .'

'Eight isn't bad.'

'. . . in the morning.'

'Oh. Yeah. That's bad.'

'It ain't good. Hold on again.' Abbey hears Cheryl rustle around, flick a lighter, then inhale deeply. She can't figure out how the hell her friend manages to sing like an angel while smoking a pack a day. Cheryl asks, 'So what's up?'

'I took a ride last night. Well, this morning, I suppose.'

Cheryl coughs. 'Seriously? Aerial?'

'Seriously. Aerial.'

'Shit. Murphy problems?'

Abbey admits to her friend what she couldn't admit to her boss. 'Yeah. Murphy problems.'

'I'm not surprised. Spill.'

After she graduated from Northwestern, Abbey went back home for a few months to figure out how or if she could make use of her degree in American Literature.

While she puttered around Buffalo for a few months – and realised that American Lit qualified her for exactly nothing – Abbey lost touch with most of her college friends. She wasn't upset about it; they were nice people but not the be all and end all. Besides, she wasn't the kind of girl who needed a posse. Cheryl was enough.

By the time winter rolled around, Abbey decided she was bored with Buffalo – understandable, as Buffalo isn't what you would call a booming metropolis – and since she'd loved her college years, she decided to plant roots in the Chicago area. Gary had a friend who had a friend at the downtown Chicago law firm of Roscoe, Belmont, Paulina & Addison, and it just so happened that Roscoe, Belmont, Paulina & Addison was in dire need of paralegals, and it just so happened that Abbey had the brainpower to become a paralegal in about two minutes. *Ta-da*, just like that, Abbey had a job, and an apartment, and a semblance of a life.

Abbey didn't need a lot of friends, but she needed *somebody*; during her first six months in Chicago, there was nobody, and she was lonely as hell. The lawyers and her fellow paras were perfectly nice, but there was a fundamental disconnection there – like she dug indie music, oddball films, and sci-fi novels, and they dug Coldplay, *Spiderman*, and *The Secret*. Once every couple of weeks, she joined her co-workers for some enjoyable happy-hour boozing, but it never went beyond that.

It wasn't a tragic life, by any means. She was making decent money, so when she wanted to take herself out to a nice dinner, or see a play at the Steppenwolf Theater, or catch some classical music at the Ravinia Theater, she could do so without having to consider the cost. Cheryl – who had just signed a deal with a small indie record label – was in town at least once every other month, singing her songs and strumming her guitar at some local shithole or another, so there was always that to look forward to. And Dave had just started his freshman year at DePaul University on the north side of the city, so there was always some family around . . . even if this particular family member spent most of his days in an I-just-went-away-to-college-and-I'm-going-to-drink-at-every-given-opportunity-because-my-parents-can't-stop-me-induced haze.

No, Abbey's life was far from tragic; it just wasn't *enough*. The problem was, she didn't know what *would* make it enough.

It was another lonely winter day when she got his email:

Hey, Ab,
I called your mom, and she told me you're back in Chicago. I am too! We should get together. I am sorry I got so weird. I want you in my life. Call me, if you are so inclined.
Yours,
Murphy Napier
(312) 612-xxxx

Abbey was indeed so inclined. Murphy might not be the perfect person to hang out with, but at least they had history, and thanks to said history, there was a certain comfort level there. Right about then, history plus comfort equaled appealing.

They met at a yummy, justifiably trendy dessert bar called Hot Chocolate. So as not to send him any romantic signals, Abbey wore one of her work outfits, which weren't the least bit provocative; her loose-fitting black pullover and shapeless black slacks screamed out, *Let's be buddies!* Sure, it would've been nice to have a warm body to cuddle up next to, but Murphy wasn't that body.

He strolled in fifteen-ish minutes late, and she could tell right away that he was still the same old nerdy Murphy. Okay, he'd changed a little: he'd put on a few pounds of what appeared to be muscle; his hair was longer than she'd ever seen it – it had a slight wave that she'd never known about, as his trademark bowl-cut hadn't left anything available for waving – and he had a thin mustache that wasn't the most flattering facial hair she'd ever seen. Most egregiously, he was wearing a bow tie. (We're not saying there's anything wrong with a bow tie in and of itself; we *are*, however, saying that a red-and-green plaid bow tie paired with a yellow-and-black plaid shirt is . . . simply . . . *wrong*.)

Abbey stood to give him a hug, but before she could wrap her arms around him, he offered up his hand for shaking. 'Ab,' he said formally, 'you look well.'

Nonplussed, she shook his hand. 'As do you, Murphy.'

'Thank you.' He sat down. 'It is wonderful to see you.'

'Um, you too.' His speech pattern was clipped and officious, which was also new.

He said, 'Wonderful, wonderful. How goes it at Roscoe, Belmont, et cetera?'

She blinked. 'How do you know I'm there?' Then it clicked. 'Oh, Mom told you.'

'That is not correct. I learned about it myself.'

Strange, Abbey thought. 'And how exactly did you learn about it yourself?'

'That is my job,' he explained. 'I am paid to learn things.'

'Aren't we all?'

He shot her a humorless smile. 'Not the way I am, Ab. For you see, I am an employee of the United States Government. A little branch you might have heard of called the Federal Bureau of Investigation. To you, we are the FBI. To me, we are The Company.'

Abbey, who'd read a few spy novels in her time, said, 'I thought the CIA was The Company.'

Murphy pouted defiantly. 'Oh, they like to think they are The Company. The reality is that the Central Intelligence Agency is a bungling outfit. They make mistake after mistake after mistake. For instance, are you familiar with a failed mission called the Bay of Pigs?'

She rolled her eyes and shot him a sardonic half-grin. 'Yes, Murphy, I've heard of the Bay of Pigs.' Then it dawned on her. 'You tried to get a job at the CIA, didn't you? And they passed.'

Murphy blushed. 'I interviewed with them six times, Ab. *Six!* If you get interviewed by somebody six times, and, each time, they tell you what an asset you'd be to them, and they start discussing salary and benefits, you make certain assumptions.'

'Well, at least they helped you get a job at The Bureau.'

'The Company.'

'Whatever.' She suddenly felt the urge to make him feel better about himself, because that's the kind of thing Abbey does: you make people feel better and you save the world, one person at a time. 'I bet there aren't too many people your age at your office. I'm sure you're totally ahead of the curve.'

Murphy allowed himself a tiny grin. 'That is kind of you to say so, Ab. I do appreciate that.'

'Don't think I'm saying it just to say it. You're a smart guy, Murphy. Smarter than me.' She picked up a packet of sugar and threw it at him. 'And I'm pretty smart.'

His tiny grin blossomed into a real smile. (Abbey thought, *He should smile like that more often.*) 'Ab, you are correct. I am indeed smarter than you.'

After they ordered a pair of haute dessert creations – him: a deconstructed Snickers bar; her: a five-inch sculpture of banana, caramel and butterscotch – they fell into their old pattern of geeking out on geeky stuff. They discussed the zombie craze that was sweeping the country's bookstores and movie theaters; they argued about the merits of the new *Dr Who* versus the old (she was for the remake, he defended the original); and they talked about Chicago's impressive array of comic book stores. All in all, a pleasant evening that Abbey would've been happy to repeat.

Which she did.

Twelve times.

And then Murphy Napier made his move.

Abbey says, 'You want me to spill?'

Cheryl says, 'Yes, Bynum, I want you to spill.'

'Fine.' Abbey sighs. 'I mean, it's not like he's stalking me, or anything.'

Cheryl says, 'Whoa, who said anything about stalking?'

Abbey ignores her. 'He's not obsessed. He doesn't call me *all* the time.'

Cheryl asks, 'Who said anything about obsession?'

Abbey says, 'Maybe it wasn't the best idea.'

'Maybe *what* wasn't the best idea?'

'Maybe I shouldn't have told him.'

'Told him what? Told *who* what? Who are we talking about? *What* are we talking about?'

'I should've kept it going the way it was going. It was fine. Okay, it wasn't *fine*, but it was what it was, and it could've been worse.'

'Kept what going? What wasn't fine?'

'I mean, it wasn't *not* fine. It was okay. But it was safe, you know?'

Cheryl takes a deep drag of her cigarette, then says, 'No. No, Abbey, I *don't* know.'

Abbey checks her clock: 9.57. Staff meeting time. 'Crap. I've gotta bounce.'

'Wait,' Cheryl says, 'please tell me what the fuck you're talking about.'

'I told him.'

'Told who?'

'Murphy.'

'What did you tell him?'

Abbey cups her hand over the phone's mouthpiece and whispers, 'I told him the one thing that I should never tell a guy.'

'Wait, you told him *that*?'

'Yeah. I told him *that*. He kind of figured it out himself. But I told him everything.'

'Oh. Shit.'

'Yeah. Shit. Exactly.'

'Why?'

'I had to,' Abbey moans. 'He didn't give me any choice. He kept pressing for an answer, and pressing, and pressing, and . . .' She sees Suzanne give her the high sign. 'Shit. I'll call you after my meeting.'

'Cool. I'll be waiting. And don't forget, you have to pick—'

Abbey hangs up.

5

At first, sex with Murphy Napier was, well, let's call it less-than-time-consuming.

After their first attempt – which lasted approximately forty-nine seconds from initial penetration to Murphy's completion – he said, 'I know you are not going to believe this, Ab, but I am no longer a virgin.'

Trying to keep the frustration out of her voice, Abbey pointed to the full condom dangling off the end of his penis and said, 'That's pretty obvious, Murphy.'

He blushed. 'No, let me rephrase that. When I bedded you just now, I was not a virgin.' He puffed up his chest. 'As a matter of fact, you are the *third* woman I have made love to.'

'Here's a tip for you, friend,' she said. 'It's a bad idea to give a girl you've just slept with for the first time your sex statistics—'

'Ah,' Murphy interrupted. 'That makes sense. Thank you for the advice.'

'. . . especially a girl whom you've been macking on for since college, which is like five years ago—'

'Five years, six months, and eighteen days, to be precise.'

Abbey blinked. 'Five years, six months and ... and ...'

'Eighteen days.'

'Right. Eighteen days.'

Abbey knew that Murphy was into her big time, but she figured that between the time he disappeared from her life and now, he'd let it go. Wrong.

Four days after their evening out at Hot Chocolate, Murphy invited Abbey to the symphony. Being a sucker for a good string section, Abbey accepted without hesitation, a decision she regretted at the end of the night, when he tried to convert his chaste-good-night-kiss-on-the-cheek to a horny-good-night-snog-with-his-tongue-on-her-tonsils.

Right in front of Symphony Center, right on Michigan Avenue, right in front of a bunch of tuxedo-clad music lovers, Abbey put her hands on Murphy's chest and shoved him. Fortunately for everybody involved, she pulled back at the last millisecond; had she gone all out – had she shoved him with her full strength – Murphy Napier would've ended up somewhere in the Chicago River, three or four miles away.

She said, 'What the fuck, Murphy? What the fuck?' (Abbey Bynum wasn't one to drop an F-bomb, so you knew she was more than a little irked.)

'I am sorry, Ab. I just thought ... I just thought ... I just thought ...'

'You just thought *what*?'

'Well, our thighs were brushing up against each other during the show, and . . .'

Abbey pointed to historical Symphony Center and said, 'Murphy, this place was built a zillion years ago for people who were *way* smaller than we are. My thigh was brushing up against the woman who was on my other side, and you don't see her trying to jam her tongue down my throat.'

'But . . . but . . . but . . .'

'No buts, pal. I'm taking a cab home.'

She ran from him, and hopped into a waiting taxi. As the car pulled away, she looked out the window.

Murphy was crying. She'd made nerdy old Murphy Napier cry. And that broke her heart a little bit. *But*, she reasoned, *he started it*. That made her feel a little better. But just a little.

The next morning, at 9.01, Abbey was delivered the biggest bouquet of flowers she'd ever received, by far: dozens of red roses, and white orchids, and pink tulips, and ivory calla lilies, and purple hydrangeas. The card read simply, 'Please forgive my impertinence. Sincerely, Murphy Napier.' She smiled despite herself; who else but Murphy used both his first and last name, and the word 'impertinence' on an I'm-sorry-for-mauling-you-after-the-symphony card.

Out of curiosity, she turned to her computer and surfed over to the florists' website to find out how much something that ornate, that beautiful, and that *big* cost:

$419. Abbey (correctly) guessed that the FBI didn't pay its newbies particularly well, and she (correctly) estimated that the flowers cost Murphy half of his weekly salary.

Suzanne sidled over. 'Holy Christ. Now *that*'s a bouquet. Somebody must love the hell out of you.'

Abbey stood up and sniffed one of the roses. 'Yeah. I think you're right. Unfortunately.'

'And you don't feel the same way?'

'And I don't feel the same way.'

'Bummer. Care to talk about it?'

They went into Suzanne's office, where Abbey gave her boss the Bynum/Napier backstory. After Abbey finished her tale of semi-woe, Suzanne asked, 'A plaid bow tie with a plaid shirt? Is he being ironic?'

Abbey shook her head. 'No. He's being Murphy.'

'Ah.' She paused. 'So do you want my advice?'

Suzanne had been happily married for nine years, so Abbey figured she had some idea of how love worked. 'Sure,' she said.

'Give him a shot.'

'Really?'

'Yep. Really.'

'Why?'

Suzanne shrugged. 'Why not? It's not like you have anything else going on.'

'Don't remind me. But the thing is, I'm totally not attracted to him.'

'Is he unattractive?'

'He could use a makeover, but he's okay.'

'Is he grossly overweight? Does he smell?'

'No. And no.'

'Is he mean?'

'No. Uptight, but not mean. He can actually be pretty sweet sometimes.'

'Would he call you the day after?'

'The day after what?'

'The day after . . . you know.'

'Oh. Yeah. Absolutely.'

'So give him a shot.'

'I mean, I get your point. I don't necessarily agree with it, but I get it.' Abbey blew a stray ringlet out of her eyes. 'Okay, just for the hell of it, let's say I do it. Let's say I do it, and let's say it sucks. What then?'

'Then you either stay friends, or you don't. Which begs the question, how much do you value his friendship?'

Abbey was quiet for a bit; eventually she took a deep breath and said, 'If I'm being honest with myself, I'd miss him, but it wouldn't kill me.'

Suzanne said, 'Okay, then. Worst case scenario, you have shitty sex, and you move on. Best case scenario, you have great sex, and you've got a boyfriend. Or at least a fuck buddy.'

Abbey laughed. 'You're the best boss ever, boss lady. Barry Belmont wouldn't talk to me like this.'

'Oh, he *totally* would. Problem is, he'd get a hard-on halfway through the conversation.'

Picturing the firm's senior partner pitching a tent, Abbey said, 'Ewwwwww!'

'Yeah,' Suzanne nodded, 'I saw it in the swimming pool at last year's company retreat. *Ewwwww* is right.'

So Abbey Bynum took her boss lady's advice and had sex with Murphy Napier. Which, as noted previously, lasted forty-nine seconds.

To his credit, over the next few months, Murphy did his best to compensate for his lack of lasting power. He worked on his oral skills, which, Abbey was pleased to note, improved over time; he even learned how to make her come on a semi-regular basis. (They weren't the best orgasms, granted, but they were orgasms nonetheless.) Also, at his own behest, Murphy made a trip to the Pleasure Chest, Chicago's finest sex toys emporium, and bought a couple of battery-operated gizmos that helped immensely, so much so that Abbey kicked herself for not picking them up for personal use years ago. He even doubled up on condoms, which helped him to last longer. At least a little bit.

After eight months of mediocre sex and slightly above-average dates, Abbey started making excuses to not go out – or, for that matter, to stay in – with Murphy:

Typical excuse number 1: 'I have an early meeting at work.' (That was a lie. Suzanne never asked her to come in early.)

Typical excuse number 2: 'I'm going out with the girls.' (Another fib. Cheryl was Abbey's only 'girl', and she was on tour. As usual.)

Typical excuse number 3: 'I'm going to my spin class.' (The most ridiculous story of them all. The last thing a girl with insanely fast metabolism and the ability to lift a car without breaking a sweat needs is a trip to the gym.)

It took a few months for Murphy to get the hint. In a move that Abbey suspected he made to save face, he broke up with her over a plate of steak frites at a cute little French bistro on the north side of Chicago. Any face he saved was lost over the next two years. Two years in which he pursued Abbey almost religiously.

He tried to win her heart with flowers, and candies, and offers of spa weekends, and gift certificates to bookstores, and jewelry. Time and again, Abbey told the poor man to save his money because she wasn't interested. He didn't listen, and the gifts kept coming.

Every so often, Abbey met an interesting guy, and every so often, she'd go out on a date, and once in a rare while, she'd accept an offer to spend the night. But nothing popped. Nobody stood out. It was all very . . . average. It felt blah. It felt ordinary. Everything felt ordinary.

Abbey was bored and lonely, and Murphy was persistent and flattering, and finally, after a particularly well-timed, well-chosen gift – a membership to the Exotic Fruit of the Month Club that was delivered on the third day of a particularly gnarly menstrual cycle – she succumbed. They had dinner, then they went back to Abbey's condo, then they had fast sex, and then they went to sleep. It was what it was: safe, uneventful, and easy.

They soon fell into a pattern, which consisted of two nights a week together, a weekday night at her place (even though Murphy's apartment was within walking distance from Abbey's office, she hated to break her morning pre-work routine), and a weekend night at his. They only had two ground rules: they could see other people – which Abbey did, and which Murphy didn't – and if somebody had to cancel one of their nights together, the other party wasn't allowed to pout.

Yes, it was what it was: safe, uneventful, and easy.

But it wasn't enough for Murphy.

A bbey speed-walks into the staff meeting, and since she arrives late, she's forced to sit on the windowsill. (RBP&A has been doing well over the last few years, and, rather than funneling all their extra cash into the partners' pockets like 99.999 per cent of the other law firms in the United States would likely do, they've chosen to hire more lawyers. Unfortunately, they haven't expanded the conference room to account for the expanded staff, so if you're late for a meeting, you're sitting on either the sill or the floor. Considering her tardiness, Abbey counts herself lucky that she's not dirtying her black pants on the carpet.)

The meeting, which is compulsory, is, as usual, boring as hell for the paras who aren't deeply entrenched in a high-profile case, and Abbey – who's kicking herself for not grabbing some coffee – is having trouble staying awake. She has to pay attention, though, because, like the hated high school teacher with the uncanny knack of knowing when you're zoning out, Barry Belmont gets off on calling on one of the paralegals to answer a random, sometimes tangential question about a case that might or might not be on the meeting's agenda. There isn't any punishment for missing a question, just public ridicule, something that fifty-something male lawyers like Barry seem to get off on.

Abbey decides that if she gives herself something to focus on – something other than the snoozy legal stuff – she'll have a better chance of remaining alert, so, for the second time in the last twenty-four hours, she decides to use the Weird Stuff.

She looks around the room and makes brief eye contact with Giselle. Abbey learns that Giselle and her boyfriend had sex last night on the roof of their building, a not-uncommon occurrence, because Giselle is somewhat of an exhibitionist, and is thrilled by the notion that her next-door neighbor might jerk-off to the scene. Giselle's boyfriend has told her repeatedly that he's not into this, but he'll do it because he loves her. Giselle loves him back, but not as much as he loves her, and she's considering breaking up with him, but he has the biggest thing she's ever put into her other—

Yikes, Abbey almost says aloud. This falls under the category of too much information, so Abbey closes her eyes, and the spell is broken.

Accidentally, Abbey, with her mind wide open, makes eye contact with Suzanne. She would have never knowingly set foot into her boss's psyche, but now that she's there, she might as well take a look around.

Much to Abbey's delight, Suzanne is exactly who she

portrays herself to be: a considerate, kind woman, whose thoughts drift from the matter at hand (a case involving a young computer whiz whose program was ripped off by a massive software conglomerate, a clear case of trademark infringement), to that evening's plans (she can't decide whether to take her husband to Tru or Moto for his half-birthday), to concern for Abbey (Suzanne thinks, 'That girl doesn't eat enough, or sleep enough.'). Abbey is touched; a lump forms in her throat. But even though her nerves are raw and her emotions are right up at the surface, she manages to keep from crying. Barely.

Two hours of yakkity-yak later, the meeting is over, and everybody files out of the conference room except for Abbey, who stares out the window at the Chicago skyline she so loves: the Hancock Building, the Sears Tower (they renamed it Willis Tower in 2009, but she refuses to acknowledge the change), the Prudential Plaza, the astounding Trump Tower, and One Magnificent Mile, one structure next to the other, next to another, creating a single, lovely whole. She wishes she could fly from building to building, and become part of the skyline herself, to somehow disappear into the architecture. Abbey looks over her shoulder. Seeing nobody's in the room, she cracks open one of the windows, sticks her face outside, and breathes in the morning city air. (Okay, it's not as sweet as the night-time suburban air, but it's still better than office air.) Without thinking, with her body and brain working on autopilot, she opens the window wider and dangles her foot over the ledge.

'Abbey, what the hell are you doing?!'

It's Suzanne.

Abbey says, 'Nothing! Getting air!' She brings her foot back inside.

Suzanne says, 'Was it my imagination, or were you dangling your foot out of the window?'

Abbey gives Suzanne a distinctly false laugh. 'What? Dangling? What do you mean? That's crazy talk. Why would I dangle? Stop being silly. Of course it was your imagination. I mean . . . I mean . . . I mean . . .' Abbey points to Suzanne's eyes – 'you're not wearing your glasses!'

Suzanne shoots Abbey a suspicious look. 'Just getting air?'

'Yes. Just getting air.'

'You weren't going to, I don't know, drop your legal pad out the window? I know the meeting was boring, but it wasn't *that* bad.'

Abbey chuckles. 'You're messing with me, aren't you?'

'Yes, I'm messing with you.' As the two women head back to their desks, Suzanne asks, 'You sure you don't want to go home? You're pretty out of it, sweetie.'

'I'm sure I don't want to go home. If I go home . . .' Abbey's voice trails off.

Suzanne says, 'If you go home, *what*?'

Had Abbey finished the sentence, it would've gone something like this: *If I go home, I might go for a daytime fly, and somebody would see me, and all hell will break loose, and I kind of don't care*. But as it was, she said, 'Nothing.'

Back at her desk, Abbey sees she has a voicemail: Cheryl.

'Okay, bitch, here's the deal: you're going home now, you're putting on comfy clothes, and you're driving to O'Hare. I'm on American Airlines, flight 402, landing, symmetrically enough, at 4.02. I'll see you at baggage claim. I know you didn't remember I was coming, and even though that's pathetic, I forgive you, because I only mentioned it once, and that was in passing, and I forgot to email you my itinerary, so it's sort of my fault. So, you know, whatever.'

Abbey smiles, and again remembers why she only has one true friend: because nobody will ever treat her as well as Cheryl . . . even when she forgets about her visits.

She writes down the flight information, then pokes her head into Suzanne's office and says, 'Actually, I'm going to take you up on your offer, boss lady.'

Suzanne looks up from her laptop. 'That offer being . . .?'

'Being me going home.'

'Great! Get out of here. Come in late tomorrow, if you want.'

Knowing Cheryl will want to either go hear a bunch of local bands, or go out drinking, or stay up all night blabbering, or all of the above, Abbey says, 'I'll take you up on that, too.'

'Great. Text me when you're on your way in. Now get out of here.'

Which is exactly what Abbey does. Which gives her an hour of walking and train-riding to think about the Murphy situation. Which she doesn't want to do. But she does. She has no choice.

The argument started innocuously enough: Abbey wanted sushi, and Murphy wanted pizza, but within five minutes, it had become an onslaught of, 'You always get what *you* want', and, 'All you ever want is what's best for *you*', and, 'You don't feel the same way about *me* that I feel about *you*', and 'This is the best I can do', and so on, and so on, and so on. Like much of their relationship, the argument was dull and uninspired. Unlike much of their relationship, however, it was *loud*.

The truth of the matter was that this had been building up for a while. Murphy was frustrated with Abbey's lack of emotion, and Abbey was frustrated with Murphy's neediness. Murphy was fed up with Abbey never wanting to do anything fun or new, and Abbey was fed up with Murphy always blabbing about his job, his job, his job.

There was no question that Abbey cared for Murphy, and vice versa, but they'd hit a wall. On a certain level, hitting a wall happens to most every couple; the question becomes, when you arrive at the wall, do you break through it, or bang your head against it? If you want your relationship to work – or even simply to *continue* – you put on your protective gear and fight your way through. But on this day, at this hour, at this minute, Abbey

Bynum and Murphy Napier chose the headbanging route.

Twenty-three minutes into the scream-fest, Murphy crossed the line: 'You have been leading me along. All this time, Ab. Leading me on. Playing me, even.'

Her mouth fell open. 'Are you kidding me? I've been nothing but honest. *Nothing*. I've told you every step of the way what you can and can't expect of me, and what I will and won't give you. You heard what you wanted to hear. And you know what? It's never been about me, or what I want. It's always about you, you, you.' She paused. 'Let me ask you a question: Do you even like me, or am I some sort of . . . of . . . of *trophy* for you to show off, or to make you feel better about yourself, or whatever?'

Like a naughty child whose parents told him he was grounded for the weekend, Murphy kicked the wall. 'You are a cock tease, Ab.'

As if to mock him, Abbey kicked a folding chair. The chair flew across the room as if it was jet-propelled, crashed into the wall, and broke into six pieces. Abbey was surprised it didn't fly *through* the wall.

Murphy gawked at Abbey, then gawked at the chair. 'Wow, Ab. I did not realise I had angered you that badly.'

Abbey's immediate instinct was to get Murphy's mind off the chair, so she walked across the room and tenderly rested her hand on his cheek. 'I care about you, Murphy. I really do. And I never wanted to hurt you. But I'm giving you all of myself that I can give. If that's not enough for you, I respect that. I understand that. I've been in your shoes, you know. Several times.'

Murphy offered her a tiny, tiny smile, then took her hand in both of his. 'I appreciate that, Ab. I really do. It is just hard for me. Most of the time, a little of you is enough, but sometimes it is not.' He kissed her hand, then turned around, pointed at the chair, and said, 'Those spin classes are doing wonders for your leg strength, am I correct?'

'Yeah. Right.' Abbey chuckled weakly. 'I guess they are.'

'I mean, *wow*! That was *crazy*! That chair had to be going twenty-five, maybe thirty miles per hour. Look at how badly it broke! I'm impressed, Ab. *Quite* impressed!'

Abbey shrugged. 'I've got good legs, I guess.'

'You have *great* legs. But I didn't know they were *that* great.'

'Yeah. Well.' She clapped once. 'I'm starving. I can live without sushi. How about we meet in the middle and order some Thai food?'

Murphy said, 'How about we sit down and talk?'

'I'm kind of hungry.'

'And I am kind of curious.' He pointed to the sofa and, in a commanding, distinctly un-Murphy-like tone, growled, 'Sit.'

She sat. Even though she could send him through the window with a flick of her finger, Abbey was suddenly a bit frightened. Usually, Murphy wasn't much of a presence, only slightly more charismatic than a lamp-post. Now, he filled up the room. She understood why the FBI would find Murphy Napier to be a great asset.

Pacing up and down the living room, he said, 'Listen, Abbey . . .' (This was the first time he'd called her Abbey rather than Ab in, well, *forever*.) '. . . we have known each other for quite a while, and we have spent hours upon hours in each other's company, and I have noticed some things about you that I find odd, and I have yet to comment on them, because I did not believe they merited mentioning.' He pointed at the pieces of the folding chair. 'Now, Ab, *now* it merits. *Now* it must be mentioned. Now talk to me.'

Stalling, Abbey asked, 'What do you mean, you've *noticed some things*?'

'Back at Northwestern, remember the day you refused my advances?'

'No,' she lied.

He continued to pace. 'I remember it well. I remember you ran from me. I remember you ran from me *fast*. Blindingly fast. Or at least it appeared that way. I found it odd, how fast you seemed to be moving, but I chalked it up to a trick of the light, compounded by my distress. In my, I guess you could say, *discomfit*, I believed my perception was altered, that you only *appeared* to be moving more quickly than you actually were moving. So I filed it away. I forgot about it until . . .' He trailed off, then stopped pacing, and gave her an intent stare. 'Do you recall the night at the symphony? The night when I unfortunately and rudely attempted to kiss you without your approval, an act I still regret? Do you recall?'

Abbey couldn't worm her way out of that one. 'Yes. I recall.'

'Ah. Fantastic. Do you also recall when you pushed me away?'

'Yeah.'

'Do you recall that you shoved me hard?'

'I don't recall doing anything *hard*. I remember I pushed you away.' She thought, *But I held back*.

'That is correct. But what you are neglecting to mention is that after you pushed me, you *pulled* me.'

Now she was legitimately confused. 'What do you mean, pushed then pulled?'

'I kissed you, then you placed both of your hands on my chest, then thrust your arms forward. The wind was knocked out of me. I felt like I was leaving my feet. But before I fell over, or flew backwards, or whatever would have happened to me, you grasped my shoulder in your right hand, and my shirt collar in your left, and held me firm.'

'I did?'

'Yes, Ab. You did. Again, I thought nothing of it, because I was so distraught at my behavior, as well as your reaction to my behavior. I blamed the strength of your shove to adrenaline. Again, I filed it away.' He stopped pacing, and kneeled down directly in front of her. 'I want you to think hard now. Do you remember the evening we went to Alinea?'

'Most of it.' What with its imaginative, molecular gastronomical approach to cooking, Alinea was one of the coolest restaurants in the world. (How Murphy managed to afford the eighteen-course prix fix extravaganza, she'll never know.) Their wine pairings were brilliant and plentiful, and by the time they left the restaurant, Abbey was hammered. Everything from dessert until she woke up with a splitting headache at noon was a pleasant blank.

Murphy said, 'Most of it, you say. Well, Abbey, I recall *all* of it. So you do not remember taking the cab to your apartment.'

Abbey shook her head.

'Which means, obviously, you do not remember arriving at your front door.'

Again, she shook her head.

'So clearly, you do not remember your inability to hold the keys tightly enough in your hand to utilise them in their proper manner.'

'Um, *what*?'

'Putting it simply, you were too drunk to open the door.'

'Oh. Right. That's been known to happen. So what?'

'*So*, I offered to take the keys from you, and you tossed them to me, but the toss was, well, errant, I guess you could say. Quite errant, for that matter. Errant to the point that the keys ended up in the middle of the street, halfway down the block. While I was retrieving said keys, I heard a loud noise. When I turned around, the door was open. As we walked through the threshold, I inspected the door itself. It appeared that somebody had torn the lock apart.'

Abbey didn't remember ripping open the door, but she did remember a locksmith working on it when she went down to get her newspaper the following morning. She said to Murphy, 'I don't know what to tell you. The door was probably broken when we got there. What're you trying to say?'

'What I'm trying to say, Abbey, is that I believe you are an inordinately strong woman, and I would like to bring you to Washington. There are some people whom I believe you would enjoy meeting, and who would enjoy meeting you.'

'Murphy, you're being ridiculous.' Abbey tried to stand up, but he placed his hands on her shoulders and rudely guided her back to the sofa. She pushed his hands away, being careful not to use anything close to her full strength. 'Cut it out, Murphy. Stop playing G-Man. This isn't funny any more.'

He nodded. 'You're right. It's not.' And then he walked across the room, picked up a wooden end table, and threw it directly at Abbey's head. Strictly on instinct, inches before it would've smacked her in the face, Abbey swatted away the table with her right hand. It flew across the living room, crashed through the window, and landed approximately 150 yards away.

They stared at each other for a bit, unmoving, breathing heavily. Murphy finally broke the silence: 'Talk to me, Ab. *Now.*'

She talked. She had no choice.

It took her only thirty-ish minutes to tell her story – learning about the powers, figuring out how to control them, and why she hates them – and the fact that she could tell it so quickly made her realise that there wasn't that much to tell. If Carin and Gary were aliens from another dimension, that would've made for an interesting tale, but this was merely a story about a young woman who lost the genetic lottery and ended up with something she didn't want. She might as well have told him about why she had to wear a retainer for most of her childhood, because on a certain level, it was equally unexciting.

After she finished, she asked, 'Now what?'

He said, 'Before I answer that, I would like to apologise profusely for throwing furniture at your face.'

She said, 'Yeah. About that. Not cool.'

'I would not have done it if I was not a hundred per cent certain you could protect yourself.'

'You were a hundred per cent certain? How could you be a hundred per cent certain? What if you were wrong? What if I didn't have the reflexes and the muscles? What if you smashed my face in?' He sat down next to her on the sofa and put his hand on her shoulder. She took a deep breath, knocked his hand away, and said, 'Don't touch me, Murphy. You're not allowed to touch me. Ever. Got it?'

He nodded. 'Yes, Ab. I have it. And now I will answer your question with another question that may seem odd: what do you think of me?'

Abbey asked, 'What do you mean, what do I think of you?'

'Here is what *I* think you think of me: I think you feel that I am intelligent, but I also believe you view me as a bit of a fool. I think you underestimate me as a person, *and* as an FBI agent. You may not believe this, but I know what I am doing. I am quite observant, and I can intuit with the best of them. There have been other tell-tale signs, Ab. Sometimes while we were making love, you would throw me around as if I was a rag doll.'

Abbey thought, *Oops*.

Murphy continued, 'And sometimes when we were running after a taxi, you picked up speed a little *too* quickly. Taken individually, one might write off those events as anomalies, but if you add them together, well, suffice it to say that I have seen enough weird stuff out of you over the last couple of years to feel comfortable about throwing a table at your head.'

She winced when he said, 'weird stuff.'

'That's wonderful,' Abbey hissed. 'Now call me crazy, but I'd never feel comfortable throwing a table at the head of somebody I had feelings for. But that's me. I'm strange like that.' She stood up. 'I'm getting some wine. You want something?'

'Water, please. Thank you.'

She uncorked some Chardonnay and took a long swig right from the bottle, then said, 'Get it yourself.'

Murphy put on a pained expression. 'Ab, I am not

here to cause trouble. I want to help you. Let me take you to DC. For two days, three at the most.'

She took a wineglass from her cabinet, filled it almost to the top, took three huge gulps, belched, then said, 'Do you know what'll happen if I go to DC, Murphy? Do you?'

'Of course I do.'

'No, of course you don't. I will be *disappeared*, Murphy. I will become a non-person. They'll grab my whole family, then they'll tell Cheryl we were all murdered, and they'll suck me dry until they figure out why I am the way I am.'

'That will absolutely not happen. I discussed it with—'

'You *discussed* it?! Goddamn it!' She polished off the rest of the wine, then threw the glass into the sink; it shattered, and shrapnel flew everywhere. 'I'm *screwed*, Murphy. You screwed me. Royally.'

'Calm down, Ab. I did not tell anybody your name, or your location, or any of your specific powers. I merely spoke to my superior in speculative fashion, and he informed me that the protocol for a situation like this is simple, and set in stone: you would be interviewed, then examined by a physician, then tested in a casual, pressure-free environment. Nothing would be done without your approval. *Nothing*. Everything will be put in writing. You may have as many witnesses present as you wish during every phase of the process. It will be safe. You will be protected, as will The Company.'

'You mean The Bureau.'

'The Company. Are you interested?'

Abbey kneeled down, took a roll of paper towels from under her sink, and began cleaning up the shattered wineglass. 'Why, Murphy? Why couldn't you just ask me like a normal person instead of getting all Jack Bauer on me?'

'Would you have told me the truth?'

'No, probably not. But it would've been my decision. But no matter what, it's none of your damn business.'

'It is *very* much my damn business. I care about you very much, Ab.' He examined his fingernails, then said, 'It is safe to say that I love you.'

'You love me? This is how you treat somebody you love?'

'I want to protect you, Abbey. I want to put you in touch with people who can take care of you, should the need arise . . .'

'For future reference, Murphy, throwing a table at somebody isn't necessarily the best way of expressing your love. I'm just saying.'

He ignored her. '. . . and I want you to reach your full potential.'

'What do you mean, my full potential?'

'I mean, you could take those powers of yours and use them to be an honest-to-goodness protector of justice. You could make a difference. You could be a true-to-life superheroine, an inspiration to little girls all over the world.' He took a deep breath. 'An inspiration to us all.'

She examined the countertop and the floor for any rogue pieces of wineglass; it looked clean. 'Sounds like that's a fancy way of saying you want to recruit me.'

Murphy nodded. 'I cannot argue that, Ab. I mean, I would be honored if you would work with us.' He paused, then repeated, 'You could make a difference. A true difference.'

Abbey understood where he was coming from, but the question was, *Did she want to make a difference?* The answer was a tenuous *no*. For Abbey Bynum, simplicity was peace, and trying to catch bad guys – or whatever it was that Murphy and his people would want her to do – was far from simple. All she wanted out of life was to have as much time as possible with her family and Cheryl, to have enough money so she could have a nice meal, and not to think about the Weird Stuff.

And now here comes Murphy Napier, getting all up in her business. Murphy Napier was messing with her groove. Murphy Napier was killing her buzz. And that wouldn't do. It was time for Murphy Napier to be gone.

Abbey sighed. 'Okay, friend, here's the deal. Here's what's going to happen. You're going to leave this apartment. You're never going to call me again. You're not ever going to mention my name to anybody you work with. You're not going to say another word about me to *anybody*. From this moment on, forget me. At best, I should be a trace memory to you. You and me, we're *done*. Now leave. Please. And I don't want to hear a peep out of you. You know what I can do, and I won't hesitate to do it.' (She wouldn't think of hurting him, but he didn't know that, now did he?)

Murphy left without a word.

Two hours later, soon after midnight, she went up to her roof, then she jumped off, then she flew all over the city without a scrunchie, then she returned home at – according to the glow-in-the-dark Mickey Mouse clock on her living-room wall – 4.27, then she went to work, then she went to a boring staff meeting, then her boss sent her home, and then she went to the airport to meet Cheryl.

Yes, it was quite a day for Abbey Bynum.

When Cheryl Sheldon sees her bestest buddy in the whole widest world over on the far end of the baggage claim area, she drops her acoustic guitar and runs into her friend's arms, and people gawk. But if you saw a pink-haired girl wearing a sleeveless Lou Reed baby-doll tee, no bra, a short black skirt, fishnets, and black boots with four-inch-heels sprinting past the baggage carousels screaming 'Abbeeeeeeeeeeey' at the top of her lungs, you'd gawk too.

Abbey has no problem with Cheryl's intrinsic loudness when they're at a smaller, grungier venue – if Cheryl wants to get loud in a bar or a club, no problem – but in a place as massive and busy as O'Hare Airport, it's sometimes . . . disconcerting. Today, however, Abbey is perfectly content to have the outside world pay attention to Cheryl, and completely ignore her.

In the car, Cheryl skips pleasantries and says, 'Okay, Bynum. Spill it all.'

So Abbey spills it all.

After absorbing the Murphy story silently for a bit, Cheryl says, 'I never liked that dude.'

Abbey points out, 'You never *met* that dude.'

'True. But I still don't like him. Do you think he'll stay away from you? I mean, if you threatened me with violence, I know *I*'d stay away. But I'm wacky like that.'

'I don't know, Cher. He's a jerk, but he's not an asshole.'

'From where I'm sitting, he's a jerk *and* an asshole. *And* a douchebag. *And* a pissant. And a—'

'He's not *that* bad.'

'No, he's worse. He betrayed you.'

'He didn't betray me. He didn't tell anybody my name.'

'Maybe he did, maybe he didn't. But he *did* throw furniture at you. Not cool.'

Abbey nods. 'There's that.'

Cheryl chews on a strand of her hair. 'Here's something I'm wondering: are you worried that the Men in Black might come by in the middle of the night and kidnap you?'

Abbey disregards the question and says, 'Are you hungry? I'm dying for sushi. We were going to have it last night but—'

'Don't blow me off on this, Bynum. Are you worried about some government guys taking you in to wherever they take people like you in to?'

'Nobody's taking me anywhere. If anything, I'm probably better off now than I was before.'

'Yeah? How do you figure that?'

'Well, I mean, like, an FBI guy is aware of me, so if some baddie from, like, Afghanistan or something finds out about me, and I disappear, the Feds will come after me.'

Cheryl shakes her head. 'You just go right ahead and keep telling yourself that. If that helps you sleep at night, more power to you.'

Abbey pulls off of the highway, and into the parking lot of Akai Hana, Wilmette's best sushi joint. After they're seated at the bar, and, after each downs a saki bomb in record time, Abbey says, 'I can move to a new apartment or a new city all I want to, but Murphy'll find me. He has the whole goddamn Company at his disposal.'

'What's The Company?'

'It's what Murphy calls The Bureau.'

'I thought the CIA was The Company.'

'I did too. But what do I know? Point is, these guys arrest bad guys who're trying to hide from them every day, and I'm not hiding. If they wanted me, all they'd have to do is grab me at Union Station after work.'

Cheryl flags down the waitress and orders some edamame and two miso soups. 'Yeah, but then you could kick those guys to the curb with, like, your fingertip.'

'Great, sure, right there in the middle of the busiest train station in Illinois, I'm going to get into a fistfight with a bunch of law enforcement officials. They'd bring in the Army.'

'And The Company.'

'Right. And The Bureau.'

'And the President.'

'And the Prime Minister of England.'

'And the Queen of Cleveland.'

'It'd be a mess.'

Cheryl asks, 'So you're not going to do anything? You're going to go about your business like nothing happened? You're just going to let it lie?'

Abbey orders another saki bomb, then says, 'I don't think I have a choice.'

On the way back to Abbey's apartment, they stop at a liquor store and pick up a six-pack of Guinness and a bottle of Gray Goose. Three hours later, they're drunk as hell.

Cheryl slurs, 'I wanna go.'

Abbey slurs back, 'Y'can't go. You jess got here.'

'No, I wanna go *up*.'

'Up where?'

Cheryl staggers to the window and points to the sky. 'Up *there*. With *you*. Fly me, Bynum! Fly me to the moon. Let me play among the stars. I wanna go, I wanna go, I wanna go!'

Abbey throws herself face down on the sofa. 'Noooooooo. No, no, no, no, no. I'm never going to go up there again.'

'You've been saying that for, like, a million years now. You say, *I'm not going to go up there*, and you go up there, and you never take me.'

'You live' – Abbey points to her left, then her right, then her left – 'that way.' She then points to the floor. 'And you don't live here.'

'I don't live where?'

'You don't live in Illinois. Plus you never asked me to take you up, and how'm I supposed to know you want to go up if you never asked me to take you? Hunh? Answer me that, Miss Smarty Pants.' She pauses, then says, 'I haven't been this wasted in forever.'

'Me neither . . . if by *forever* you mean *last Thursday* . . .' Cheryl giggles, then says, 'I'm here now. I'm asking now.'

Abbey sits up. 'I dunno. I've never flown drunk before.'

'It might be fun. The cold air'll sober us up, I bet.'

'I dunno. It might mess us up worse. Like you might get airsick or something. You might puke. Like on some poor, unsuspecting pedestrian.'

Cheryl points at the Mickey Mouse clock. 'It's, what, 3.30 and we're in Wilmette. The only pedestrians out are squirrels and bunny rabbits. Now go put on your cape and tights, and let's fly the fuck out of here.'

Abbey stands up. 'I don't have a cape. Or tights. Well, I have tights. But I don't fly in 'em.'

'What do you fly in?'

'Usually my jammies. Sometimes my lucky Chicago Bears sweatpants.'

'You still have those?'

'They're almost broken in just right. A few hundred

more runs through the washing machine, and they'll be the perfect level of softness.'

Cheryl laughs. 'Okay, what should I wear?'

'I dunno. Something warmer than that.'

' 'Kay. Gimme the Bears pants.'

' 'Kay. I'll also get us scrunchies. When you fly, you *gotta* have a scrunchie. Trust me, I know.'

Cheryl's right about one thing: the cold air sobers them up. She peers over the edge of the roof and says, 'Shit, I don't know about this, Bynum. I think I'm changing my mind.'

Abbey says, 'Hey, *you* asked *me*. We can go to bed, as far as I'm concerned. Remember, I only got about an hour of sleep last night.'

Cheryl sits down. 'You won't drop me, will you?'

'No way. I took Dave up a zillion times. I never dropped him.'

Again, Cheryl peers over the edge. 'Fuck it. Let's do this.'

'You sure?'

'You only live once.'

'If you want out, I won't blame you.'

'I want it.'

'Okay, but if you're going to puke, you have to give me some notice so I can get you over the lake.'

'You want me to stick my finger down my throat right now? Get it out of my system?'

'No, that's okay.' Abbey opens up her arms and says, 'Get over here. I'm going to pop your flying cherry.'

Abbey and Cheryl are exactly the same size, but even if Cheryl were nine feet tall and weighed four hundred pounds, Abbey would be able to pick her up with no effort whatsoever. She hugs her friend tightly to her chest and says, 'Ready?'

'Shouldn't I be facing the other direction?' Cheryl asks. 'If we're face-to-face, I'll be looking at you, not the rest of the world.'

'Right. Good point. Let me take you from behind.'

'I'm not that kind of girl, Bynum.'

'You're *totally* that kind of girl, Sheldon.' She spins her friend around, wraps her arms around her waist, then counts off, 'Five . . . four . . . three . . . two . . . one . . . *blast off*!'

They don't move.

Cheryl says, 'What the hell. Are you okay?'

Abbey says, 'Oh my God. It's gone. I can't do it any more.'

'Oh my God. Do you, I dunno, want me to take you to the hospital or something?'

'I don't know.' Then Abbey yells, '*Psyche!*', jumps off the roof, and takes to the sky.

Cheryl screams, 'Yoooooooouuuuu biiiiiiiiiitch! I fucking *hate* yoooooooouuuuu biiiiiiiiiitch!' Then she cracks up, laughing like a loon. A drunk, pink-haired loon.

Abbey says, 'Pipe down. You're going to wake up the whole neighborhood. Now steel yourself. We're going higher. *Way* higher.'

And they go higher.

They don't speak, because the wind in their respective ears has all but rendered them deaf. At two thousand feet, Abbey slows down to float, and Cheryl gasps. 'Holy shit, Bynum. This is . . . this is . . . this is . . . *fuck, wow.*'

Abbey looks at the stars, the skyline, the street. '*Fuck, wow* sums it up pretty nicely.'

As they head slowly south towards downtown Chicago, Cheryl asks, 'How can you not do this every day? If I'm you, I'm waking up, flying, eating breakfast, flying some more, eating lunch, flying some more, eating dinner, flying some more, then sleeping. That'd be my day.'

'No it wouldn't. No way.'

'Why do you say that?'

'Because if you were flying all the time, you'd miss writing songs, and performing, and hearing bands, and having sex. The novelty would totally wear off, and you'd get tired of it, and you'd want to be normal again. You'd want to be like everybody else. You'd fly when you wanted to get away and be alone for a while . . . but maybe you wouldn't. Maybe you'd go to a café, or a bookstore, or a quiet bar.' She turns slightly to the East, so that they can fly over Lake Michigan for a while. 'You might even be embarrassed.'

Cheryl says, 'C'mon, Bynum. You know me. I don't get embarrassed.'

'You don't get embarrassed on stage, playing your

songs. You don't get embarrassed screaming my name at the top of your lungs in an airport. But I bet you'd be embarrassed having this Weird Stuff that nobody else in the world has. It's like . . . it's like . . . it's like having a third nipple. Maybe it feels good once in a while, but if you go to the beach in a bikini, people'll stare, and you'll feel like an idiot.'

'You are *soooo* wrong. First of all, nobody knows about the Weird Stuff.'

'*I* know about the Weird Stuff. And that's all that matters. Now quit talking and look at how pretty the city is.'

Cheryl takes it in. 'It's gorgeous. Thank you for bringing me. Thank you so much. It means a lot.'

'You're welcome. Now put a sock in it.'

Abbey takes them over the downtown skyscrapers, to the museums just to the south of the Chicago Loop, then back over the lake, then she accelerates to almost top speed – actually, she doesn't know what top speed is, because she's always been afraid to open it up too much – and, in five minutes, they're in Indiana. Since Indiana is an industrial area, and thus smells like rotten eggs, they turn round and head home.

Ten miles away from Abbey's apartment, Cheryl says, 'Drop me.'

Abbey says, 'Ha ha ha. Relax, we'll be home in, like, five minutes.'

'I'm serious. I want you to go higher, then I want you to drop me, then I want you to fly down and catch me.'

Suddenly completely sober, Abbey says, 'I would never, never do that, Cheryl. *Never.*'

'You're *going* to do it, Bynum. I trust you. You'd never let me fall. You'd take down an airplane to save my life. You can do it, and you *will* do it.'

'No way.'

'*Yes* way. You need to learn.'

'I need to learn what?'

'You need to learn how to save people. Do it now, or I swear to God, I'll never speak to you again.'

Knowing full well she can easily do this without anybody getting hurt, Abbey climbs up another five hundred feet, says, 'Fine. See you in a minute', then opens her arms and lets her best friend fall into the night.

Hearing Cheryl simultaneously laugh and scream at the top of her lungs, Abbey quickly dives through the sky and gets herself into position to keep her friend from becoming road pizza. Several hundred feet from the ground, Abbey comes to an abrupt halt, holds out her arms, and easily catches the still-giggling Cheryl Sheldon.

As they float towards Abbey's apartment, Cheryl babbles. 'Oh my God, that was *amazing*, like the best thing *ever*, the wind was *sick*, and I couldn't hear anything, but I heard *everything*! *Woooooooooo!* I love you, Abbey Bynum! *Woooooooooo!* Till death do us fucking part! *Woooooooooo!*'

Abbey chuckles despite herself. They touch down on the roof, and she says, 'If you're happy, then I'm happy.'

'I'm happy as hell.'

'Then I'm happy as hell.'

'And you're going to stay that way.' Cheryl squirms out of Abbey's arms, turns towards the sidewalk, cups her hands over her mouth, and yells, '*Fuck Murphy Napier!*'

Abbey lightly smacks Cheryl on the back of her head. Through gritted teeth, she says, 'Cut it out.'

'Nope. Not until you say it, too.'

'*No*. We're going in. Now.'

Cheryl again cups her mouth, and again yells, '*Fuck Murphy Napier!*' A trained, professional vocalist, Cheryl Sheldon has some serious pipes, and when she lets it go, it *goes*. 'Say it with me now, girl.'

Abbey sighs, then says in a perfectly normal tone, at a perfectly normal volume, 'Fuck Murphy Napier.'

'Seriously? That's the best you've got? You don't have, like, super voice powers or something?'

Abbey says, 'Fine', then, raising her voice incrementally: 'Fuck Murphy Napier.'

'No. *Fuck Murphy Napierrrrrr!*'

'Fuck Murphy Napier!'

'No. *Fuuuuuuuuck Murrrrrphy Napierrrrrrrrr!*'

'*Fuck Murphy Napier!*'

'*Fuuuuuuuuuuuuuck Murrrrrrrrrrrrrrrphy Napierrrrrrr rrrrrrr!*'

'Right.' Abbey laughs. 'What she said.'

'Okay. Good enough. Are you purged now?'

After a quick internal inventory, Abbey realises that

she does feel somewhat lighter. 'Actually,' she says, 'I kind of am.'

Cheryl wraps her arm around Abbey's waist and says, 'Excellent. Now let's go enjoy the first day of the rest of our lives.'

Part Two

It's two years later, and things have changed. Some a little. Some a lot. And some a *whole* lot.

Cheryl Sheldon is now a viable third-tier rock star, and we mean no disrespect when we say 'third-tier', especially since, if she hit the first tier – and by first tier, we're talking, say, U2 and Lady Gaga – she'd be a put-upon stressball who wouldn't be able to leave her house in New York City without being accosted by autograph seekers, worshipful little girls, lustful big boys, and assholes with cameras. If she was second-tier – like, say, Sheryl Crow or Elvis Costello – she'd be able to live some semblance of a normal life, but there'd still be paparazzi around and, goodness knows, she doesn't need that. But Cheryl is more on the level of her heroes the Indigo Girls, an act with an intelligent, loyal audience who'll stick with her through thick, and thin, and an album of Dusty Springfield covers. Cheryl probably won't move up another tier because her songs are too clever for mass-acceptance, and that's just the way it is, and that's just the way she likes it.

Suzanne Addison and her husband Joseph adopted a baby, a healthy little girl from Vietnam whom they named Eloise Rachel. (Eloise was Suzanne's grandmother's name. Suzanne loved her grandmother, but hated her moniker, so they call the kid Ellie, which she thinks is lovely.) She took some time away from the office, but not much, because Suzanne likes being a lawyer almost as much as she likes being a mommy. She's doing an excellent job balancing home and work, but she's tired all the damn time, and has a new-found – and, in her mind, unfortunate – tendency to snap at her employees, but, Suzanne being Suzanne, she then apologises profusely for the rest of the day. On the plus side, her brand-new crankiness has served her well in the courtroom.

Dave Bynum graduated from DePaul with a useless degree in Political Science, a piece of paper that qualifies him for exactly six jobs in the Chicago area, all of which are already filled by people at least eleven years older than him. After much pavement-pounding, he landed a gig as a marketing writer for a small, funky software company. (Being that he met about two of the job's ten requirements, nobody's quite sure why he was hired, and Dave isn't saying. Abbey thinks that he either seduced the Human Resources girl who'd interviewed him, or he's selling weed to his new boss. Abbey's too nice of a sister to bust out her ESP and fish around his mind for the answer.) He has a super-nice apartment in the West Loop, so he doesn't feel compelled to crash at Abbey's place during one of his still-too-regular drinking binges.

Carin and Gary are still Carin and Gary, still working their nine-to-fives, still enjoying their periodic nights out with their friends, still worrying about their kids, that sort of thing. Being that Abbey and Dave can't find the time to come home, they make a quick trip to Chicago every six or eight weeks, sometimes crashing with Abbey, sometimes crashing with Dave. (It's a good thing they switch it up, too, because if it weren't for the parental visits, Dave wouldn't *ever* clean his apartment.)

Just for the hell of it, Abbey tried to find her old college flame James Caraway, but she gave up after none of the forty-one James Caraways on Facebook were *that* James Caraway.

Barry Belmont was busted for sexually harassing one of his assistants, and was summarily dismissed; the only reason his last name is still on RBP&A's letterhead is that his father was one of the founding partners.

Abbey's fellow para Giselle Collins is going to law school, and she's not doing well, but she's trying, and trying *hard*, and all the junior and senior partners are doing everything they can to help her get over the hump. (In case you're curious, Giselle still has outdoor sex with her boyfriend, who's finally gotten used to it; for that matter, he now kinda digs it.)

Abbey's upstairs neighbor Mrs Vance passed away last summer; she lived a good life, and she died peacefully, and Abbey sometimes misses her smile.

RBP&A hired a whip-smart new lawyer named Jon Carson. More about that in a bit.

Murphy Napier is missing in action. And Abbey isn't trying to hunt him down.

And as for Abbey? Well – surprise, surprise – she's a superheroine.

Abbey Bynum never asked for much out of life. When she was a kid, something as small as a new cute top every once in a while, or an iTunes gift card, or a faster wireless Internet connection in her bedroom would keep her happy for weeks. When she was at Northwestern, little pleased her more than having her friends over for a dinner party . . . a dinner party during which nobody chose to discuss how shitfaced they'd gotten the previous weekend. As an adult, a decent date with a decent guy was lovely; she wasn't even asking for fireworks, just decentness. Today, she's thrilled when she has twenty-four straight hours with no plans: no work, no errands, no laundry, no nothin'. She cherishes those days. She wishes there would be more of them.

Sadly, that's not in the cards. Especially now.

Naturally, it was Cheryl – impulsive, vibrant, do-gooding Cheryl – who convinced her to take the plunge, to use the Weird Stuff for something other than late-night flights and moving furniture from one side of the living room to the other. 'You have to do something, Abbey,' she told her friend the morning after Abbey dropped Cheryl down from the heavens, then caught her before she crashed.

Abbey, who was nursing a bitch of a hangover, said, 'I *am* doing something. Taking more Advil.' After downing a couple more pain relievers, she said, 'And stop yelling.'

'I'm *not* yelling' – she wasn't – 'you just drank too much last night' – she had – 'I'm speaking in a perfectly normal tone of voice' – she was – 'and I'm telling you that you have to do something.'

'And I told you, I just did something. The Advil . . .'

'I'm being serious, here. You need to do something with your Weird Stuff. *Something.*'

'Like sell it on eBay? That'd be the best.'

'No, Bynum. *Help* people. Fuck it, you know, go ahead and be Wonder Woman.'

Abbey put her hands over her face and groaned, 'Nooooo. Can we not talk about this now? Or ever?'

Cheryl said, 'We're talking about it.'

Abbey stood up and padded towards the bathroom. '*You*'re talking about it,' she said. '*I*'m taking a bath.'

'Fine. You're taking a bath. *Then* we're talking about it.'

'Fine.'

'Fine.'

'*Fine.*'

It wasn't like she hadn't ever considered using her powers for the forces of good. While Abbey soaked in the hot, bubbly, coconutty water, she recalled that when she was thirteen or fourteen, she'd often imagine scenarios in which she used the Weird Stuff for . . . for . . . for *something*. She'd picture herself swooping in on a crime scene of some sort – a bank robbery was her favorite setting, but sometimes it was a murder scene, or a mugging – then catch the bad guy and save the day, then get a medal from the Mayor, then the Mayor would declare her birthday (21 September) as Abbey Bynum Day, then she'd get invited to the White House to meet the President, then she'd get invited to a film premiere with Mark Ruffalo, then she'd become Mark Ruffalo's girlfriend, then she'd become Mrs Abbey Ruffalo. Or maybe *Ms* Abbey Ruffalo. Maybe she'd keep her name. She'd figure that out later.

Aside from The Event – that infamous afternoon in which she saved Dave from getting beat down by Jerry Feinberg – Abbey had used the Weird Stuff only one other time for superhero-y purposes. It was a simple, subtle moment, and Abbey probably would've forgotten about it altogether, if Cheryl hadn't put her mind on this superhero-y track.

She was seventeen. It was summer, a Friday afternoon, and she was wandering around at the mall, killing time before meeting Cheryl for dinner. She had no agenda, so her modus operandi was to poke into a store, and if nothing caught her eye in the first two minutes, poke right on out again.

Old Navy was having a ridiculous sale – buy one pair of jeans, and get a second pair for a penny – so the place was a mob scene, but Abbey wanted in. (She liked Old Navy, because it didn't pretend to be anything it wasn't.

They sold you jeans that fit well and looked nice, but you knew they were only going to last you two seasons. But Old Navy knew exactly how long their jeans lasted, and *they* knew that *you* knew it, which was why they had sales like this.) She worked her way through the crowd, snared two pairs of boot-cuts in her size, then navigated back through the throng, and got into line. While she waited, she futzed around with her BlackBerry – she checked her email, then posted a status update on Facebook, then Googled her own name, then checked her email again – when out of the corner of her eye, she noticed a skater-kid stick a pile of jeans under his baggy T-shirt, then head quickly towards the exit. Without thinking, Abbey put her to-be-purchased jeans on a shelf and whooshed to the exit in one second flat, coming to a stop right in front of the kid.

The kid crashed into her and fell flat on his ass. As Abbey helped him up, he said, 'Whoa. Dudette. Didn't see you there.'

Once he pulled himself upright, Abbey reached under his shirt and yanked out the jeans, then said, 'You were going to pay for these, right?'

The kid paled and said, 'Whoa.' That was all. Just 'Whoa.'

Abbey said, 'You're leaving now, right?'

The kid said, 'Right.' And then he left.

When she got back into the line – a line that had almost doubled in size in a mere two minutes – she thought about whether or not she'd handled the situation well. She did stop the theft, yes, but she'd let the kid go. She'd saved the store, but she doubted the kid learned a lesson. As far as the thief was concerned, Abbey was some random chick who happened to notice the lump under his shirt, no big deal, he'd try ripping off another place on another day. A temporary fix at best.

The thing is, if she'd have hauled the kid over to a guard, they probably would've looked at the security tape, and the tape would've shown what would appear to be Abbey materialising out of thin air, and that could've caused problems. And this was the crux of the issue: could she use the Weird Stuff to do good stuff without drawing attention to herself?

Abbey dunks her head under the water, comes up wearing a faceful of bubbles, then leans back, closes her eyes, and thinks, and thinks, and thinks some more.

These days, what with everybody's cell phone equipped with video capabilities, it would be difficult, if not impossible to stay anonymous doing superhero work. If she did happen to thwart a bank robbery in broad daylight, the whole thing would be on YouTube within twenty minutes, and she'd be besieged by reporters, scientists, secret agents, terrorists and guys from high school who'd blown her off, but now wanted a taste of the flying chick. If she saved somebody from a mugging, the victim (and – if the cops let him go, which would likely be the case – the mugger) would blog about it that very night. And some sort of identity-hiding costume wouldn't do any good; somebody somewhere would take a picture and post it online, then somebody else would do some Photoshopping, then somebody else would somehow figure out it was her. Her life, as she knew it, would be over. As much as she liked helping people, she couldn't see herself sacrificing *everything*.

On the other hand, maybe she *could* stay underground. Maybe she *could* keep her identity a secret. Maybe if she moved quickly enough during a robbery, or a mugging, or whatever – and goodness knows, Abbey Bynum can move quickly – she could get to the scene, save the day, and get the hell out without anybody getting either a good look or, more importantly, a photo. It dawned on her that if she worked only at night, it might actually be feasible.

She grabs a washcloth, wipes the bubbles from her face, then rubs her temples. *This is ridiculous*, she thinks. *Who the hell do you think you are? You're not some girl who went to the police academy. You don't know a damn thing about criminology. You don't know the proper way to subdue somebody. You're a boring girl who has a boring job and dates boring guys . . . and you're perfectly fine with that. Let's keep it that way.*

Cheryl taps on the door. 'You okay, Bynum?'

Abbey calls, 'Yeah, I'm fine. Why?'

'You've been in there for almost an hour. Are you diddling yourself or something?'

Abbey looks at her hands: *Wrinkle City*, she thinks. *Guess I have been in here for a while*. 'No, Cheryl,' she laughs, 'I'm not diddling myself.' Although, now that she has mentioned it, that might not have been a bad idea; at the very least, it would've calmed her down. Too bad the sex toys in her nightstand were all associated with Murphy, because they were *awesome*. She'd have to get a new batch of machinery, ASAP. She tells Cheryl, 'I'm just thinking.'

'About what?'

'About things.' She steps out of the tub, wraps herself in a towel, then says, 'You can open the door, if you want.'

Cheryl steps into the bathroom, puts down the toilet lid, then sits down. 'What kind of things?'

'The kind of things we were talking about before.'

'You mean the kind of things like saving humanity from itself?'

'Yeah,' Abbey sighs. 'I guess.' She pauses. 'Hey, did I ever tell you about that kid at Old Navy?'

'What kid at Old Navy?'

'The guy who was trying to steal some pants, and he would've, if I hadn't stopped him with the Weird Stuff.'

'Um, no Bynum. You never mentioned that.'

'Yeah, I didn't think so.' After Abbey has relayed the story, she says, 'So. How do you like them eggrolls?'

'I don't. I'm pissed that you didn't tell me about it until now.'

'I'm sure I was embarrassed to say anything at the time, and I totally forgot about it until now. Swear.'

Cheryl points her pinky at Abbey. 'Pinky swear?'

Abbey takes Cheryl's pinky with her own, then

shakes it up and down. 'Pinky swear.' She pauses, then asks, 'Do you think I did the right thing there?'

Cheryl shrugs. 'Who the hell knows? There's no right or wrong in that situation. What you did was good. And at least you did *something*. But was it right?' She shrugs again, then repeats, 'Who the hell knows?'

Suddenly, Abbey feels a lump in her heart that moves quickly into her throat, and she bursts into tears, sobbing and hitching. She backs up against the wall, then slides to the floor and buries her face in her hands. Cheryl sits down next to her friend, then wraps her arms around her shoulders and pulls her into her chest. Rubbing Abbey's wet head, Cheryl cooes, 'It's okay, sweetie. It's okay. You'll be okay. You don't have to do anything you don't want to do. It's okay.'

When she was able to speak, Abbey says, 'Murphy said I could help the country.'

'Yeah, I know he said that,' Cheryl says. 'It bothers me that that tool and I were on the same wavelength.'

'He may be a tool, but I think he means well. And he's smart. And so are you. Maybe you're both right.'

'Or maybe we're both wrong. Maybe you should just keep doing what you're doing. You have a nice life, so enjoy it. You'll find a great guy, and start a great family, and you'll be an awesome mom, and it's all good. It's not either of our jobs to save the world. I sing stupid songs, and you do stupid legal crap . . .'

'Your songs aren't stupid,' Abbey points out.

'Whatever. Point is, if you're a good person, and

you're nice to your friends, and your family, and your co-
workers, and random animals on the street, that's good
enough for me. It should be good enough for *everybody*.'

'Well, not *everybody*. I don't think the folks at The
Company will be too pleased.'

'You mean The Bureau.'

'I mean, let's go get some breakfast.'

Cheryl left two days later, but Abbey can't get her advice out of her head: *You need to do something with your Weird Stuff . . . You need to do something with your Weird Stuff . . . You need to do something with your Weird Stuff . . .* It's driving her nuts, so she decides to call the two people who can always talk her off the ledge.

As usual, Carin picks up on the first ring – for some reason, Abbey's mother always had to have her phone within reaching distance – and, as usual, she gives a nervous, tentative 'Hello?'

'Hey, Mom.'

Carin perks up immediately. 'Hi, honey. What's going on?'

'Lots.' Abbey gives her the salient points of the Murphy mess, then tells her about Cheryl's suggestion. 'What do you think?'

'Oh, that's easy: do whatever makes you happy.'

This is Carin in a nutshell; all she wants for her children is for them to be content. Salary and status mean nothing to her. If being a garbage collector is fulfilling for her children, great. If being a biophysicist is fulfilling, that is equally great. A sweet sentiment, no doubt, but it doesn't help Abbey's current situation one iota.

Abbey says, 'Let me talk to Dad.' Gary is the pragmatist, and Abbey is certain he'll give her a straight answer.

She's wrong.

'It could be amazing,' he says, 'or it could be a disaster. You could do a lot of good, but what if, say, you see a robbery of some sort—'

'Like a *bank* robbery?' Ah, the bank robbery dream . . .

'Yeah, sure, like a bank robbery. And you see somebody leave the bank, and you go after them, and you tackle them, and hurt them badly, and then find out you got the wrong guy. You're not a police officer or a detective. These guys go to school for a long time, you know.'

'I know. Believe me, I know.'

'On the other hand, it could be amazing,' Gary reiterates. 'You know what? What the heck, I say give it a shot.'

Abbey blinks. 'Really?'

'Yeah. Really.' He pauses. 'Remember that time you took me flying?'

'I think about it almost every time I go up myself.'

'Me, I try not to think about it at all, because to be honest, Sweet Pea, I'm kind of scared of heights, and the whole thing made me kind of queasy. But when I *do* think about it, I think about how, I don't know, how *special* it was . . . in kind of a nauseating way.'

Abbey laughs. 'Thanks a lot, Dad.'

'But seriously, it was magical. *You*'re magical. You're one of a kind. You're unique, and special, and it might be good for people outside of your family, your friends, and your law firm to realise that.'

'But what if when people find out about me, they call me a freak?'

Gary says, 'You're a smart girl. You'll figure it out. Maybe you could just make sure you move fast, and fly high. That should be enough, right?'

'I don't know. Possibly.'

'Listen, whatever you do, it doesn't have to be forever. Fly around and see what you can see. Maybe you'll see some criminal activity, and maybe you won't. Maybe you'll stop one gangbanger from murdering another, and you'll feel so good about it that you'll call it a day and go back to your normal life. You can always walk away, and nobody will pass judgment. But try it. Why not? Who's it going to hurt?'

Abbey says, 'Um, possibly me.'

Abbey Bynum's first foray into superherodom was unspectacular, but sweet nonetheless: she rescued an elderly lady's cat from a tree. (Afterwards, with her Siamese purring away in her lap, the woman offered Abbey a reward, which she graciously refused, then some hard candy, which she also graciously refused.) It was nothing a fireman, or somebody with a tall ladder, couldn't have done, but Abbey was on her way home from work, and the street was empty, and the woman was wearing Coke-bottle glasses – thus making it impossible for her to identify Abbey, should the need arise – so she figured, *What the hell*. It made her feel good . . . but of course it did; if you're a nice person – which Abbey is – and you have an affection for kitties – which Abbey does – how could it *not* make you feel good?

When Abbey finally started getting proactive about stopping crime, the primary issue was *finding* crime. She couldn't see what was going on down on the ground from the lofty height at which she generally flew, and she was afraid to fly any lower for fear of being spotted, so searching for bad guys via the skies was out. She couldn't cover any significant ground wandering around the area, and she didn't want to run like a maniac up and down each block because, once again, she was concerned about being noticed, so searching for bad guys via the ground was also out. So Abbey did what most amateur crime fighters did: she bought herself a police scanner.

Abbey's Uniden BCD396XT Handheld TrunkTracker IV didn't come cheap – we're talking $524.52 plus shipping and tax – but that walkie-talkie-looking thing *worked*. On her first night, she listened to the dispatchers around the area talking about a bunch of 240s in Hyde Park, and a 10–62B on the north side, and a big 11–51 bust in Chinatown, and she had no frigging clue what any of it meant. After several hours of listening to this gibberish, Abbey got online, Googled the phrase 'police radio codes', and *boom*, over four thousand pages of info that would turn the gibberish into something at least semi-understandable, were right there on the screen of her laptop.

She thought it best to start her crime-fighting career slowly, so she kept her ears peeled for any 211s (robbery, which she figured she could handle), or 415s (disturbance, ditto), or 510s (speeding or racing vehicles, which she figured might even be fun). She'd avoid the 187s (murder), the 245s (assault with a deadly weapon), and the 314s (indecent exposure) until she got her feet wetter.

Finally, at 2.51 a.m., she heard this from the Evanston P.D.: 'Attention personnel in the downtown area. We have a two one one S in progress at the Dominick's grocery store at one nine one zero Dempster, repeat, a two one one S in progress at one nine one zero Dempster. Over.' (The 'S', Abbey learned, meant a silent alarm had been sounded.)

And then: 'Unit one two one, on the two one one, ETA seven minutes, over.'

And then: 'Unit thirty, also on the two one one, ETA five minutes, over.'

And then: 'Attention personnel in the downtown area. Units one two one and thirty on the one nine one zero Dempster two one one, ETA seven minutes and five minutes, over.'

Abbey allowed herself a tiny grin and thought, *Unit Abbey Bynum, on the two one one, ETA one minute, over*. She opened up her window, flew out at full speed, then, sixty seconds later, she was kneeling on the roof of Dominick's, peering down below to see what she could see, which turned out to be a whole lot of nothing. There were a couple of customers in the parking lot, so she zipped over to the other side of the roof: empty, thank God. She flew down to the ground, then sped around the building to the front door; as far as she could tell, nobody saw.

With as much stealth as possible, Abbey eased her way into the store. She peered around the corner: about twenty yards away, there was a heavily tattooed young man – a boy, really; he couldn't have been more than eighteen – pointing a handgun at a pretty, pale, shivering, obviously scared-as-hell teenage girl. The boy yelled, '*For the fifth time, open the fucking safe!*'

Through chattering teeth, the girl said, 'M-m-m-my b-b-b-b-boss is the only one who h-h-h-h-h-has the k-k-key.'

'*Then for the fifth time, fucking call him, bitch!*'

'I d-d-d-d-did. That b-b-b-button I pushed. That called him. I d-d-d-d-d-don't know where he is.'

Abbey thought, *I bet she pressed the silent alarm. Good for her*. Then Abbey got on her high horse, ran the twenty yards that separated her and the gunman in .0003 seconds, tackled him, took his weapon, then stepped on his foot *hard* so he wouldn't be able to run away when the police came – she thought she felt some crunching bones, but that might've been her imagination – and made herself scarce.

From soup to nuts – from the time she began her sprint, to the time she was out of the store – the whole thing took twenty-one seconds. It wasn't caught on CCTV, and neither the gunman nor the poor cashier were able to tell the cops what the hell had happened.

Abbey flew east towards the lake; when she was over the water, she removed the bullets from the gun (something else she'd learned how to do online; how much do we love the Internet?), hurled them out to sea, then threw the gun straight down into the lake. If nothing else, she got one firearm off the streets, which was a triumph in and of itself. Ten minutes later, she was home, jazzed beyond believe.

Cheryl was on a quick tour through Northern California; since it was just after 1 a.m. out West, Abbey knew her friend would be awake, so she rang her up on her cell. Cheryl answered on the sixth ring, right before Abbey's call would've gone to voicemail. She cleared her throat and grunted, 'S'up, Bynum?'

'Did I wake you?'

'Li'l bit.'

'Isn't it early for you?'

'I drank my ass off after the show last night, and I'm still feeling it.'

'Okay, well, you don't have to talk. You can just listen.'

'Great. Thanks. Go.'

At a million miles per hour, Abbey said, 'So I bought a police scanner, and I learned police codes, and I heard about an armed robbery, and I flew over, and I tackled the dude, and I got the gun, and I threw it in the lake, and I saved the store, and it was *awesommmmmme!*'

'Are you serious?' Cheryl laughed, then coughed again.

'I'm serious.'

'Holy shit! You're, like, fucking Wonder Woman! You're Batgirl! You're Aeon fucking Flux! Son of a bitch, I wish I was there! What were you wearing?'

'It doesn't matter what I wore. I was in and out of there in under a minute. Nobody even saw me.'

Cheryl said, '*I* want to know what you wore. I need to picture this in my head, and I want to make sure I get it exactly right.'

Abbey looked down at her outfit. 'Shorts and a T-shirt. I would've worn jeans, but it's pretty hot out.'

'Which T-shirt?'

'A red one with black trim, with a small yellow flower on the back, in between my shoulder blades. But it doesn't make any difference, because *I stopped crime!* I'm a real crime fighter! I *rock!*'

'You rocked *before* you were a crime fighter, Bynum.'

Abbey shrugged. 'Maybe. But definitely not as much. And I have to thank you. If it wasn't for you, I never would've done this. Hell, if it wasn't for you, I never would've even *considered* doing this.' She paused. 'Oh, I also got somebody's cat out of a tree.'

Cheryl said, 'Now *that*'s what I'm *talking* about! Barbarella in the house!'

Over the next several weeks, Barbarella, er, Abbey continued her night-time do-gooding, but she was wise enough to pick her spots. She never went out on more than two calls a week, and she never went on a call that she couldn't get to or from within a minute. (She loved calling them 'calls'. It made her feel, like, *official* or something.) After two months of quashing petty robbers and moronic drunk drivers, she decided it was time to step it up.

And stepping it up, in this case, meant answering a 487.

That's grand theft.

As in a bank robbery.

Abbey guessed that the night-time attack of the Fifth Third Bank on the 1700 block of Main Street in Evanston had been well designed and carefully planned, not the kind of thing that was slapped together by a couple of slackers who woke up one day and thought, *Yo, if we could knock over the bank, we'd never have to work again.*

When she heard the call on her scanner, her first thought was, *If you're a guy planning to hit a bank at night, you have to know how to get in, and how the alarm works, and how you open the safe (or safes), and how to get out.* On the way to the bank, it dawned on her that the only people who could've pulled it off either used to work or were currently working at the bank. It would be almost impossible for some schmuck off the street to navigate their way through the locks, the alarm, and the safe without foreknowledge of the building's inner workings.

But figuring out how it happened wasn't Abbey's expertise, or, frankly, her problem. All she cared about was busting the bad guys.

It wouldn't be easy. Even though only twenty-seven seconds elapsed from the time she heard the call to the time she was perched on the bank's roof, the perpetrators – or 'perps', as she'd become fond of calling them, because what's more fun than police lingo? – were probably long gone.

Then Abbey had an idea: she would take to the air, and fly in concentric circles, and search for a car that was moving a little too fast. Yes, that would require her flying lower than usual, but it was 3.31, and she guessed (and hoped) that the public would be so distracted by the police sirens – and the police would be so distracted by the hunt for the thieves – that nobody would look up.

She was right. Nobody spotted her. It took her five minutes of circling to spot a possible suspect.

The car was a black Chevy Malibu. It wasn't old, it wasn't new, and nobody would've given it a second look had it not been weaving around the neighborhood, going down random side streets, then doubling back around, then speeding up, then slowing down. If you didn't know better, you'd have thought it was a little bit drunk, out on a little bit of a joyride, but if you looked closer, you could tell the driver knew what he was doing, that there was a method to his madness.

Abbey drifted higher a few hundred feet, low enough to still see the car, but high enough to feel comfortable that nobody would spot her. The car continued to wind through the city, faster, slower, north, south, east, west. Phalanxes of cop cars drove up and down the bigger streets, sirens blaring, but Abbey's suspect remained out of their sight.

Finally, after about five more minutes of weaving, the Malibu turned on to Sheridan Road – a main street that ran parallel to Lake Michigan – and headed south, towards Chicago, moving at what looked to Abbey like the exact speed limit. She dived down three hundred feet and looked up and down the street: empty.

Just the way the robbers wanted it.

Just the way Abbey Bynum wanted it.

Once she felt she was in the clear, Abbey didn't mess around. She swooped towards the car from the side, then, flying only inches off of the road, lifted the Malibu from the bottom, picked it up, and carried it into the sky, towards the lake. The men in the car screamed, and the almost palpable fear in their voices was music to Abbey's ears, almost as lovely as the latest Cheryl Sheldon album.

Unceremoniously, she dropped the Malibu on to the sand, close enough to the water so that it would be nearly impossible for the bad guys to escape either on foot or in the car, and far enough away so that the money wouldn't get wet. The second the car hit the ground, the two front doors and the driver's-side rear door flew open. Three slender but muscular men – all dressed in black T-shirts, black jeans, black trainers and black baseball hats – flew out of the car, and all three promptly fell face first into the wet sand. Working faster than she'd ever worked, Abbey stripped them naked, tied together their T-shirts and pants into a long rope, which she then used to secure the three robbers to the car. Then, just to play it safe, she covered them with sand up to their necks. (She could've suffocated them, but she felt that you deserve jail time for robbing a bank, not the death penalty.) She then ripped the car's trunk from his hinges and gazed at four duffels. A quick peek inside confirmed that, yes, this was the money, so she grabbed the bags, flew straight to the bank, kicked a hole in the south-facing wall, threw the four bags in, then zipped home.

After downing almost half a gallon of water in a single gulp, Abbey staggered into her bedroom, and fell into an immediate, dreamless sleep. She awoke ten hours later, starving like crazy, and happy as hell.

Jon Carson breezes into the offices of Roscoe, Belmont, Paulina & Addison for his first day of work like, well, like a breeze. A fresh, subtly cologned breeze. Abbey barely registers his first appearance in the office, however, because the night before he came in for his first interview with Suzanne, Abbey had her most harrowing call yet.

The bank robbery that Abbey had thwarted was the biggest crime she'd come across since she'd unleashed the Weird Stuff, and she was pretty sure that was about as big as it would get in the sedate northern suburbs. There were a couple of murders in the bad part of Evanston each year, but Abbey wasn't ready to deal with death just yet. Robbery, sure. A brandished weapon, no prob. But a corpse, not so much.

But she *was* ready for the opportunity to fix larger problems, to solve more important crimes, thus, in terms of how far she'd fly to get to a crime scene, Abbey started taking more chances, extending her radius past Evanston, and into the city of Chicago itself. The primary benefit of the new strategy, of course, was that now she had a wider array of crimes to choose from.

It was fall, and, this being Chicago, the weather was sometimes an issue. This particular November morning, the wind was whipping around at twenty-eight miles-per-hour, and the temperature was in the low thirties, so the wind chill factor was . . . ahhhh, who cares about the numbers. All you need to know is that it was friggin' cold.

Just after midnight, Abbey was jolted out of a doze when the scanner piped up: *'Code one zero at Diversey and the lake! Repeat, Code one zero at Diversey and the lake! All personnel in the area report immediately! Confirm receipt of this call!'* Code ten, as Abbey had learned, was an alert for the local SWAT team to prepare; it was what they dubbed a 'pre-call'. Code eleven was an *actual* call and Abbey wouldn't touch one of those, but if she could beat them to the scene of the Code ten, take care of business, and get out of there before the cavalry showed, it might not escalate to a Code eleven, and how cool would that be?

She grabbed a thick black wool cap and her puffy black winter jacket, and flew off, making sure that the window she'd exited from was closed before she took to the sky, because who wants to come home to an ice-cold apartment after a night of saving Chicago?

When she arrived at the harbor in just under two minutes later, she was kind of astounded at the tableau: there was a line of men wearing woolen caps and flannels that stretched from the end of the pier to a snazzy speedboat; the men were passing wooden crates from the land to the sea like an assembly line. Abbey had never seen anything like it – she didn't have a boat, and she wasn't a pirate, so when would she have? – and to her barely trained eye, it looked like a movie. She thought, *This might be one of those times where it would've helped to have gone to the police academy.* As she hovered a hundred yards or so above the boat, she tried to formulate a plan.

Idea number 1: She could swoosh down, pick up the boat, fly it out to sea, and let the cops and/or the SWAT team sort it out when they arrived. (That wouldn't work, she decided, because she'd be taking the evidence with her.)

Idea number 2: She could knock each of the pirates unconscious, hopefully long enough for law enforcement to show. (That wouldn't work either, because what if one of them woke up before than the rest? Or worse, what if she accidentally killed somebody?)

Idea number 3: She could grab a few of the crates from the beginning of the assembly line, then they'd be distracted, then they'd be sitting ducks for the police. Perfect. Unless the boxes were filled with explosives. Then she'd be screwed. (Then it dawned on her: if it was dynamite, the guys wouldn't be tossing them so quickly and casually.)

So Idea number 3 it was.

Abbey went into a blurry-fast nosedive, snatched up a wooden crate, stuck it on the ground behind a nearby tree, and laughed to herself as the pirates let out a collective, *What the hell?!* In the confusion, before the cops rolled up, she grabbed two more of the boxes, piling one on top of the other. Quickly, she ripped open the crate and checked out the contents. Underneath a couple layers of packing bubble-wrap, there were at least two dozen big plastic bags filled with white powder. Abbey wasn't a druggie – some weed here and there didn't constitute druggie behavior – but she was far from a naïve little girl, and she was pretty certain that she was looking at about a bajillion dollars' worth of heroin.

Yikes.

Abbey heard sirens. She looked up, and was thrilled to see that the bad guys were freaking out, realising they were on their way to being seriously busted. All by her lonesome, little Abbey Bynum from Buffalo, New York had kept kilos and kilos of heroin off the streets. In one fell swoop, she and her Weird Stuff had saved countless lives.

But there was one downside to the evening: Abbey was spotted. However, it could've been worse. *Far* worse. Like they could've found her in the air. As it was, she was spotted behind the tree where she'd hidden the boxes. She quickly put the cover back on the top crate and tried to affect an air of innocence.

Two of the officers ran over, the taller one calling, 'Miss, Miss, please don't move, we need to talk to you!'

Instinctively she raised her arms in the air and said, 'I'm sorry! I'm not moving! I'm sorry!'

The shorter one said, 'Don't worry, ma'am. At ease. We just want to know what you saw.' He paused, then noticed the three crates by her feet. 'And maybe you could also tell us your relationship with these boxes.'

Abbey kicked the bottom one. 'These? They, um, were here when I got here.' Abbey was a lousy liar, and had it been daylight, the officers would've seen the tell-tale blush.

The tall cop said, 'Would you care to tell us when you got here, ma'am?'

She looked at her watch and told them the truth: 'Four minutes ago. About.'

The tall cop grunted, 'Ah. So. What did you see?'

She looked at the boxes, and told them some lies: 'Well, I was going for a walk—'

The short cop interrupted, 'A walk at this hour? In this weather?'

'. . . because my boyfriend just dumped me, okay?' *Not bad*, she thought, giving herself a mental pat on the back.

The tall cop cleared his throat, then said, 'We're sorry, ma'am. Do you have any ID on you?'

Abbey never took her wallet with her during her crime-fighting jaunts, because what was the point? It's not like she was going to get pulled over for speeding. She said, 'I left it at my boyfriend's place.'

The short cop said, 'Your ex-boyfriend, you mean.'

She sniffled, hoping it would make her sound teary and distraught. 'Right. My ex.' She briefly considered trying to manufacture some tears, but Abbey Bynum knew she was a lousy actress, so she didn't bother. It would've been embarrassing for everybody.

The noise of a dozen helicopters burst through the sky; the SWAT team had arrived. The tall cop said, 'Could you give us your name, ma'am? We might want to get back in touch with you to ask some questions.'

Abbey wanted to remain anonymous, and what with her legal training, she was aware that she didn't have to tell the cops anything. She said, 'I'd prefer not to.'

'Are you sure? It would be a great help to us. We sure do appreciate it when a civilian helps us out.'

If only they knew. 'I understand,' she said, 'but I didn't see anything that could help you.' She held out her pinky, then said, 'Pinky swear.'

The short cop looked like he was going to take Abbey's pinky with his own, but a SWAT officer started yelling fancy SWAT-isms out of his bullhorn, so both officers gave Abbey a brusque goodbye, and went towards the boat to finish the job that Abbey had started.

This all being the case, it was understandable the following morning, when Jon Carson breezed through the office for the first time, all fresh and subtly cologned, that Abbey didn't register him.

But she sure as hell did the next day.

Hollywood would say that Jon and Abbey 'met cute'.

Abbey is heading out of Suzanne's office, precariously carrying a two-foot-high stack of files. Jon is heading into Suzanne's office, precariously carrying two large mugs of coffee. Neither is paying attention, so next thing you know, there's a *boom*, then some curse words, then there's java and paper all over the damn place. Both kneel down simultaneously, and, naturally, their heads conk.

Is it love at first sight? Abbey doesn't believe in that sort of thing . . . which, if you think about it, is kind of odd, because you'd think that somebody who had the singular ability to defy the laws of physics and gravity would believe in *anything*. But when it comes to matters of the heart, Abbey's pragmatic streak – a streak she has inherited from her father – takes over. So it isn't love at first sight.

Is it lust at first sight? Abso-frigging-lutely.

Abbey hasn't had sex in five months, and she hasn't had *good* sex in, well, she can't remember the last time she had good sex, so she is on hair trigger. The funny thing is that, until that moment, she hasn't even *realised* she's on hair trigger, likely because on the surface, she feels the crime-fighting is satisfying enough to fill the void in both her heart and her bed. But when she gets a gander of Jon Carson's dancing cocoa-brown eyes, full lips, super-straight teeth, and broad, muscular shoulders, it dawns on Abbey that she's lonely. Not to mention kinda horny.

Jon wipes his hand on his suit pants, then, satisfied it's coffee-free, offers it to Abbey. 'Jon Carson. I'm the new lawyer guy.'

Abbey shakes his hand. 'Abbey Bynum. I'm the old paralegal girl.'

'Lovely to meet you, Old Abbey Bynum.'

'Right back atcha, New Jon Carson.'

Jon asks, 'So what do you do here?'

'Aside from wipe coffee off my skirt, I'm a paralegal.'

Jon chuckles. 'Oh, right, you just told me that. Duh . . .'

Suzanne clears her throat, then says, 'I don't want to be the bitchy boss here, Abbey, but I have to bring Jon up to speed on a few things.' She points to the mess on the floor. 'Don't worry about that, Abbey.'

'I dirtied it. I'll clean it up.'

Jon says, 'It's partly my dirt, too.'

Suzanne waves them both off. 'We'll get one of the custodians. Abbey, you can come back later for your files.'

Abbey says, 'I, um, I need all this stuff for this morning.' She doesn't; she just wants to stay in the room and get a good gander of the new guy.

Jon stands up and says, 'We'll talk later, Old Abbey Bynum. Lunch today?'

Abbey asks Suzanne, 'Is that cool with you?'

Suzanne gives the two of them a knowing smirk. 'Yeah. Sure. Lunch.' She points at the chair in front of her desk. 'Jon. Sit. Talk.'

While Suzanne and Jon go on to discuss the minutiae of an intellectual property case that Abbey is well out of the loop on – and, frankly, not the least bit interested in – she checks out Jon as best she can from her awkward angle on the floor. He's wearing a nice suit that might be way expensive . . . or might not; she isn't up on men's fashion. (She *can* tell that it is extremely well tailored. *Extremely.*) He has a light sprinkling of gray throughout in his dark hair, but his face is smooth and unlined; he could be anywhere from twenty-eight to forty-five. Age isn't an issue for Abbey – one of her best-ever boyfriends was eleven years her elder – so she doesn't care one way or the other. Her thinking has always been, *Why discriminate? Why let age – or, for that matter, race or religious beliefs – get in the way of what might be a wonderful relationship?* Actually, scratch that. Abbey does have one prejudice: wilfully stupid people. She really, really hates the wilfully stupid. If Jon Carson is working at Roscoe, Belmont, Paulina & Addison – specifically for Suzanne Addison – there's no way he's wilfully stupid . . . or unwilfully stupid . . . or stupid on any level. So brains won't be an issue.

Physical attraction won't be an issue either, as Jon is flat-out, ice cream-meltingly, tummy-tingling hot. *Man*, Abbey thinks, examining her shapeless gray sweater and uninspiring black skirt, *I wish I lived closer to my apartment so I could go home and put on something less lame*. She briefly considers flying back to Wilmette, changing, then flying back to work – it would take ten minutes, tops – but she quashes this thought immediately, simply because it would be wrong on so very, very many levels, the most obvious one being that she'd be busted.

Abbey has milked her file-picking-up as long as she can, so when there is a break in Jon and Suzanne's conversation, she says, 'Jon, my cubicle is right outside Suzanne's office' – she points out the door – 'so come and grab me when you're ready.'

He checks his watch. 'One o'clock?'

She confirms, 'One o'clock.'

Jon is swamped with work and can only get away for a quick bite, so he and Abbey go to a Mexican take-out place across the street from the office called Chipotle. (This is Abbey's choice, because it's yummy, it's fast, and everybody's on an equal footing when eating a sloppy burrito with their hands.) The restaurant is loud, echoey, and chaotic, so the two of them have to yell to be heard over the din. About 40 per cent of their conversation is thus rendered useless, which Abbey considers to be fortunate, as she feels that she'll come off like a giggly teenager. But Jon mustn't see it that way, because on the way back to the office, he asks her if she wants to meet him for drinks after work on Friday. She says yes, but is a little disappointed he doesn't shoot for dinner.

That night, around midnight, Abbey calls Cheryl, who is on yet another one of her North American tours. Cheryl picks up after half a ring and, without preamble, says, 'That's great, Bill, just great . . . Hey, listen, I have to take this call, it's my manager . . . Okay, great meeting you too . . . Sure, just email me through the website . . . No, sorry, I don't give out my personal email, no offense . . . Yes, I see all the emails from the site . . . Okay, great, b'bye.' She takes a deep breath, then says, 'Thank God. Good timing. You saved my ass, Bynum.'

'I'm your manager?'

'For the moment. My ass needed saving.'

'From whom?'

'From this douchebag producer who wants me to be in his flick . . .'

'Cool!'

'. . . but wants me to fuck him first.'

'Not cool.'

'*Totally* not cool. So what's going on? What's happening that merits a midnight phone call?'

'Okay, so this new guy has started working with us, and he's super-cute, and he's a lawyer, and he seems really smart, and we went out to lunch today, and *he* asked *me*, and it was totally stupid because we couldn't hear each other, but I think he likes me, because he asked me out for drinks, but it wasn't for dinner, but that's okay, because maybe we won't like each other, and we can bail after, like, an hour, but if we go out to dinner, that's always an option, and—'

Cheryl interrupts, 'Christ, Bynum, you sound like you're fourteen.'

Abbey squeals, 'I know, right? It's pretty sweet.'

'If you make it through drinks and to dinner on Friday, are you going to let the dude bang you, or what?'

'I have a question for you, Cheryl.'

'Shoot.'

'You write these gorgeous love songs that have the most lovely lyrics, and I'm describing what could be the start of something beautiful, and you ask me if I'm going to bang the dude? That's the best you can do?'

Cheryl says, 'Whatever. Now answer me. Are you going to let the dude bang you?'

Abbey pauses. 'I am *totally* going to let Jon Carson bang me.'

Abbey is so hyped about her night out with Jon that, for the first time in forever, she has bought herself an outfit that is neither for work, nor practical: a black long-sleeved pullover top that clings to her midsection in such a way that her boobs look enormous (which they aren't); a tight black and red skirt that makes her butt look high (which it isn't); and a pair of funky black heels that make her look tall (which she isn't). Hopefully, if or when it gets to the point where she takes off her clothes in front of Jon, he won't be disappointed with the reality of Abbey's nice, but unspectacular body.

The news of her and Jon's date has spread around the firm like wildfire – *Thanks a lot, Suzanne*, Abbey thinks – so nobody is surprised by Abbey's unprecedented fashion statement. When she strolls into the office clad in her new duds, she is met with good-natured wolf whistles and catcalls. Blushing wildly, she sits down at her cubicle and attempts to focus on her job, something that, over the last few days, has become increasingly difficult to do.

Jon Carson isn't the sole reason Abbey is spacing out at work. Ever since she started proactively using the Weird Stuff to save the universe (or at least her tiny part of the Midwest), Abbey's interest in the machinations of the law has dwindled each day. She understands the importance of making certain that the country's big, moneyed businesses are punished when they try to screw over a sole proprietor who hasn't had the means to defend himself, but after you've actually enforced the law on the street – after you've stopped an armed robbery, after you've launched a drug bust – enforcing the law in an office is dull, dull, dull. Had it not been for Suzanne, she would've seriously considered leaving RBP&A. (Actually, let's amend that: had it not been for Suzanne, *and* her relatively fat weekly paycheck, *and* her three weeks vacation time, *and* her five personal days, she would've considered seriously considered leaving RBP&A. You see, the economy wasn't in the best shape, and the average superhero salary was exactly nothing, plus superheroes aren't unionised, so the benefits are nonexistent.)

Every time Abbey thwarts a criminal, she becomes hungrier. Hungrier for action, and drama, and physical stimulation (not *that* kind of physical stimulation, although *that* kind would be nice), and the thrill of a hard job done well. It is fulfilling in a way that paralegaling would never be. But now with Jon Carson in the picture, Roscoe, Belmont, Paulina & Addison might be a slightly more interesting place to be.

12

Abbey and Jon meet up at a place a few blocks from the office called Bar Novo, which Abbey has chosen because it's more of a lounge than a bar, replete with soft chairs, nice music and no tourists. Abbey arrives right on time, at 5.15; Jon two minutes later.

Abbey doesn't know if Jon has dressed up specifically for their meeting, or whether he always dresses this way, but he looks *good. Real* good. Real *real* good. Like good enough to eat, good. He smiles when she waves him over, a warm, sincere smile that sets off bumper cars in her chest. 'You look smashing, Abbey,' he says as he signals over the waiter. 'What're you drinking?'

'Something red. You decide.'

He nods, then asks the waiter to bring over the wine list. After some deliberation, Jon chooses a bottle of 2005 Cakebread Chardonnay from the Napa Valley. Accidentally on purpose, Abbey peeks at the right side of the wine list: that single bottle cost $80. She thinks, *This guy either has money, or class, or he's trying to impress me, or all of the above*. The bumper cars in her chest pick up speed.

After the waiter pours the vino, they clink glasses, and Jon says, 'Tell me everything, Abbey.'

She takes a dainty sip. '*Everything?*'

'Well,' he says, 'not *everything*. Everything you'd be comfortable telling somebody on a first date.'

'We're on a first date?'

'Not really.'

'Oh,' Abbey says, doing a decent job of hiding her disappointment.

'No, this is our *second* date. I count Chipotle as a date. And if you don't – and I don't mean *you*, Abbey Bynum, I mean the *royal* you, the world at large – you ain't right in the head. Chipotle equals date.'

Abbey laughs, then gives him a gentle (and, in her mind, bold) touch on the thigh and says, 'I have to be honest with you, Jon – *everything* about me isn't that interesting. But here I go . . .' And there she went.

Naturally, she can't tell him *everything*, but she tells him a lot. As she recounts her life story – family, college, work, Cheryl, old boyfriends, and the like – she again realises that the most noteworthy thing about her – the thing that separates her from every other attractive-but-not-beautiful, very-smart-but-not-a-genius girl out there is the Weird Stuff. And that's the one thing she can't share with him.

By the time she finishes blabbing about herself, the bottle of wine is empty, so Jon signals for the check and asks, 'Where should we eat?'

'Ah,' Abbey says, 'so the date continues.'

'Of course it does. How do you feel about Italian?'

'I like it, and it likes me, so let's do it.'

Jon asks, 'What do you mean, it likes you?'

Abbey says, 'Okay, for instance, Indian food doesn't like me.'

Jon nods wisely. 'Ah. Understood. Noted for the future.'

Abbey thinks, *A future! Yay!*

They hop into a cab and Jon directs the driver to Little Italy, specifically an old Chicago favorite called Francesca's. As Abbey's condo is in a far-north suburb way the hell on the other side of the city, she's never been to this part of town, and is properly psyched. After they order – he: roasted veal medallions with wild mushrooms, prosciutto and a brandy sauce; she: roasted swordfish with a spicy cherry tomato sauce, capers, garlic and white wine – Jon says, 'Okay, it's my turn.'

'Your turn to what?'

'To spill my guts. Here goes . . .'

Born in Greely Center, Nebraska (population: 531), Jon Carson's full name is Johnny Carson – not Jonathan, just Johnny – and he started going by Jon in high school, because he was tired of all the references to the venerable talk show host who was his namesake. 'I was skinny,' he says, 'like *crazy* skinny, up until I got my ass kicked by David Kritzman during my sophomore year of high school. Then I started weightlifting – kind of obsessively, really – and I got *really* big, *really* quickly. I went through a phase where I was bullying the other kids. I'm not proud of it, but there it is.'

The teachers at Jon's high school weren't exactly the cream of the crop, so anything he wanted to know about beyond their bare-bones curriculum, he had to figure out himself. 'Our library sucked, so I got a library card for the library four towns over. It wasn't great, but it wasn't awful. I also spent a ton of time online, researching stuff.'

Abbey asks, 'Like what?'

'Like *everything*: government, and astronomy, and American history, and European history, and social sciences, and books, and sports, and movies, and, you know, *everything*. I taught myself French, Italian, and Spanish. My school had such a bad reputation that even though I got good grades, I wouldn't have gotten into a good college if I hadn't kind of kicked ass on the SATs and the ACTs.'

'How hard, exactly, did you' – here she does finger quotes – '*kind of kick ass*?'

He shrugs. 'I did okay.'

'You got perfect scores, didn't you?'

'Not perfect.' He gives her a modest, cockeyed grin. 'But almost.'

'Where did you end up going to college?'

'I got a full scholarship to this private institution outside of Washington.'

'Washington state, or Washington DC?'

'DC.'

'What was it called?'

'Inmann Tech.'

'Never heard of it.'

Again, Jon shrugs. 'Nobody has. But I got a great education, then took a year off to, um, travel in the Midwest, then I took advantage of a free ride to Harvard Law—'

Abbey interrupts, 'Ooh, a *Harvard* man. My mother will be *so* impressed. How was it?'

'Great learning, crappy environment. Competitive. Snobbish. Pretentious. I missed Inmann. More personal attention. More cutting-edge learning. More, I don't know, *coolness*, I suppose.'

Abbey asks, 'Did you have a girlfriend? Or girlfriends?'

'There were a few. Some serious. Most not.'

He leaves it at that, and she knows better than to press. She asks, 'What did you do after Harvard?'

'Puttered around Boston for a while.'

'Doing what?'

'Puttering.' (Again, she knows not to press.) 'I finally got bored, then I went back to Inmann and started teaching some classes but, in typical Inmann fashion, they weren't typical classes. I don't know, I guess you could call them pre-law, but it covered a lot of other junk. It was fun. I made some good connections. Learned a lot. I got kind of burnt out after four years of that, so I got a gig at a firm in San Francisco.'

'Why San Fran?'

'I was fed up with the East Coast. The San Fran guys offered to make me partner early on, but it wasn't working for me; they defended white-collar criminals, and I couldn't get with that. As far as I was concerned, those bastards they were defending deserved to fry. Bilking your stockholders to have fifteen million in your bank account instead of fourteen million? Come on. That got old, fast.'

'And then what?' Abbey is riveted. The story isn't *that* interesting, but Jon's eyes sure as hell are.

'Then one of my buddies from Inmann called me up and told me about you.'

'About me?'

'Well, about your firm.'

'I didn't even know we were hiring.'

Jon shrugs. 'Maybe I was the guy they were looking for, whom they didn't *know* they were looking for. You know what I mean?'

Abbey smiles. 'I know *exactly* what you mean.'

After dinner – Jon picks up the check, natch – Abbey says, 'It's early. Want to go hear some music or something?'

'What're you thinking?'

'Maybe Double Door?' Double Door is a rock club in a funky part of Chicago called Bucktown where Cheryl used to gig regularly before she moved to New York. It generally presents five or six alternative-ish bands a night, some good, some not so much, but they have a quality selection of beers, and nice-sized dance floor, and a manageable douchebag-to-nice-person ratio.

Jon points at his suit and says, 'I'm not really dressed for clubbing.' He pauses. 'But we can stop by my place, and I can run up and change.'

'Works for me,' Abbey says.

Jon's place is at the Trump International Hotel and Tower.

Damn.

Here's the thing: the Trump International Hotel and Tower is the fanciest, schmanciest, most exclusive address in Chicago. The hotel rooms are astounding in and of themselves – a couple years prior, Cheryl's record label put her up there while she was in town for some promotional event or other, and Abbey had never forgotten their night there – but the apartments, well, she couldn't imagine.

Turned out she doesn't have to.

Walking across the ornate lobby – which looks like the hippest, funkiest high-end furniture store you've ever seen – Abbey asks, 'How long are you staying here?'

At the elevator bank, Jon jabs the 'up' button and says, 'Until my lease is up. Longer than that, if I decide to buy.'

'Wait, you're *renting* here?'

'For the time being.'

As nonchalantly as possible, Abbey says, 'Oh. That's cool.'

Jon Carson's apartment is . . . is . . . is *wow*, so *wow* that Abbey can't even come up with a decent adjective to describe it.

It's on the forty-third floor – only fifteen floors from the top – and has a south-east-facing view – which offers a look at both Lake Michigan and the skyline (two of Abbey's favorite things in the world) that's breath-taking. The living area and kitchen are open, a huge room that is probably as big as Abbey's entire condo. Jon's living-room furniture is high-end and tasteful, similar to that in the lobby. As for the kitchen, even though Abbey doesn't know much about appliances, she's watched enough Food Network to recognise that the stove, the fridge, and the dishwasher are above top-of-the-line.

Before she can stop herself – before she realises the possible implications of saying this – Abbey blurts out, 'Can I see the bedroom?'

Jon smiles. 'Ms Bynum, are you trying to seduce me?'

Abbey blushes. 'Um . . . um . . . um . . .' And then she says the boldest thing she's ever said to a boy in her entire life: 'Not yet.'

The lights are too low for her to see if Jon blushes himself, but he does emit an audible gulp, then he clears his throat nervously, so he definitely catches her drift, and, most importantly, is turned on by it. At least that's how she reads it. But when he says, ' "Not yet",' she says. 'Good to know. Noted', she knows she's read it right. 'But yeah,' he continues, 'come see the bedroom. But the bathroom's better.'

Abbey thinks, *The bathroom's better? Way to kill the moment.*

Turned out he's totally right. The bathroom is better. *Way* better. But first, the bedroom.

She's seen king-size beds before, but has never slept in one. (Abbey has always gravitated towards less professional gentlemen – e.g., musicians, writers, hot waiters, nerds, etc. – so nary a one of the boys she's slept with has had a living space big enough to house a king-size.) She believes Jon's bed, which, since it sits atop a two-foot-high platform, requires steps to get on to it – is a king . . . but it might be bigger, a king-plus, if there's such a thing. The matching nightstands on either side of the bed are tall and sleek – as the bed is so far off the ground, they have to be tall – and the matching dresser and armoire are huge – she wonders if they're filled, and what they are filled with – and the view, as is the case in the living room, is mind-blowing.

But that bathroom. Oh, that bathroom.

Abbey guess-timates it's about four hundred square feet, but she's not good at measuring, so if somebody asked her the specific size, she'd probably just say, 'Fucking huge!' (And we know that Abbey isn't one to casually drop an F-bomb, so we know that the room is, well, fucking huge.) Floor-to-ceiling marble. Tub big enough for two (*oh, boy!*), elevated just like the bed. A steam shower that can fit a basketball team. Two sinks on the vanity with gold faucets. And, wait, what's that?

'Jon,' Abbey asks, 'is there a television embedded *in* the mirror?'

Jon smiles. 'It came with the place. Not the kind of thing I'd ever get for myself. But I'm not going to lie: it's kind of fun watching football highlights while I'm shaving.'

'Oh, I'm sure. So. Nice pad.' Then she gets bold again: 'We don't have to go dancing, if you don't want.'

Jon says, 'Dancing could be fun.'

'Or we could stay here. And, you know, cuddle.'

'Oh.' Again, he gulps and clears his throat. 'Yeah, that could be fun, too.'

She says, 'Yay!' She doesn't mean to say, 'Yay!', she means to say, 'Can I have a glass of wine?' But something between her mouth and her brain gets kinda screwy.

Abbey is not an aggressive woman, and rarely makes the first move, probably because the first time she made the first move – Perry Hardaway, musician, brainiac, junior year, high school – she was rebuffed. (She found out later that Perry was into her, but he freaked out when she jumped him during a party at Esteban Gomez's house, because Perry had never been kissed before, thus the rebuff. It was too bad, because Abbey herself had only kissed one other boy – Michael Jahns, painter, brainiac, sophomore year, high school – so she and Perry could've helped one another get past the awkwardness. *C'est la vie, c'est l'amour*.) Besides, she enjoys watching the kisser-to-be work his way into kissing position: will he try and play it cool, and casually put his arm around her as if he's been doing so for years, then lean right in and plant one on her mouth? Will he rest his thigh against hers during the movie, then snuggle closer to her, then kiss her on the neck during the closing credits? Or will he just go for it, just grab her around her waist, pin her against the nearest wall, and dive right in?

With Jon Carson, she doesn't wait to find out.

The second they sit down on his plush wheat-colored living-room sofa, she drapes her thigh over his lap and says, 'I'm going to kiss you now.'

Jon puts his hand on her hip. (*Whoa, this guy has some big hands*, Abbey notes.) 'I can get with that,' he says.

She puts her hands on his cheeks, pulls his face towards hers, and locks his lips with her own. When it comes to smooching, she normally likes the build-up – short closed-mouth kisses, leading to long closed-mouth kisses, leading to short open-mouth kisses, leading to long open-mouth kisses – but what with those eyes, and hands, and teeth of Jon's, Abbey goes straight to tongue.

He tastes wonderful, like wine, and honey, and opulence.

He smells wonderful. She doesn't know the brand of his musky, sweet cologne, but she'll find out, and buy him a gallon of the stuff.

He feels wonderful, muscular, but not *too* muscular. She hasn't liked *too* muscular ever since she hooked up with a hard-core weightlifter right after she started at RBP&A. It was kind of gross.

Jon's like the Baby Bear's porridge: he isn't too hot, he isn't too cold; he's just right.

As he explores her neck with his tongue, she runs her fingertips down his chest; when he shivers, she takes off his tie, unbuttons the top four buttons of his shirt, licks her index finger and thumb, and uses the lubricated fingers to rub his nipple. Again, he shivers; this time, he also moans.

Jon lets her play with him for a while, then he decides to take over. He lifts her from his lap as if she's a tiny doll – oddly enough, she doesn't remember getting on to his lap in the first place – then lays her down gently on the sofa. He kisses her forehead, her eyes, her nose, her cheeks, her lips, her earlobes, the nape of her neck, and her chin. Before he gets to her breasts, he wiggles down to her waist, lifts up the bottom of her shirt, and runs the tip of his tongue around her belly button. She gasps so loudly that she apologises.

Jon says, 'Don't say you're sorry. Just say, *Keep going*.'

Abbey moans, 'Keep going.'

He says, 'Beg me.'

'Please, baby. Please keep going.'

He chuckles warmly. 'That's begging?'

She returns his laugh. 'Please, Jon, for the love of God, don't stop licking me. Don't stop. *Do. Not. Stop.*' Abbey Bynum isn't one for dirty talk – she actually prefers silent sex – but right then, the moment is right, and when the moment's right, you go for it. You have no choice.

Jon says, 'That's better', and he resumes exploring her midsection with his mouth. When he makes it to the bottom of her bra – which seems to take forever; the guy is a total tease – he asks her, 'Could I have a hand?'

Abbey thinks, *Why isn't it ever like the movies? Why can't my bra just fall off all by itself?* Then she sits up, yanks off her shirt – *I hope I didn't rip anything there* – reaches behind her, and unclasps her bra. 'You can take it from here,' she says.

'Gladly.' He slides her bra off her shoulders, then throws it across the room. As she giggles, he simultaneously kisses her shoulder blades, and runs his fingertips down her side, which she loves. How he knew she loves it, she has no idea . . . nor does she care. He runs his hand from her stomach to her breast, which makes her gasp. He traces her breast with his index finger, then asks, 'Do you want me to touch your nipple?'

Again with the dirty talk . . . and she would answer in kind, but she seems to have lost the power of speech, so she nods. And nods. And nods some more.

He says, 'My pleasure.' And then he brushes her nipple with the back of his hands, while at the same time kissing her ear. Gradually, he increases the pressure on her breast, until he's practically squeezing it. Nobody has ever done that to Abbey, and she likes it. Who knew?

She pulls away from him, stands up, kicks off her shoes, wiggles out of her skirt, then blushes as Jon gives her an appreciative, unabashed once-over. 'Abbey,' he says, 'your body is incredible.'

Abbey laughs, then rolls her eyes. 'No it's not. It's okay. It's not incredible. But thank you.'

He says, 'No, it *is* . . .'

She cuts him off. 'Whatever. Shut up and take off your shirt.'

Jon shuts up and takes off his shirt, and Abbey goes to town on his chest, running her fingernails, and tongue, and lips from his neck to his waist until he's a quivering mess. After he lets out a particularly loud groan, she says, 'You all right up there?'

He pants, '*God*, yes.'

Abbey laughs, then leans over and takes off his shoes and socks, then reaches up and unbuckles his belt. He's wearing tight boxer briefs that have pinned his erection to his abdomen. 'You look uncomfortable,' she says. 'Can I help you with that?'

Again, Jon pants, 'God, yes.'

Abbey says, 'I'm happy to do so . . . but only when we get on that big bed of yours.' Then she pops up, runs to the bedroom, and jumps on to the raised bed, careful not to take off into the air and through the ceiling. A surprise flight would've put a dampner on the evening.

She gets under the cover, takes off her panties, then, as Jon enters the bedroom, throws them over his head. He says, 'I see where you're going with this. And I like it.'

'I thought you might. Now get over here.'

Jon removes his underwear – she's impressed: not too hot, not too cold, just right – then he climbs on to the bed, straddles her, and asks, 'What can I do for you?'

Suddenly, her mind goes blank. 'Um . . . um . . . um . . . surprise me!'

He gives her an evil grin. 'Glad to. But either you need to get out from under the covers, or I need to get in there with you.'

Tapping slightly into her Weird Stuff, she pushes him off – if he notices she is stronger than your ordinary girl, he doesn't react – then throws the covers to the bottom of the bed. 'Do your worst.'

'My worst, or my best?'

'Your best worst.'

'Will do.' Then he spreads her legs apart, dives in between her thighs, and she loses her mind.

His technique is lovely, but what makes it special – what elevates it above and beyond your normal very good bout of oral sex – is Jon's intuitiveness. He knows how to deliver the perfect lick, the perfect tweak, the perfect rub, the perfect *everything*.

She has orgasm after orgasm after orgasm; she loses track after three. The only other time she'd multipled was with James Caraway, and that was intense. This, however, is INTENSE. Capital I, capital N, capital T, capital E . . . you get the point.

Again utilising an iota of the Weird Stuff, she sits up,

rolls him on to his back, and says, 'Now what can I do for you?'

'Fuck me.'

Abbey blinks. 'Whoa. Okay, then.' She takes him in her hand, guides him inside of her, and for the next nineteen minutes and twenty-one seconds, she again loses her mind. Considering how much she's teased him, he lasts a long time – 19.21 ain't bad – but Abbey wouldn't have cared if he finished in slightly over ten seconds – okay, she would've cared a little, but it wouldn't have been a tragedy – because she's satisfied. Big time.

While he catches his breath, she hops off the bed, pads over to the bathroom, and closes the door. (Some people, after they've been intimate with one another, are comfortable leaving the bathroom door open in front of their lover. Abbey Bynum is not one of those people.) After she does what she has to do, she washes her hands and stares at herself in the mirror. Her hair is messier than usual – which is saying something – and she's flushed, and there are beads of sweat dotting her neck and chest. She looks like she's been well fucked, and she likes it.

When she comes back out, Jon says, 'Feel like having a sleepover?'

Abbey shrugs. 'I don't know, Jon. I have a lot to do tomorrow morning. I have to go to the farmers' market, and I have to clean the apartment, and I need to get my hair done.' She then runs to the bed, hops in, and lays her head down on his chest. 'But I guess I can put that off for another day.'

He fiddles with one of her curls. 'Good. Great.' And then he falls right the hell to sleep.

She would've awoken him, had she not fallen right the hell to sleep herself.

Like most law firms, Roscoe, Belmont, Paulina & Addison is a veritable gossip factory, except more so. The lawyers themselves are catty enough, but the paralegals are like a bunch of high school kids, always all up in each other's business, always asking inappropriate questions, always spreading distorted versions of the truth, sometimes accidentally, sometimes on purpose, which is why Abbey is inclined to keep the whole Jon thing quiet. But Jon is an affectionate, thoughtful man who likes buying her flowers and candy, and, when his increasingly hectic schedule allows for it, taking her out to a nice lunch. Even if she wanted it to, it's not going to stay secret, so she embraces it.

The irony is that since they've put their relationship in the office's public eye, the office's public eye has become less inclined to gossip about it, which makes absolutely zero sense to Abbey. *That*, she thinks, *is some truly weird stuff*.

Jon wants to meet Abbey's brother, and being that the general public – okay, not the general public, just

RBP&A – has demonstrated that they believe the Abbey/Jon twosome is acceptable, she okays a get-together, so on a sunny Sunday winter morning, the three of them go out to brunch at a cute place on the north side called Sola. Dave shows up fifteen minutes late, apologising profusely before he even sits down. He says to Jon, 'I'm totally sorry, dude. I got in at, like, four last night, and I'm fried. I even took a cab here, and Abbey'll tell you that that's a big deal, because I'm a cheap-ass motherfucker.'

'I appreciate it,' Jon says.

'No problem, bro. This is the first time in a million years that Abbey's introduced me to one of her dudes. She usually keeps me on the D.L.'

'Late, foulmouthed, and disheveled,' Abbey says, mussing Dave's already messy hair. 'Why would I ever want to keep you on the D.L.?'

Dave pushes her hand away. 'Hell if I know. I'm a goddamn amazing brother, and if I were my sister, I'd totally bring me around.' He turns to Jon. 'I'm charming as shit.'

Jon laughs. 'I couldn't agree more, Dave. You *are* as charming as shit. Just like your sister.' Then he guides Abbey's face towards his and gave her a this-close-to-being-too-intense-for-a-public-kiss kiss.

Dave says, 'Okay, I'm officially grossed out. I need a Bloody Mary. Yo, waiter . . .' After ordering, and receiving, and taking a huge gulp of his drink, Dave says, 'You know what, Abbey, come to think of it, this is the first time you've *ever* introduced me to one of your dudes.'

Abbey asks, 'Is that right?' She ticks through her mental Rolodex: Billy Rogan, no. Carlton Serris, no. Elliot Warren, no. Murphy Napier, *God* no. 'Hunh, I guess it's right.'

Dave says to Jon, 'You must be doing something right, dude.'

Jon rubs his hand up and down Abbey's back, between her shoulder blades. 'I'm just being me. She's the one that's doing everything right.'

Abbey squirms. 'Jeez, you're going to give me a big head.'

Jon says, 'Just calling it like I see it.' He scrunches up his face, then pulls his iPhone from his pocket. 'Ah, crap,' he says. 'Have to take this one. It's about that Wilson development thing. You know about that one, right?'

'Er, sure.' She has no clue.

He smiles. 'You don't know a *thing* about that one, do you?'

'Not really.'

'It's one of Suzanne's things. It's a mess.' Abbey isn't surprised Suzanne hasn't put her on a messy case. As much as she'd slacked when she was consistently ridding Chicago of bad guys, it had gotten even worse when she started seeing Jon. 'I'll make it quick, I promise.' Then he heads off to the quietest part of the restaurant, which turns out to be a corner of the bar.

When he's out of earshot and wrapped up in his phone call, Abbey says, 'Soooo?'

Dave says, 'Sooooo? So what?'

'So what do you think?'

Dave smirks. 'He smells rich.'

Abbey snorts. 'He *is* rich.'

'That's cool. He's nice to you?'

'He's very nice to me.'

'He'll pick up the check?'

'Most likely.'

'Then I give him a thumbs-up.' Dave downs the rest of his drink. 'You tell him about the Weird Stuff yet?'

He says it a little too loud for Abbey's comfort, so she smacks him on his bicep and hisses, 'Shut *up*.'

He rubs his arm. 'Um, *ow*.' He pauses. 'What's the problem? It's not like anybody knows what Weird Stuff is.'

'Dave . . .'

'I could stand up on the table and be all like, *Weird Stuff, Weird Stuff, Weird Stuff*, and nobody would give a damn. They'd probably think I was a freak or whatever, but they wouldn't give a damn.'

She rolls her eyes and says, 'Sometimes you are *such* a little brother.'

'Yeah, but I'm charming as shit. So you didn't answer my question. Did you tell him?'

'No, David, I didn't tell him. And I'm not *going* to tell him.'

'He might find out anyhow.'

'How would he find out?'

'Like, remember when you hit me on the arm three seconds ago? That kind of hurt. You might accidentally do something, I don't know, *strong* to him.'

Abbey thinks about the times – the *many* times – she's thrown Jon around in bed like he was a feather. He's never said anything about it, so she assumes he thinks she's simply a strong girl. She doesn't think she's done anything else that would've raised any suspicion. 'I wouldn't do anything *that* strong to him.'

Dave leans in and whispers, 'What about that shit with your period, and the mind-reading?'

'It's under control,' she says.

That's true. Sort of.

The ESP still comes on to the scene each month at the same time as her cramps – a wonderful one-two punch if there ever was one – but, fortunately, she's still able to rein (mostly) it in when it's out on its own. So that's a plus . . . but for most every plus, there's a minus, the current one being that last month during period time, while she was on the train, with her iPod cranking a lovely Stax Records compilation, she heard somebody say, 'Damn, I'd totally fuck that chick with the curly hair.'

Abbey wondered, *That guy must be yelling, if I can hear him over the music*. She looked over to her right and met the eyes of a forty-something gentleman; he blushed, turned away, and stared out his window.

Her stomach sank to her feet, because, immediately, she *knew*; over the past ten years, she'd come to realise that the Weird Stuff never lies. If she heard somebody's thoughts without looking them in the eye, it wasn't an isolated incident. *Great*, she'd thought. *Another thing I'm stuck with. Another problem that has to be dealt with. And nobody can deal with it but me.*

Sometimes having superpowers can make you feel like the loneliest person in the world.

But that wasn't the only Weird Stuff-related thing to pop up that needed dealing with: during her last period – the second period after she'd started messing around with Jon – she realised that if she squinted in just the right way, she could see through walls.

That all started, awkwardly enough, while she was in her favorite bathroom stall at work, futzing with her tampon. After she flushed the toilet, she yawned, then, as she opened her eyes, she saw William Roscoe's new assistant – Abbey hadn't bothered to remember her name yet, because Roscoe went through assistants like tissue paper, so what was the point? – in the next stall peeing. It should be noted that there was an oak floor-to-ceiling partition in between the two stalls.

Abbey gasped. Loudly.

The girl called over, 'Everything okay in there?'

Abbey cleared her throat, which turned into a coughing fit. 'Yeah . . .' *cough, cough* – 'everything's . . .' *cough, cough, cough* – 'fine . . .' *cough, cough, cough, cough*.

'Are you sure? You don't *sound* fine.'

Abbey squinted at the partition to see if this was some

sort of hallucination . . . but, deep down, she knew full well it wasn't. Sure enough: Abbey could see the new assistant, staring at her side of the partition, a concerned look on her face.

'I'm okay,' Abbey said. 'Really. I'm fine. Thank you.' She then left the stall and gave her hands a cursory wash, then headed straight to the elevator so she could go outside and get some air. As she walked around the block, a single phrase ran through her head over and over and over again, like a mantra:

This sucks.

She experimented with this whole X-ray vision thing at home; it took her about two hours to figure out how to properly squint her eyes so she could see through solid objects of any thickness. Like all of the Weird Stuff, it felt natural, as if it was a part of her.

But that made sense, because, whether she liked it or not, it *was* a part of her.

Abbey chooses not to mention this to Dave. She'll tell him eventually. But not yet.

Jon wanders back to the table, plops on to his chair, and puts his hand on Abbey's thigh. (Even after two months, his touch still gets her engines revving.) 'What a load of crap. I understand the guy's paying us a lot of money, and I understand why he's upset, but that doesn't mean he can take it out on me. Listen, he's the one who cut the corners. He's the one who hired the lousy contractors. If he hadn't have half-assed it, it wouldn't have gotten to this point. This is why I left that firm in

San Fran, because—' He stops himself, then looks at Dave. 'I'm sorry. This is probably boring the hell out of you.'

Dave can be a dork but, most of the time, he's a polite dork. 'Nah, man, it's cool. My job sucks, too. I'm getting another Bloody. You want one?' Jon nods. He points to Abbey. 'You?' She also nods. Dave flags down the server, and tells him, 'Bloodies all around!'

By the time the check comes two hours later, they've gone through a total of eleven Bloodies, and are all pleasantly bombed. Best of all, there's no more discussion of the Weird Stuff. All in all, Abbey considered the brunch a rousing success.

14

Abbey Bynum hasn't moved out of her condo.
Abbey Bynum hasn't changed jobs.

Abbey Bynum still keeps that same ridiculous morning schedule.

That all being the case, the guy could've easily snatched her up whenever he wanted to, without breaking a sweat, but he didn't, and she forgot about him. By the time he reached out, she hadn't thought of him in nine months, three weeks and two days.

He'd found her phone number even though she'd changed it two, no, *three* times, and currently, the area code was that of Buffalo, New York.

He doesn't call, which she thinks is nice . . . sort of. No, he texts her on one of the rare evenings she isn't at Jon's place:

> ab . . . would like to talk to u . . . it's important . . . better 2 talk in person . . . r u willing 2 meet? i promise 2 b normal . . . sincerely yours, murphy napier . . .

Despite her annoyance at having been tracked down, she allows herself a tiny inward chuckle. *Who else but Murphy Napier would end a text with a 'sincerely yours' and a full name*, she thinks. *Still dorky after all these years.*

Wanting to nip it in the bud while still keeping things on a polite plane, she texts him right on back:

No, thank you. Stay well.

Three seconds later:

this is important, ab . . . you should talk 2 me before somebody else finds u . . . sincerely yours, murphy napier . . .

This catches her attention. Ten seconds later:

Fine. We can meet after work tomorrow. 15 minutes only.

One second later:

we can meet now . . . and we will speak as long as it is necessary . . .

And then her doorbell rings.

She trudges over to the intercom and tentatively says, 'Yeah?'

'Hi, Ab.'

Which means that he was standing outside of her building the whole time. Swell.

Fearing another furniture-throwing incident, she says, 'I told you we'll get together tomorrow. Go away.'

Murphy says, 'No. That does not work. Can I come up, please? Now? It is better we discuss this in private.'

'I disagree. It's better we discuss this in *public*. Very public.'

'Fine. Can we do it now?'

'Yeah, whatever. Go to the Alchemy on Fifth and Linden.' The Alchemy, which is about a hundred yards from her front door, is Abbey's favorite coffee joint. 'Get a table and order me a double espresso. I'll be there in fifteen minutes.'

'Ab, I really think—'

'No discussion, Murphy. It's there or nowhere.'

'Fine. Fifteen minutes. If you are not there, I will enter your building myself.'

'Really? Is that legal?'

'It is if I say it is. It is if The Company says it is.'

'You mean The Bureau.'

He lets out an exasperated sigh. 'Fifteen minutes. Over and out.'

Abbey doesn't feel the least bit compelled to put on a nice outfit; for that matter, she thinks it's best if she uglies herself up, so as not to send any kind of signals at all; she wants to turn Murphy Napier off.

She goes to the bathroom and wipes off all her make-up, then opens her bedroom dresser, digs deep, and fishes out a pair of paint-splattered green sweatpants and an oversized purple long-sleeve T-shirt with a Northwestern University logo on the front. For good measure, she takes a Chicago Bulls baseball cap from her closet and slaps it over her curly mop, and then it's off to the Alchemy.

Save for the barista behind the counter whose nose is buried in an issue of *Rolling Stone*, the café is empty. The barista looks up and says, 'You Abbey?'

Abbey nods.

The barista points at the bathroom in the back of the café and says, 'Dude's in there.'

'Thanks,' she says. 'Kind of quiet tonight.'

Again, he points at the bathroom. 'Dude threw everybody out. I'm bolting when he gets out of the can.'

Abbey blanches. 'Why?'

'Dude showed me his G-Man badge and said he'd throw me in jail if I didn't close for the night and make myself scarce. Least he's giving me some cash-ola to fill the register. Lots of it. Boss'd be pissed if we didn't make our nut. He's throwing me some extra cabbage, too. Cool dude.' Abbey hears a rustle in the back of the shop. 'Okay,' the kid calls over Abbey's shoulder, 'I'm outta here. You'll drop the key back at my house like you promised, right?'

'Right.'

''Cause I'm fucked if you don't.'

'I showed you my identification. You spoke to my

superior on the phone. I will be true to my word.'

'You still got my address?' the kid asks.

'I still have your address. Now disappear.'

The barista disappears.

'Ab, you can turn around. You can look at me. I will not hurt you. I am not here to hurt you. I am here to help you.'

Finally, reluctantly, she faces Murphy, and gasps.

Turns out Murphy Napier cleans up nicely.

Gone are the bowl haircut, the dweebie bow tie, the ridiculous mustache, and the cut-slightly-too-high pants; it's all replaced by a mostly shaved head, a cool patterned tie, and a perfectly tailored suit. Not to mention it looks like Murphy has spent a whole lot of time in the weight room . . . but not too much. Abbey is impressed, and against her better judgment, she says, 'You look good, Murphy.'

Murphy says, 'You do too, Ab.'

'You think so?' She points to her ratty sweats. 'You like these? You think this is a good look for me?'

He gives her a rueful smile. 'As far as I am concerned, you could turn a burlap sack into a good look.' He winces. 'I apologise for that comment, Ab. I promised myself that I would keep this meeting strictly professional.'

She takes a seat at the nearest table. 'That would be for the best.' She points to the coffee-making equipment behind the counter. 'Did they teach you how to make espresso at the FBI academy?'

He hits his forehead with his palm. 'I was supposed to order you a double espresso, wasn't I?'

'Yep.'

'I will make it myself.'

As she watches him fiddle silently with the espresso machine, she considers his physical transformation, wondering if it was something he did on his own, or if one of his bosses said, 'Agent Napier, you look like a weenie, and you're ruining our image. Here's five thousand dollars. Buy yourself some new clothes, get a decent haircut, and join a gym.' She would ask him, but she doesn't want to engage him on a personal level. Like he said, *Keep this meeting strictly professional*.

He slowly – and, she notes, almost gracefully – carries their drinks to the table, careful not to spill a drop. They sip for a bit, then Murphy says, 'What do you know about the Fifth Third Bank robbery in Evanston?'

With as much innocence as she can muster, she says, 'What Fifth Third Bank robbery in Evanston?'

Murphy snorts, then shakes his head. 'I wish you could see your face right now, Ab. It is bright pink. You are a horrible, horrible liar.'

'I'm not lying.'

'Yes you are. And we are going to sit here until you tell me what you know, even if it takes all night.'

She says, 'Seriously? You're not going to let me go home?'

'That is correct. And if you continue to be difficult, I

will take you into the office for questioning first thing tomorrow. Believe me, that is the last thing I wish to do. But I will do it.'

She remembers one of Suzanne's favorite legal phrases is 'Lying by omission', and Abbey now wonders how much she can omit here without getting caught. She decides the answer is *Very little*, so she says, 'You know what, Murphy? Go ahead and take me in. I don't have to tell you anything unless you arrest me, and you can't arrest me without cause. You can question me all you want to, but you're going to do it in front of my lawyer.' (Finding a lawyer would be easy – Suzanne, of course – but explaining the Weird Stuff to said lawyer, well, that would be a bit more problematic.)

Murphy says, 'I will not arrest you, Ab. Do not be so dramatic.' He pauses. 'But I think it is fair to tell you that I will not let our personal history get in the way of me doing my job, so if that is the way you want to play it, then that is the way we will play it, Ab.'

Abbey nods, then, mimicking his clipped, formal voice, says, 'That is the way I want to play it, Murph.' She gets up. 'Text me the address where you want me tomorrow. I'll be there at nine.'

Before she gets to the door, he pounds the table with his fist; both cups fall and espresso flies everywhere. '*Sit down,*' he roars. '*This meeting is not over until I say it is over!*' He takes three deep breaths, then says, 'I apologise for my outburst. I have been under a lot of pressure. There are several cases that are . . .' He trails off, then stands up and walks back behind the counter. 'Would you like another drink?'

'No,' she says, more than a little freaked. 'I want to go home. I want to be away from you.'

He ignores her. 'Let me tell you what I think happened with the bank, Ab. You heard about the robbery on your Uniden BCD396XT Handheld TrunkTracker IV . . .'

In spite of herself, she blurts out, 'How the hell did you know about the scanner?'

'At The Company—'

'You mean The Bureau.'

'. . . we can scan for scanners. That is a professional piece of equipment, and you should consider yourself lucky that nobody went into your house while you were at work and took the darn thing. I mean, do you feel it is wise for the general public to have access to this sort of information, access to whatever crime may be happening in their neighborhood at any given time?' Without waiting for Abbey's answer, he says, 'Absolutely not. That too often leads to blown cases and dead civilian vigilantes.' He glares at her and says, 'Vigilantism is a bad, bad idea. Do you know anybody engaging in that sort of behavior? Because it is punishable by arrest.'

She shakes her head, knowing that if she speaks, her voice will betray her freaked-out-ed-ness.

Murphy sucks in another huge lungful of air and says, 'Now, as I said, I believe you heard about the incident on your Uniden, then made your way to the bank at a remarkable speed. Since you are still driving your Honda Fit, there is no way you could have possibly gotten there via your automobile in such a timely fashion, so I believe you ran. You see, I am well aware of how fast you can run, Ab.'

I didn't run to the bank; I flew, Abbey thinks, then wonders, *Is it possible he doesn't remember that I can fly? I doubt it. He never forgets anything.*

He continues, 'I know for a fact that, at some point in the evening, you tracked down the perpetrators – I am not certain specifically how – then dumped their car into Lake Michigan. Your fingerprints were all over the automobile.'

She thinks, *Damn it, I have to start wearing gloves.* Abbey asks, 'How did you get my fingerprints?'

'That is not germane to this conversation. Suffice it to say that if we need access to somebody's prints, we are able to procure them. Now, back to the matter at hand, I believe that you took the stolen items – the cash, specifically – and returned it to the bank.' He gave her a hard, mirthless smile. 'My fellow co-workers and I were quite impressed with the hole you made in the side of that building. Nice work. And we were also pleased – as were the bank officials, naturally – that you did not remove a single cent. Admirable. *Very* admirable. Most vigilantes take their own reward, and sometimes the reward is almost equal in value to the stolen property. So. That is all I have on the Fifth Third Bank robbery.

Anything you would care to add?'

Abbey says, 'I'll talk to you about this after I discuss it with my lawyer. Can I go now?'

Murphy says, 'Yes . . .'

Abbey stands up. 'See you tomorrow.'

'. . . but not until I say this one more thing.'

She plops down again. 'Of course you have to say one more thing.'

'I know you will not believe this, but I am here to help you. I do not know the full scope of your powers, but I know that it's probably quite frightening for you to deal with them on a day-to-day basis and have nobody to discuss it with. What I propose is that when you come in tomorrow, we broaden the scope of this conversation, and we discuss how we can help you, and how you can help us . . .'

'I don't need any help.'

He ignores her. '. . . and I bring Dr Paul Walton into the loop. Dr Walton heads our Paranormal Division. He is in Washington, but I am certain he will be more than willing to see you here in the morning.'

'Murphy, I told you the last time I saw you—'

'Yes, I remember exactly what you told me. Word for word. But the game has changed. There are other paras out there, you see . . .'

'Paralegals?' Abbey asks. 'What does that have to do with anything?'

He winces. 'No, not paralegals. Paranormals.'

'Swell,' she says, 'Paranormals. I've been categorised.'

'Yes. You have. Maybe someday we'll find another para for you to speak with—'

'Swell. A superhero support group,' she interrupts.

Murphy nods. 'Okay, yes, that is indeed apt. If you have support, you might be able to accept it. You might be able to live a happier life.'

Abbey says, 'Yeah, and I bet I might be able to help you guys fight whatever questionable wars you have to fight.'

'You would never, ever have to do anything you did not want to do. *Ever*.'

She stands up and says, 'Good. That starts this very second, because right now, what I don't want to do is be here with you. I'll see you tomorrow.' She stomps out the door. He doesn't try to stop her.

15

Abbey wants to take an Ambien, crawl under the covers, and sleep like a drugged-up baby, but she knows she has to tell somebody about this new development, because if she ever disappears due to some Weird-Stuff-related event or some FBI-related-idiocy, she has to make sure her friends and family know where to start looking for her.

As much as she'd like to, she doesn't want to get her parents or her brother involved just yet; she'll talk to them after the interview tomorrow, when she has a better idea of what Murphy and/or the The Bureau – not The Company, *The Bureau* – has planned for her. Cheryl, on the other hand, would be a great sounding board.

She looks at Cheryl's tour schedule, which is hanging on the fridge: tonight, she's back in New York, doing a pair of shows at Webster Hall. Abbey knows that the afterparties following hometown gigs are outrageous, and Cheryl won't be in a quiet location to speak until the morning. *Crap.*

Abbey's not ready to spill the beans to Jon, so she

rings up the one person who's going to find out tomorrow anyhow.

Suzanne picks up her cell on the third ring. 'Are you okay, Abbey? Why the hell are you calling this late? Do you need the day off tomorrow or something?'

'No,' she says, 'but I'll be coming in late.'

'No problem. You certainly could've emailed me, and that would've been—'

'. . . and you'll be coming in late too.'

Suzanne chuckles. 'What're you talking about, Abbey? Are you taking me to a belated birthday breakfast?'

'Wait, when was your birthday?'

'Five months ago.'

'Oh. Right,' Abbey says, 'but no. No breakfast. Listen, can I come over?'

And then Abbey Bynum loses her shit.

Suzanne says, 'Honey, don't cry. Are you okay? Are you hurt? Do you need something?'

Between sobs, Abbey says, 'Yeah. I need a lawyer.'

'I'll be right over.'

'No. I'll come to you.' She pauses. 'I need to be away from my place. Can I stay the night?'

'Of course you can. But I don't want you driving in this condition. I'm coming to get you.' Suzanne lives in Deerfield, an insanely affluent suburb three towns over from Wilmette.

'No, don't do that. I'll cab it.'

'Abbey, I can—'

'I have to pack an overnight bag. I'll be there in half an hour. No discussion.'

'Okay, fine. I'm leaving the front door open so the doorbell won't wake the kid.'

Suzanne won't give a damn how sloppy Abbey looks, so Abbey decides to leave on her sweats. Abbey doesn't give a damn how she'll look at the FBI meeting tomorrow, so she grabs a backpack, throws in a pair of jeans and her venerable Black Flag T-shirt, leaves the house, jogs over to the cab stand, then thinks, *Fuck it*, and punches a hole in the sky.

If Abbey flew at full force, she would've been at Suzanne's doorstep in three-plus minutes, and that kind of speed would require a lot of explaining, so she slows down. *Then again*, she thinks, *I already have plenty of explaining to do, so why not get started?* So she puts on the afterburners, and, in no time flat, is on Suzanne's porch.

She opens and closes the front door as gently as she can, then tiptoes through the entryway and into the living room. She's only been to Suzanne's house two other times and doesn't remember the lay of the land, so she accidentally wanders into the piano room. She looks at the instrument and thinks, *It'd be fun just to start bashing the hell out of that thing right about now*. But she restrains herself, and goes to find her boss.

Turns out Suzanne is in the kitchen, making coffee. Abbey says, 'Hey, boss lady.'

Suzanne flinches. 'Jesus, Abbey. You scared the shit out of me. How'd you get here so quickly? Were you calling from outside, or something?'

'No. It's kind of a long story.'

'I figured. You want some coffee?'

'No thanks. I'm wide awake. But you know what I'd love?'

'What?'

'Vodka. A double. No, a triple.'

Suzanne turns off the coffee machine. 'I'll join you. I mean, who doesn't love drinking on a school night?'

As the two women sip their drinks – actually, Suzanne sips, and Abbey guzzles – Abbey fesses up about the Weird Stuff. About ten minutes in, Suzanne slips into lawyer mode, and asks, 'Can we stop here for a second so I can get some paper and take some notes?'

The last thing Abbey wants is to have any of this documented, but she realises that, whether she likes it or not, it has to happen; it was going to happen eventually, and now it's time. Through a lump in her throat, she says, 'Go ahead', and then she polishes off her drink.

Abbey has never been this thorough in telling the Weird Stuff story; once she gets on a roll, she can't stop, and ends up giving Suzanne more than the mere facts. She tells her boss about how she feels like an outcast almost every minute of the day, and what it's like to shut off an entire part of her brain so she doesn't accidentally read somebody's mind, and how she wants to quash her compulsion to go on random flights over the neighborhood, and how unbelievably fulfilling it is to keep a store from being robbed, and how she wishes it would all go away, but how devastated she'd be if it actually did.

After Abbey finishes up, Suzanne is quiet; the only noise in the kitchen is the ticking wall clock, and the sound of Suzanne's pen tap-tap-tapping on her legal pad. Finally she says, 'I don't disbelieve you, Abbey, but I need to see something. I hate to ask you to do this, but can you . . . can you . . .'

'Can I do some Weird Stuff? No problem. Pick a number between one and a million.'

Suzanne says, 'Okay. Got it.'

Without hesitation, Abbey says, 'Three.'

Suzanne blinks. 'Um, yeah.'

Abbey squints and peers at Suzanne's waist. 'Jesus, Suzanne, you're wearing spanks. Why in God's name would you be wearing spanks at' – she looks at the clock – 'one in the morning?'

'Wait, you could see through . . . oh, hell.' Suzanne blushes. 'I'm probably the only person in the entire world who find spanks comfortable.'

'Do you wear them to sleep?'

'Sometimes.'

For the first time since Murphy Napier re-entered her life, Abbey smiles. 'Now that, boss lady, is weird stuff.'

'Well, now you know one of my secrets. You keep mine, and I'll keep yours.'

'You *have* to keep mine. Lawyer–client confident-iality. Me, I'm starting a website called Suzanne Wears Spanks To Bed dot com. Pictures and all.'

'Ha ha ha.' Suzanne thoughtfully chews on her pen. 'I hate to tell you this, Abbey, but the best thing to do at the meeting tomorrow is to tell the truth. Tell them everything. If *they* found out about you, somebody *else* could find out about you.'

'Yeah, but they had their eye on me. I mean, *Murphy* had his eye on me. It's not like some random terrorist cell is going to track me down.'

'Probably not, but a lot of countries have intelligence agencies that're far better than ours.' She sighs, then repeats, 'Somebody else could find out about you.'

'You think?'

'Yeah. I do. And they won't be as nice as Murphy.'

'Murphy wasn't nice.'

'My point exactly. All the stuff you're scared the American Government might do to you? All the poking, and prodding, and testing? A foreign government would *definitely* do it to you, and they *definitely* wouldn't let you bring a lawyer. Right now, this is the lesser of two evils. The devil you sort of know is better than the devil you don't know at all.'

Abbey rubs her temples. 'Will they take me away? Will they try and hurt me? Will they kill me? Will they think I'm, I don't know, a threat to humanity or whatever?' She barks out a harsh sob. 'What's going to happen to me, Suzanne?'

Suzanne puts down her pen, stands up, and pulls Abbey into an embrace. 'I don't know, Abbey. I just don't know.'

16

The Federal Bureau of Investigation's building in Chicago is located on the south-west side of the city, right off of the highway, and, as every window is made of one-way glass, the thing looks like a giant rectangular mirror. As Abbey and Suzanne walk through the parking lot towards the front door, Abbey nervously says, 'Not *too* intimidating, is it?'

Suzanne gives her a playful slap on the shoulder. 'You have nothing to be intimidated about, *nothing*. Remember, you can lift this dump out of the ground without even trying, probably with one hand.'

'There's that, I suppose.'

'Don't worry. I'll be with you the whole time. Remember, I'll be taking notes, and recording the entire interview.'

Abbey says, 'I really truly hope I don't have to Weird Stuff anybody.'

At the front desk, Abbey asks to see Murphy Napier in suite 507. The receptionist jabs at her keyboard, reads something on her computer screen, then says, 'Agent

Napier is expecting you.' She waves over a bland gentleman in a bland suit standing on the other side of the lobby. 'Please go with Agent Bronstein,' she says. 'He'll prepare you for your visit.'

Abbey chuckles. 'That's what you guys call this? A visit?'

The receptionist ignores her. Bronstein puts his hand on the small of Abbey's back. 'Right this way, Ms Bynum, Ms Addison.' He leads the women to a small room which has three blank walls and a thick partition made from what Abbey assumes is bulletproof glass, then points at the two folding chairs. 'Please sit down. The Duty Officer will be right with you.'

Suzanne says, 'Agent, we already have an appointment with—'

'I know. This is the way it works. Everybody talks to the Duty Officer. Even the President would talk to the Duty Officer. Shouldn't take more than ten minutes.'

It takes an hour.

The Duty Officer – a smiling young woman who never offers her name – grills Abbey and Suzanne about everything from their current occupations to the names of their respective first-grade teachers. Just when Abbey is going to shatter the glass partition into smithereens, the officer says, 'Please go back to the front lobby. Agent Bronstein will escort you to Agent Napier's office. He and Dr Walton are waiting for you. Have a great day.'

Abbey gives the officer a toothy, wholly phony smile.

'Oh, it's been *great* already. If it gets any greater, my head's going to explode.'

Through gritted teeth, Suzanne whispers, 'Be nice. These people are your friends.'

'Maybe they are. Maybe they're not.'

Murphy meets them at the elevator on the fifth floor, wearing a huge grin; he looks happier than Abbey has ever seen him. 'Thank you so much for coming, Abbey.' He offers her his hand for shaking; she refuses. Unfazed, he turns to Suzanne and says, 'Counselor Addison, I presume.'

Suzanne nods. 'Agent Napier.'

'Good to meet you,' he says.

'I wish it could've been under happier circum-stances.'

Murphy says, 'Ms Addison, I think you will see that these are some very happy circumstances, indeed.' He says to Abbey, 'You have made a wise decision, Ab. This will change your life for the better.'

Abbey says, 'Yeah. Sure it will.'

As they walk down the hallway, Suzanne whispers to Abbey, 'I thought you said he was a dork.'

Abby says, 'He *was*. Now, not so much, I guess.'

'He looks pretty good.'

'If you say so.'

When they arrive outside of Murphy's office, he introduces Suzanne and Abbey to his assistant, a pretty young girl named Kelly, who looks to be fresh out of high school. Abbey asks, 'So how do you like it here at The Bureau?'

Murphy says, 'You mean The Company, Ab.'

Kelly says, 'What the hell're you talking about, Murphy? We're The Bureau. Those bumblers at the CIA are The Company.'

Triumphant, Abbey claps, then points at Murphy. '*Ha!* I *told* you.'

Murphy shakes his head. 'Kelly's new. Let's go.'

His office is small, nondescript, and barely decorated; his college and FBI diplomas hang on the wall opposite the window, and that's it. No family, no friends, no pets, no nothing. Murphy points to the elderly, bearded gentleman seated on the well-worn leather sofa. 'Abbey Bynum, Dr Paul Walton. Dr Walton, Abbey.'

'Please, Abbey,' says the doctor, 'call me Paul.' He stands. 'It is a pleasure, a *true* pleasure to meet you. I look forward to working with you.'

Paul seems like a nice man, but Abbey is thrown by that whole 'look forward to working with you' thing. Before she can protest, Murphy says, 'Dr Walton, Ab will not be working with us unless she chooses to do so. She has not yet made that choice. Please keep that in mind during today's discussion. Okay?'

Paul nods. 'Of course, Murphy.' He says to Abbey, 'Sometimes my brain and my mouth don't work in tandem.'

Abbey says, 'I know what you mean.' Then, to Murphy: 'Okay, let's get this over with. We've already been here forever. I want to get home and watch *Days of Our Lives*.'

Murphy says, 'I did not know you watched soaps . . . oh. You were joking.'

'Yep. Joking. I'll give you credit, Murphy: at least you can recognise a joke now. You still don't laugh at it. But at least you recognise it.'

Suzanne places her hand on Abbey's forearm and says, 'Abbey. Please. Be cool.'

After the four sit down, Murphy says, 'Can we start from the beginning, Ab?'

Suzanne says, 'Hold on', then pulls her digital voice recorder from her briefcase, places it on the table, hits the red button, and says, '*Now* we can start from the beginning.'

Eyeing the recorder, Murphy says, 'This is highly irregular, Ms Addison.'

'Well, Agent Napier, this is a highly irregular situation. We record, or we take off.'

Murphy thins his lips. 'Fine. I'll need you to sign a non-disclosure agreement before you leave the building.'

'Done,' Suzanne says. 'Go ahead, Abbey. Just like you did for me last night.'

For the second time in less than twelve hours, Abbey tells her story, and this time it's a smoother ride. *The tale becomes easier with each telling*, she thinks.

When she finishes, Paul takes her hand and says, 'If you choose to let us help you, Abbey, we'll help you. *I'll* help you.'

Abbey takes her hand back – gently, so as not to

offend him; he actually seems like a decent fellow – and says, 'I appreciate that, but I don't feel like I need any help.'

'You do not?' Murphy asks. 'It does not bother you when a new power pops up during your menstrual cycle?'

'It doesn't *bother* me. It's just . . . weird.'

Paul says, 'But we can make it less weird. We can help you harness it.'

Abbey says, 'Okay, two things: first, it's pretty well harnessed, and second, what are you trying to harness it for?'

Simultaneously, Paul says, 'So you can be happier', and Murphy says, 'So you can help us.'

Murphy blushes, then says, '*And* be happier, of course.'

Abbey glares at Murphy, then, without removing her gaze from his face, says, 'Suzanne, Paul, can Murphy and I have a moment alone, please?'

Suzanne says, 'You're not going to hurt him, are you?'

'No. We just need to chat.'

After Suzanne and Paul take their leave, Abbey turns off Suzanne's recorder and says, 'Okay, Murphy, here's the deal: I think I'm going to do something with you. Like I told Suzanne last night, it's time. I'd like the Weird Stuff to disappear, but that's not going to happen, and I think I'll need some protection, and whether I like it or not, you guys are probably my only choice. So what I need from you right now is your word that you won't start acting like you did near the end of our . . . our . . . our . . .'

'Our *thing*?' Murphy asks.

'Okay. Yeah. Sure. Our *thing*. See, right now, this isn't about you. This is about me, and it should only be about me. I *never* make anything about me, and I don't want to start now, Murphy, but this is the way it is. So you need to get out of Murphy World and get on the bus to Abbey Land. Got it?'

Murphy nods. 'I have a tendency to get wrapped up in my head to the detriment of those around me. This is something I have been working on in my day-to-day life, Ab. I promise you, as we progress, I will be a better man. I will try my hardest.'

'I guess that's all I could hope for.' She gives him a half-smile – which is way better than the sneer she's been sporting since she arrived at the FBI building – then says, 'Murphy, do me a favor.'

'I will try.'

'Use a contraction.'

He screws up his face. 'What do you mean?'

'Say "can't." '

'*Can't.*'

'Say "wouldn't." '

'*Wouldn't.*'

'Now use one of those in a sentence.'

'Um, okay. Um, I cannot believe that you have decided to work with me, because I thought you would not.'

'How about, I *can't* believe that *you've* decided to work with me?'

'Isn't that what I said?'

Abbey shakes her head. 'Forget it. Let's get the rest of the gang back in here.'

Once all four are seated, Suzanne says, 'Okay, Agent Napier, let's discuss specifics. What would you like out of Abbey? And before you answer that, every single term you ask for is negotiable. If we don't like something, if there's something you want Abbey to do that she's not comfortable with, it ain't happening. And I don't want you pressing her. If you do – if you piss her off – or if you piss *me* off – she's out.'

'I will not press her, nor will I piss her off, nor will I piss you off. I promise. So. Here are our thoughts. It is the FBI's belief that it is essential for Abbey to continue to live a normal life. We want her to keep her job at the law firm. We want her to continue living in her condominium in Wilmette. We want her to keep up that anal retentive daily routine of hers. We want her to keep dating Jon Carson . . .'

Unable to help herself, Abbey says, 'Oh, gee, thanks, Murphy, I'm *so* glad you approve of my love life.'

Murphy says, 'This is not about approval or disapproval. This is about keeping up appearances. If you are happy and comfortable with Jon Carson, then continue seeing him. It will be best for everybody. Okay?'

Abbey says, 'Fine.'

'Fine.' Then, to Suzanne, he says, 'We also ask that she give up the vigilantism. She will work with nobody other than us.'

Suzanne says, 'Done. Can we discuss compensation? She won't do this for free.'

Abbey says, 'Um, yeah, that's right, I won't do it for free.' Up until that very second, she hadn't considered asking for money.

Murphy says, 'We cannot put her directly on the payroll – we do not want a paper trail – so the FBI will be hiring Roscoe, Belmont, Paulina & Addison as legal consultants. The fee that the FBI pays RBP&A will then be forwarded to Ab. She will receive one thousand, two hundred and fifty-two dollars, twenty-eight cents a week. That's after taxes.'

Abbey says, 'Now that's a pleasant surprise. When I get my first paycheck, I'm *totally* going on vacation.'

Murphy says, 'I am afraid not. For the first year or so, we'll need you in Chicago. You can visit your family in Buffalo, but that will have to be it for traveling.'

Suzanne asks, 'Why?'

'Because we are going to have Ab on twenty-four-hour surveillance.'

Abbey says, 'Excuse me? You want me to live a normal life, but how am I supposed to do that with a bunch of spooks following me around?'

'They will not be following you around, *per se*, Ab.'

'I thought the definition of surveillance was following people around.'

'They will only be in your general area. You will never see them, and they will barely see you. We do not want them in your face, but we *do* want them to keep track of you, because we are . . . concerned.'

Suzanne asks, 'Concerned about what, Agent Napier?'

'Right now, nothing specific. Nobody knows about Abbey, and we intend to keep it that way for as long as we possibly can. But eventually, no matter how hard we try to keep a lid on it, word will get out, and we need to be prepared for that eventuality, because it could happen *fast.*'

Abbey mumbles, 'This sucks.'

Murphy says, 'I agree wholeheartedly. But it is better than the alternative.'

Suzanne says, 'The alternative being . . . ?'

'The alternative being', Murphy says, 'somebody snatching Abbey without us – or *anybody* – knowing until it is too late.'

'I see your point,' Abbey says. 'Surveillance it is.'

'Agent Napier,' Suzanne says, 'you've done a whole lot of talking, but you've yet to tell us exactly what you want out of Abbey.'

'What we want out of her is one full day a week. I hope you will be willing to let her off from work. I know the firm will miss her, but her presence with the FBI will benefit the greater good of the country. How about Thursday?'

Suzanne says, 'Thursday is staff meeting.'

Abbey grins. 'Then Thursday is *perfect*!'

Suzanne grumbles, 'Fine. Thursday.'

Murphy says, 'I recommend you tell your co-workers that you are going back to school.'

Abbey says, 'Great cover story', then she asks Murphy, 'What're we going to be doing on these Thursdays?'

'Three-and-a-half hours with Paul on utilising and harnessing your powers, and three-and-a-half hours with me on law enforcement. One hour for lunch.'

Suzanne nods. 'That's fine with me. Abbey?'

Abbey says, 'Fine', then she asks, 'So why, Murphy? Why now?'

Murphy stands up, walks over to the window, and turns around. With his back to the group, he says, 'The country is crawling with supervillains . . .' He spins back around. '. . . and we need Ab to help us subdue and capture them.'

Abbey gulps. 'Me?'

Murphy nods. 'Yes, Ab. You.'

This is it, Abbey thinks. *It's official. My life, as I know it, is over. I'm a good guy. I'm a superhero. Or superheroine, I guess. God, I hope it doesn't suck.*

She looks at Suzanne. 'Before I do anything, I have to tell my family.'

Murphy says, 'No you don't—'

Abbey stands up and says, 'Excuse me?'

'. . . because they already know.'

Part Three

17

Exhausted after her fifth training session with Paul, Abbey Bynum goes to Jon Carson's apartment, ready to collapse into his bed like a house of cards . . . a ragingly horny house of cards.

It's not like her new mentor Dr Paul Walton – and Paul's a great guy, so let's just go ahead and call him a mentor/friend – is running her ragged, although he's trying his damndest. Truth be told, if she's learned one thing over the last month-plus, it's that *nobody* can run her ragged, that when it comes to the Weird Stuff, she has an inexhaustible well of energy. Whether she's hurling five hundred-pound palm-sized balls of osmium through a target that's exactly six-inches in diameter, or dodging a barrage of rubber bullets numbering in the hundreds, or doing loop-de-loop after loop-de-loop after loop-de-loop in a twenty feet by twenty feet by twenty feet glass room, she's fine. It's all easy, and, when she's honest with herself, she admits it's kind of fun, kind of like Friday afternoon gym classes at high school, when it was Free Play, and the kids could do whatever they wanted to do, so long as it got their heart rate up. Being in constant motion could be pretty damn cool.

No, the exhausting part is dealing with what Dr Paul Walton likes to call, 'the psychology of superheroes.'

'If we were to simplify,' Paul says during their first afternoon together, 'we'd say that Superman had more angst than Kurt Cobain, and Batman loathed himself to the point of self-flagellation, and Spiderman was always trying to prove *something* to *somebody* so that he could get laid. Clark Kent, Bruce Wayne and Peter Parker were not healthy people, Abbey. Yes, I know they're fictional characters, but there's a reason they have not only endured all these years, but have also touched so many people. And that reason is that they're *real.*'

Abbey says, 'I hear what you're saying, Paul, but I don't think it applies to me. I'm a normal chick. I'm not Kurt Cobain. I'm not even Courtney Love.' (She doesn't bother mentioning that she has a Hole T-shirt at the bottom of her dresser at home.)

'Right,' Paul says, 'but remember that Superman would've been a normal guy had he lived his life on planet Krypton. Peter Parker was a normal guy until he got bitten by that spider, that *steatoda grossa.* Bruce Wayne was . . . okay, Bruce Wayne was a little nuts, but he was, nonetheless, a living, breathing being who wanted the same things we all do: happiness, love and peace of mind, with a little bit of vengeance thrown in for good measure. But their respective powers – whether those powers were supernatural or man-made – made them *unstable*. I don't want that for you, Abbey. Nobody does. And it could happen when you get into the field. We want you to be as mentally strong as you are physically.'

In certain respects, Abbey has always thought of herself as a girl version of her dad: no-nonsense, practical, realistic and, yes, stable. 'I think I'm pretty earthbound,' she says. 'Pun intended.'

'So Agent Napier claims. And I have no reason to doubt him. But I've been studying the psychology of superheroes for over twenty years now, and no matter how stable you are – and no matter how stable you *think* you are – things might change once you're out there, and I want you to be prepped. I want *both of us* to be prepped.'

'But I've already *been* in the field. You know that, right?'

'Of course I do, Abbey. I know about the bank robber, and the drug bust, and the muggings. I even know about you rescuing that cat from Mrs Iris Carmody's tree.'

Abbey blinks. 'Um, how? I never told Murphy about that. As a matter of fact, I only told one other person about that.'

Paul says, 'Oh. Hmm. Interesting.'

'Oh, hmm, interesting, *what*?'

'Well, it appears Agent Napier never mentioned it to you.'

Abbey groans. 'Mentioned *what* to me?'

'That, um, that, um . . .'

'That, um, *what*?!'

Paul sighs. 'That we've been clocking you for years.'

'*Excuse me*?!'

Paul stands up and paces around the makeshift gymnasium/office that he's commandeered as his training center in the sub-sub-sub-basement of the Chicago FBI building. 'Oh, dear,' he says. 'I really thought Agent Napier had briefed you.'

'Agent Napier hasn't briefed me on *anything*. All Agent Napier does is teach me about the "routine activity theory," and panipticons, and all this other criminology crap that probably isn't going to help me, *ever*. Get him in here.'

Paul hunches over his MacBook Pro, punches a few keys, and peers at the screen. 'It appears he's in the field.'

Abbey tries to calm herself with a deep breath. Doesn't work. 'I don't want to be, like, a diva or anything, but if he's not here in sixty minutes, I'm outta here.'

Fifty-eight minutes later, while Abbey is idly practicing moving barbells with her mind, Murphy wanders into the gym. 'Good afternoon, Ab,' he calls. 'How are you progressing?'

One of the barbells flies at Murphy's face. He ducks, narrowly avoiding a trip to the emergency room and the plastic surgeon. Abbey says, 'I'm progressing wonderfully.' She points at his crotch. 'Unless you talk to me, next time I'm aiming there.'

Murphy calmly says, 'Talk to you about what?'

'Talk about how long you've been, you've been . . .' she snaps her fingers as if it will help her remember the word she is searching for, then asks Paul – 'Hey, Doc, what did you call it?'

'Um, clocking you.'

To Murphy, she says, 'Right. What he said. How long you've been *clocking* me.'

Murphy turns to the doctor and says, 'Thanks, Paul. Thanks a lot.'

'She would've figured it out eventually,' Paul says. 'She reads minds, you know.'

'Yes, but I have the cloaking agent,' Murphy says. 'You *know* that.'

Paul repeats, 'She would've figured it out eventually.'

Abbey asks Paul, 'What's a cloaking agent?'

Paul says, 'It's just like it sounds. We'll discuss that later. Agent Napier, could you please tell Abbey what she wants to be told so we can get on with it?'

Murphy points to the row of folding chairs against the near wall. 'Join me?'

Abbey is still thinking about this cloaking agent business. Guessing that it's some sort of something – maybe it's a drug, maybe it's an implanted computer chip, maybe it's a literal cloak – that blocks people like Abbey from digging into your brain, she tries reading Murphy's mind. Nothing. It's a blank.

Murphy gently shakes Abbey's shoulder. 'Did you hear me? Would you like to sit?'

'Fine.'

Once seated, Murphy touches Abbey's hand, and says, 'Ab, I apologise—'

She jerks her hand away as if his is on fire. 'Don't try and be nice to me. Spill.'

Murphy says, 'I swear to you on my life, I never told them. I never told my bosses. I never told my boss's bosses. I never said a single word to anybody about who you were, and what you were, and where you were. Had I said something – had I given them any information whatsoever above and beyond what they already had – who knows how far up the food chain I could be right now? I could probably be a supervisor by now. I could be heading my own division. But I never told.'

'Okay. Fine. For right now, I'm choosing to believe you. That doesn't mean I *do* believe you.'

Murphy looks pained. 'Why not?'

'You threw furniture at me.'

'Oh. Yeah. There is that.'

'Yeah. There's that. So how did they find out?'

He points at Paul, who is hunched over his Mac. 'He could explain the science of it far better than I, but what it boils down to is, your powers – and every paranormal's powers, for that matter – emit some sort of specific electrical charge – or discharge, really – and they have the technology to pick it up.'

'*They?* Who's *they?*'

'*Us*, really.'

'How long have *they*, or *us*, or *whoever* known about me?'

Murphy takes a deep breath. 'Since you were born. The FBI has been watching you since you were born. It *is* possible other United States agencies know – the CIA, the NSA, et cetera. We doubt it, but we cannot confirm that one way or the other. However, we are certain that nobody outside of the country is aware of you or your powers.'

'Oh,' Abbey whispers. She feels dizzy. Her forehead is dotted with sweat, and she thinks she might pass out . . . she probably would've, for that matter, had she not dug her fingernails deeply into her thigh.

Again, he touches her hand. 'Ab, are you okay?'

Again, she swats it away. 'No, Murphy. No, I am most definitely *not* okay. Would you be okay if you found out that the Government knows everything about you? About your birthday parties when you were a kid, and your first date, and the first time you made love, and how often you smoke weed? Would you be okay if you found out this has been going on for your entire life? *Would you?*'

Murphy says, 'Of course not. That is why I tried to get them to back off.'

'What?'

'One morning when we were still going out – a morning after you and I had a huge argument about something trivial – I looked up your file . . .'

'Of course you did.'

'. . . and the system would not let me in. You were classified. I could not change a single word of it. Then

I went to see my supervisor, and I asked him to lay off you. I asked him to leave you alone. I told him you should not have to be involved with anything you did not want to be involved in, but when he explained how keeping tabs on you was for your own protection, it made sense to me.'

'Yeah? How's that?'

'Our paranormal technology is far ahead of the rest of the world's, but it was only a matter of time before everybody else caught up, before you were *made*, before you became a valuable commodity to our enemies, and before you were kidnapped, and possibly tortured, and possibly drugged, and possibly brainwashed, and who knows what else. Even though it made sense to keep you under light surveillance, I kept requesting that we leave you alone. I said that you should be allowed to live your life as freely and as happily as anybody else. After the tenth "no", I asked if I could handle your case. If somebody was going to look out for you, it might as well be me. They said yes. For that, I remain grateful. I hope you will be, too.'

Abbey is stunned into silence.

Murphy says, 'Hello? Ab? Talk to me.'

Eventually, she quietly asks, 'Why didn't you tell me? All this time, you knew, and you didn't say anything. Why? I mean, we were sleeping together for a good long while. I know we weren't, like, boyfriend/girlfriend, but don't you think that people who screw regularly shouldn't keep secrets?'

'I could not tell you, Ab. I simply could not.'

'Because you would've gotten fired.' She sighs. 'It was always about the job for you, Murphy.'

'I cannot lie: that was a part of it. A small part of it, granted, but a part of it, nonetheless. If I would have divulged a national secret to you, I would have been blackballed from law enforcement, and possibly arrested for treason, and that would not have done you or me any good. But if I kept quiet, I could protect you. I could make certain that you would not be harmed.' He pauses. 'You see, somewhere, somebody is developing the power to deal with paranormals such as yourself, and there is nothing anybody can do about that, myself included. Technology will roll on in the garages and basements of the world, whether we like it or not.'

Abbey asks, 'If you wanted to protect me so badly, why weren't you nicer to me? Why didn't you treat me like a girlfriend? Better yet, why didn't you even treat me like a *friend*?'

'I tried, Ab. I truly did. But you made it clear that you did not want me the way I wanted you, and I have rejection issues – that is what my therapist calls it, "rejection issues" – and when you pushed me away, rather than fight back – rather than fight for you, rather than try and figure out how to make myself into a man worthy of not just your love, but *anybody's* love – I *pushed* back. I pushed back, and that was wrong, and I know that now.' He pauses. 'I did not know how to . . . to . . . to *nurture*. I do not know if I ever will. I do not know if it is in my make-up. If you were never properly taken care of as a child, you might not learn how to properly take care of others.'

Abbey says, 'You never told me about your parents. I could've helped you. How was I supposed to know?'

'You never asked, and I never offered, because, well, those are the kinds of things you do not bring up in discussion unless absolutely necessary. Honestly, even if you had asked, I probably would have changed the subject. It is only recently – say, within the last year – that I have been able to discuss my mother and father with any degree of objectivity, even with my shrink.' He stands up. 'But that is neither here nor there. You asked why the FBI has always known about you, and now you know why. We could not tell you everything until you were properly trained, or, at the very least, deep in the loop. And here you are. And now you know. And now you have to get back to work, as do I.' He places his hand on her shoulder; this time, she doesn't shove it away. 'I am here for you, Ab. Know that I will protect you as best I can.' He gives her a small, almost sad smile. 'I realise you have the means to protect yourself, but you can never have too many hands on deck, as they say.' He checks his watch. 'I will see you at our three o'clock class, correct?'

She nods, afraid to say anything for fear that she'll start blubbering.

18

In general, Abbey Bynum does one of two things after sex: she falls into an immediate, deep sleep, or talks until her partner wants to stick a pillow in her mouth. Tonight, after a particularly intense bout of lovemaking with Jon Carson, it's the latter.

'Honey,' she asks, 'what do you think of when you hear the phrase, "the psychology of superheroes"?'

Jon scratches his freshly shaved chest. 'Um, why?'

'No reason.' Then she thinks, *Screw it, I'll put him in the loop. Seems like everybody else is.* 'Okay,' she says, 'there is a reason.' It's after 1 a.m., and they both have to be awake in six hours, and they've both had a long day, but Abbey's revved, and Jon is a willing listener, so she opens her mouth to divulge her deepest, darkest secret . . . and Jon yawns. Abbey says, 'Okay, go to sleep. We'll talk about it another time.'

'No, no, no, I'm up, I'm up, I'm up. Let's talk about . . . what're we talking about?'

'We're talking about Weird Stuff.'

'Like what? Like Kevin?' Kevin is the new mailroom kid. He has a mustache tattooed on to his face. Apparently the dummy has trouble growing facial hair, as well as remarkably poor judgment.

'No, not Kevin, although he is *really* weird. No, Weird Stuff like this.' And then she looks into the bathroom. Three seconds later, Abbey's travel-sized bottle of Arctic Mint Listerine floats over to the bed. It drops on Abbey's chest, after which she opens it, takes a swig, and then a gulp.

Jon stares at her for a bit, then says, 'I don't know what's more disconcerting, the flying Listerine, or the fact that you swallowed it.'

She laughs. 'You know I swallow. Sometimes.'

'Yeah. You do. And I dig it.' He sits up and rubs his eyes. 'Hey, what just happened here? Am I still awake, or am I dreaming?'

Abbey kisses him on the cheek. 'You're awake. I have a long story I'd like to tell you. Can I get you a drink?'

Jon shakes his head. 'I think I should be a hundred per cent sober for this.'

'Yeah, maybe you should. So. Once upon a time, there was a little girl named Abbey. When she was a baby, Abbey ignored the maxim, *You have to walk before you can run*. For her, that line didn't really apply, because Abbey knew how to *fly* before she could walk.'

Jon looks at the ceiling during Abbey's monologue, interrupting her near the end of the story when he asks, 'What does your family think about all this? Are they scared that you're a secret agent, or whatever it is the FBI is calling you?'

Abbey says, 'Interesting you mention that, Jon. After I told Murphy I'd come aboard, I told him I wanted to tell my family before I made a final decision, and he said, "They already know." '

'What the hell did that mean?' Jon snaps, sounding legitimately angry. Turns out Jon does angry well, and Abbey's glad she's not a lawyer, so she never has to go up against him in court, because he'd wipe the floor with her.

'They were there,' she says. 'They were in the building. The night before, the FBI dragged them to Chicago: Mom, Dad and Dave. They also dragged Cheryl, who was a mess, because she'd just played two shows at Webster—'

Jon interrupts, 'Wait a minute, you're telling me that the Feds kidnapped your parents, *and* your brother, *and* your best friend?'

Abbey says, 'No. Not really. I mean, I don't know if kidnapped is the word. Mom, Dad, Dave and Cheryl all said the agents were nice and polite. But, as my dad put it, "They were very persuasive." I guess the agents didn't threaten them, but they didn't *not* threaten them. Does that make sense?'

'Yeah,' Jon says drily. 'Unfortunately, it does. I've dealt with the Feds. They have themselves some big egos.'

Abbey shrugs, and, thinking of how kind Paul has

been, says, 'I don't know about that. Anyhow, we all talked it out, and everybody was supportive. They were scared, but supportive.'

Jon punches his pillow. 'The FBI is so goddamn *dramatic*. They couldn't have let you tell them yourself? Or done a conference call? They had to drag your people out of their beds in the middle of the night? They were probably scared shitless.'

'They weren't, really. Deep down, all of us knew something like this was going to happen someday. We never discussed it, probably because we were afraid that talking about it would make it real, and if we made it real, it would come to fruition. They were cool. Nervous for me, but cool.' She smiles. 'Cheryl was a little pissed that she missed her afterparty. So.' And then she stops.

'So what?' Jon asks.

'So.'

'*So?*'

'So, what do you think?'

'I don't know. This is a lot to absorb.' And he clams up.

Abbey's a little taken aback. Thus far, everybody she's told the Weird Stuff story to has been nothing but sympathetic, and she expected the same from Jon. She looks at his expressionless face, and can practically see the gears spinning.

But she can't *hear* them.

And she wants to.

Abbey can count on one finger how many times she's

purposely and purposefully utilised her ESP to find out what somebody was thinking about her. It was two years prior – right after she figured out how to control the ESP, rather than the ESP controlling her – at Bloomingdale's, on a crowded Saturday afternoon. Abbey tried on an $899 little black dress, and couldn't decide whether or not it looked good on her, so she asked a well-dressed saleslady, who said, 'It looks *lovely*, ma'am, just lovely.' Abbey thought her 'lovely' was dripping with sarcasm, so she dug into the saleslady's brain, and found out that the woman was thinking, *Looks like shit, but I need the commission*. Abbey wasn't in the mood to get into it with her, so she vowed to never shop at Bloomie's again, a vow she broke three months later, on a Friday afternoon when she was in desperate need of a last-minute outfit for the RBP&A Christmas party, which was two hours away.

In any event, Abbey is curious as to what Jon is thinking. She's pretty sure he'll eventually tell her, but she decides to take a sneak preview. She closes her eyes, opens up her mind, and melds with Jon.

Nothing. It's a blank. Radio silence.

Odd, she thinks. *That's the second time today*. 'I have to pee,' she says.

' 'kay,' Jon says, still lost in thought.

In the bathroom, she gazes at herself in the mirror. Aside from the fact that her hair is the longest it's ever been, and she has that just-been-properly-fucked sheen of sweat on her chest, she looks the same as she always does. She stares at herself for a good two minutes, not even sure what she's looking for, but whatever it is, she doesn't find it.

Even though she doesn't use the toilet, she flushes so as not to concern Jon. Not that he's concerned right now – *He's probably still in La-La Land*, Abbey thinks – but you never know.

On the way back to bed, she again tries to peek into his brain, and again, nothing. She decides not to worry about it, and says, 'Come on, baby. Let's go to sleep.'

Jon says, 'Right.' He kisses her on the cheek. 'Good night. I have to go into the office early tomorrow—'

'It's Saturday.'

'. . . so I'm setting the alarm for six-thirty. You can stay here as long as you want.' He sounds dismissive, cold, and doesn't kiss her goodnight.

Abbey doesn't fall asleep for three more hours.

19

Two days later – a Monday, at six in the morning – Abbey's cell screams at the top of its electronic lungs. She groans, grabs the phone from her nightstand, and squints at the caller I.D. display: unknown number. She punches the green button and gives a tentative, 'Hello?'

'Good morning, Abbey, this is FBI Agent Barb Jacobs. Agent Napier is indisposed right now, so I'm your runner.'

This is news to Abbey. She sits up. 'Um, I've never heard of you.'

'I'm sitting at Agent Napier's desk right now. To confirm my identity, I want you to dial his direct line. Immediately. We have a situation. I'll expect to hear from you in no more than thirty seconds.' And then she hangs up.

Abbey calls Murphy's number, and Agent Jacobs picks up after half a ring. 'This is Jacobs. I assume you're comfortable that I am who I say I am, but if not, you can ring up Dr Walton on his cell number. He's expecting your call.'

'No, that's okay. I'm good. What's going on? What's the situation?'

'No time to explain. There's a car waiting for you in front of your house. It's a black Dodge Charger. There are two agents in the front seat; the driver is named Sapp, and the other guy is named Faulk. They'll take you to me. Leave your house quickly and immediately, but don't do anything that might be construed as suspicious.'

Abbey is wearing only a baby-doll T-shirt and an old blue thong, 'Can I at least put on some clothes?' she asks.

'Like I said, quickly. I'll see you within the half-hour.'

In the car, Sapp and Faulk say, 'Good morning' in unison, then remain silent for the remainder of the twenty-nine-minute ride. They hustle her up to Murphy's office, and there's Agent Jacobs, looking every inch the badass that Abbey suspects she is.

'Good morning, Abbey,' Jacobs says. 'I appreciate you coming in this early and this quickly.'

'Um, you're welcome, but I don't think I had much choice.'

Jacobs nods. 'Nonetheless, I appreciate it.'

Abbey gives her a quick once-over: tall, muscular, blonde, model-pretty, and exceedingly youthful-looking. She blurts out, 'How old are you?'

Jacobs gives her a tight, mirthless smile. 'Nineteen.'

'*Seriously?* Nineteen? How did you—'

'No time. Here's the deal. We're going to Tennessee immediately. A suburb of Nashville called Hendersonville, to be specific.'

Abbey asks, 'Who's *we*?'

'You, me, Sapp and Faulk. Agent Napier might meet us there, but he might not, depending on the timing. I'll brief you while we're in the air.' Jacobs grabs Abbey's wrist and pulls her out of Murphy's office, and down the hallway. 'Our transport is on the roof and gassed up. We're leaving in seven minutes.'

Abbey gets a bad vibe from Jacobs, and the thought of being cooped up in a small plane with her is far from appealing, so she's tempted to fly to Tennessee by herself via Weird Stuff Airlines. But she and Paul haven't gotten too far with their in-sky navigational lessons, and since Abbey's never flown anywhere outside of the Chicago and Buffalo areas, there's the distinct chance that if she takes to the air on her own, she'll end up in Costa Rica.

Once the plane takes off, Jacobs calms down. 'I apologise, Abbey, but I'm freaking the fuck out. This is my first time in charge of an operation, and I don't know how far from the scene Napier is, and I've never met you before, and I've never dealt with a para before, and I haven't eaten in forever, and I'm fucking hungry, and I'm fucking exhausted.' She pounds the arm of the chair with a closed fist. '*Fuck*.'

Abbey changes her mind; Jacobs seems okay. The kid is just scared . . . just like she is, so why not make a friend? After all, one scared girl plus one scared girl equals two slightly less scared girls. Abbey reaches into her purse, pulls out a Zone Bar, and says, 'Want to split this? It's chocolate peanut butter.'

Jacobs looks like she wants to kiss Abbey. On the lips. With tongue. 'Oh my God, thank you a million times. You're fucking amazing.' After Jacobs downs her half-a-bar in two bites, she says, 'Okay. Phew. My blood sugar is under control. So here's the score. Ever heard the name Baron von Stroheim? Probably not.'

'He's an old-timey movie guy, right?'

'No, that's Erich von Stroheim.' She sighs. '*Fuck*, I wish Napier had told you about this. No, Baron von Stroheim is, well, he's a supervillain.'

Abbey gives her a small smile. 'Supervillain? Yeah, Murphy mentioned there're some of them floating around. Is that, like, the official FBI word for them?'

'No.' Then she says to Sapp and Faulk, 'Boys, what does the brass call supervillains?'

In unison, the agents say, '*Masters*.'

Jacobs rolls her eyes. '*Masters*. Ridiculous, right? Our pal von Stroheim is a master. One of the lesser ones, granted, but he's a master, nonetheless. He's escalated his offensive, and we – and by we, I mean the FBI – don't have a quality protocol in place to deal with this particular escalation.'

'Okay, I'm lost here. I'm a little behind. I'm still doing Superhero one-oh-one with Dr Walton. This sounds like it's an advanced course.'

Jacobs nods. 'Unfortunately, it is. We're throwing you into the fire, Abbey, and for that, we apologise. But this is a serious situation. This is a threat to our national security.'

'Jesus,' Abbey says, 'not too much pressure.'

'I won't sugarcoat it. There's a *ton* of pressure. But we wouldn't put you' – here, she does finger quotes – ' "out there" if we weren't confident you could handle it.'

'Fantastic,' Abbey says, her voice dripping with sarcasm.

'You'll be fine.'

'Fantastic,' she repeats, and thinks, *Screw it, let's do this. I'm in it, so I may as well win it.* 'I guess you should tell me what "out there" means.'

Jacobs looks relieved beyond belief. 'Great. Thank you *so* much. So here's the deal: Baron von Stroheim's real name is Eric Simms, and he's from Muncie, Indiana.'

'Why Baron von Stroheim?'

'Fuck if I know. Practically every master gives himself a dipshit nickname. There's one guy in Los Angeles who goes by Sergeant Hollywood, and some douchebag in Texas who dubbed himself Captain Cowboy.'

Despite herself, Abbey smiles. 'That's pretty lame.'

'I know, *right*? It's *totally* lame.' (Abbey's liking Jacobs more by the second; she reminds her of Cheryl.) 'In any event, like I said, von Stroheim is a lesser master, but a master, nonetheless. Some of his computer-programming skills are so far ahead of ours that we've tried hiring him several times, but he's not having it. Physically speaking, he's developed himself with exercise and electrical stimulation to the point that he's stronger than a regular old human being, but not nearly as strong as you, which is why we put him in the *lesser* category. He's also developed some flight technology, but as far as we can tell, it's very much in its infancy. We need to take him out immediately, and we think that between you, me, Sapp, Faulk and the mob of uniforms whom we'll have on the ground in Tennessee within the hour, we can do it.'

'Why does he need to be taken out? What did he do?'

Jacobs explains, 'In general, these masters aren't the most imaginative types. They either want money or power. Their typical modus operandi is to take hostages, or threaten to destroy either a building, or a city, or the moon, unless we give them a billion dollars, or something like a seat in Congress. Von Stroheim wants the money.'

'Have any of these masters succeeded?'

'I'm afraid you don't have the security clearance that enables me to discuss that. Maybe Agent Napier can fill you in later.'

Abbey blanches. 'Isn't that the kind of thing I should know about before I dive into one of these messes?'

'Probably,' Jacobs says, 'but that's not my decision. FBI hierarchy sucks eggs, but there's nothing anybody can do about it.' She turns to Sapp and Faulk. 'Right, guys?'

They stare at Jacobs, and don't say a word.

Jacobs says, 'I leapfrogged over them, and they're still pissed.'

Abbey, who doesn't want to get involved in inter-departmental politics, changes the subject: 'How much is this von Stroheim guy asking for?'

'A billion dollars. Just like all these other assholes. It's always a billion dollars.'

'What're his threats?'

Jacobs reaches into her briefcase, pulls out a file, and stares at the paper. 'Hendersonville, Tennessee is full of rich folks who live in gated communities, and it's generally a quiet town that the Federal Government has zero interest in on a day-to-day basis, so it's kind of an ideal location for a guy like von Stroheim to set up his base, a guy who needs space, and needs easy access to civilians he can fuck with. About two years ago, he bought a house in one of these subdivisions – an expensive one, I might add – and set up his lair.' She looks up. 'Seriously. His lair. That's what the master dumbasses call their hidey-holes, so that's what *we* have to call them.' She shakes her head. 'Morons. Anyhow, cutting to the chase, the Baron has a laser weapon that can shoot out multiple beams simultaneously – like hundreds of them – and right now, he has them set to destroy every house in every subdivision within ten miles.'

Laser beams. Yikes. Abbey asks, 'Why do you need me for this? Why can't you get a bunch of agents who've done this sort of thing before?'

'Von Stroheim is a moron, but he's a smart moron, and his lair is protected like, like, like . . .' she turns to

Sapp and Faulk – 'either of you care to give me a metaphor?'

Sapp says, 'It's protected like a motherfucker.'

Jacobs says, 'Inelegant, but accurate.'

Abbey asks, 'What does *protected like a motherfucker* mean, specifically?'

'Oh,' Jacobs says, 'nothing your average paranormal couldn't fight her way through. Dozens of infra-red video cameras around the perimeter. A twenty-inch-thick partition of re-re-re-reinforced steel surrounding his lair. Landmines. That sort of thing.' She smirks. 'Oddly enough, no guards. No henchmen. That's one of the reasons you don't hear much about masters. They tend to work alone, and working alone is not what you would call a recipe for success.' She shakes her head. 'Seriously. What a moron.'

The airplane lands, and Abbey's nervous stomach turns into a ball of acid that could probably melt von Stroheim's steel wall. 'What do you want out of me? What am I supposed to do?'

Jacobs stands up and heads to the exit door; Abbey and the other two agents follow. 'Right now, there are two dozen of our agents on the way, as well as a SWAT team. Three of our guys are negotiating with the baron as we speak. He's not budging on his demands, and we won't ever accept his terms, so they're stalling until you get there. See, none of these masters know about you yet. You're not on any of their radar. Baron von Dillhole won't know what's coming.'

'And what is it that's coming?'

They walk down the stairs on to the runway, towards the waiting black van. Abbey, Jacobs and Faulk crawl into the back, while Sapp sits up front. Jacobs says, 'Von Stroheim's simple, so our attack will be simple: you go in, you subdue him, and you take him out. We think the entire operation will take no more than forty-eight seconds from the time you leave the starting point until capture.' She hands Abbey a blueprint. 'This is the layout. His command center is in the sub-basement. You'll break through the door, you'll fly down the stairs, you'll nail him with a taser . . . oops, wait, hold on . . .' She digs into her briefcase and pulls out a taser that looks more like a men's electric shaver than a deadly weapon. 'This'll render him unconscious for five minutes, which is more than enough time for you to carry him to us.' She smiles. 'We'll have you back in Chicago in time for lunch . . . which the Bureau will spring for. Aren't we wonderful?'

'Yeah. Sure. Swell.'

Abbey Bynum screws up the protocol. Royally.

The FBI's plan called for her to be in and out of Baron von Stroheim's lair in forty-eight seconds. She isn't even close.

It takes twenty-three.

Back in the plane, Abbey can't stop talking.

'Punching through that steel wall was like punching

through tissue paper. It was *nothing*. I didn't even feel it. I mean, look at my hand . . . not even a scratch! I thought it would be hard, but it totally wasn't. It was like . . . *boom!* I almost froze, because I couldn't believe it was that easy, and I thought it was a trap or something, but then I saw him, and I ran over, and I was holding the taser out, and I, like . . . like . . . like *dived* at him, and I don't even think he knew I was there. I think he was all tased up before he even realised something was wrong. And I couldn't believe he was so weird-looking, and so *small*, and that uniform he was wearing – that red skin-tight jumpsuit, and that lame-o mask – was ridiculous! I was like, *This is the guy who's going to take over Tennessee? Seriously? He's such a dweeb!* Oh my God, I'm *so* hungry now. Let's go have pizza, like Giordano's would be *awesome*. I'm totally not going into the law firm today. Hey, Faulk, Sapp, you guys should come to lunch with us. It'll be fun. I can't wait to tell everybody about this. Okay, not everybody, just my family, and my best friend, and my boyfriend. And don't worry, they're cool, they won't say anything to anybody. Oh, and Paul, I have to tell Paul. And Murphy. Murphy should know. Maybe he already knows, I don't know. This was so fun. Did you have fun?'

Agent Barb Jacobs answers, 'Apparently not as much as you did.'

After stuffing herself on stuffed pizza – spinach and mushroom with extra cheese, because after thwarting a

Master Dweeb like Baron von Stroheim, she *deserved* extra cheese – Abbey is taken to Murphy's office. She's so jazzed that she runs into his arms, gives him a sloppy, spinachy, mushroomy kiss on the cheek, and yells, 'Yo, Murrrrrrrrphy! Murphy Naaaaaaaapier! How cool are we? Look what we did! We saved, like, a million lives!'

Murphy grins. '*You* saved a million lives, Ab. Actually five hundred and one, to be exact, but it is still quite impressive.'

'It was amazing, Murphy. Amazing. I never in a zillion years thought I'd be saying this, but thank you. Thank you for bringing me into this. Thank you for letting me help. Thank you for letting me be myself. Wait, that's a Sly and the Family Stone song.' And then she sings at the top of her lungs, 'Thank you . . . for lettin' me . . . *be* mahselllllf . . . againnnnn!'

Murphy winces, looks around the hallway to make certain nobody has heard Abbey, then closes his office door. 'You're welcome, Ab. Obviously everybody at The Company—'

'The Bureau.'

'. . . also thanks you. But stay focused. This isn't over. Those damn supervillains are everywhere.'

'I thought you guys call them masters.'

'*They* call them masters. *I* call them supervillains. If they were masters – if they mastered their craft – this world would be in worse shape than it is. Fortunately, we have been able to keep them under control and under wraps, thanks to people like you.'

Abbey says, 'People like *me*? What do you mean?'

'There are other paras, Ab.'

'There are?' She smiles, relieved. 'I'm not the only one? Oh my God, that's the best news I've heard in *forever*. Where are they? Are any of them in Chicago? Can we get together?'

'I'm afraid that will never happen, Ab. *Never*. We will never introduce one para to another. It is for everybody's safety. Too many variables. Too many unknowns.'

'I understand,' Abbey says. 'It sucks, but I understand.' She stares at Murphy thoughtfully. 'You know, I could overpower you right now, and hack into your computer, and find all these paras myself.'

Murphy nods. 'You could. But you will not.'

'Why do you say that?'

'Simple. You are too sweet. That is why we trust you with this business. Your combination of sweetness, smarts and strength is . . . is . . . is *deadly*.'

He's right. Abbey is too damn nice to mess with a good guy like Murphy. A bad guy, she's happy to annihilate, but somebody who's on her side, she'll leave be. Unless there's betrayal involved. If that happens, all bets are off.

Abbey says, 'Whatever.' She checks her watch. 'Can you get somebody to give me a ride home? It's almost dinnertime.'

'You just ate lunch.'

'Saving the world jacks up your appetite.'

After Abbey gives Barb Jacobs a goodbye hug, Sapp

and Faulk drive her back to Wilmette, without saying a word . . . until they pull up in front of her condo.

Sapp grunts, 'Pleasure working with you.'

Faulk grunts, 'Ditto.'

In a lousy impression of the two taciturn agents, Abbey grunts, 'Pleasure. Ditto. Over and out.' Then she leans over the front seat and musses both of their hair. In the rearview mirror, she sees them grinning a teeny, tiny bit, and thinks, *Getting them to smile was harder than busting von Stroheim.*

Once inside, she calls her parents, then Dave, and then Cheryl. She talks until her cell's battery is down to nothing, and she's too tired to look for her charger, so she isn't able to call Jon, but she's not worried, as she's meeting him tomorrow after she's done at the office, and after he's done in court.

Abbey Bynum slides into bed at the ridiculously early hour of 9 p.m., happier than she's ever been in her adult life. Things in Superhero Land are smooth and fulfilling.

Until they're not.

I don't like it.'

So says Jon Carson.

'What don't you like about it?' Abbey asks over a home-cooked dinner – yes, Jon can cook – of slow-roasted halibut with pineapple salsa, sautéed spinach and coconut rice.

'It feels like they're using you.'

'Of *course* they're using me. They're using me the same way one of your clients uses you. I have a skill, I'm applying that skill, and they're paying me for it.'

'What are they paying you?' After she tells him, he says, 'So for just over a grand a week, you're risking your life. Does that make sense? Is your life worth that little?'

'What do I need money for? My Honda gets me from one place to another, and I'm perfectly content with my clothes, and now with this extra grand a week, I can take a nice vacation when I want to. That's fine with me.' She gestures at Jon's palatial apartment. 'This is lovely, but it's not necessary.' She spears a piece of fish, smiles, and says, 'I sure love visiting, though.'

Jon smiles, but it's not the usual Jon Carson, light-up-a-room smile; this one's all lip, and no teeth. 'I just don't want to see you taken advantage of,' he says. 'I want you to be safe. And if you use your Weird Stuff to help an organisation with as many financial resources as the FBI, you should get properly compensated.'

She shrugs. 'I've only done this one thing for them . . .'

'No,' he interrupts, 'you've spent hours and hours with Napier and Walton, and they've scouted you since you were an infant. That's more than *one thing*. That's a big deal. They should take care of you; I know how the FBI runs, and I don't think they ever will do you right, and I don't like it.'

'Okay,' Abbey says, 'for the sake of argument, let's say that I keep doing what I'm doing, and I feel like I deserve a raise, and they say no, what do I do then?'

'Simple. You go freelance.'

'Like I used to.'

'Right. Like you used to. Except bigger. *Much* bigger.'

'What does *much bigger* mean?'

'You put together a superhero start-up company. You get investors, and you get all the surveillance equipment you need, and you hire a couple of private detectives, and when you find out about some supervillain's plot, you send out an emissary to whatever law enforcement agency is handling the case, and you offer your services for a set cost. I think fifty grand a job is fair. No, more like a hundred grand. For somebody with your potential, fifty

K is chump change. And I'll help. We'll do it together.'
He smiles for real. 'We can take over the world.'

'You sound like a master.' As he laughs, she polishes
off her dinner – which is superb, better than anything
you can get at three out of four restaurants in Chicago –
then says, 'There were thirty-odd FBI and SWAT people
at von Stroheim's. And I know I handled it fine. But
here's the thing: apparently von Stroheim wasn't the
brightest bulb in the chandelier. What happens if I go
after somebody who knows what they're doing, I get in
trouble, and I don't have any back-up?'

Jon stands up and clears the table. 'That's why you
get investors, so you can have money to put people who
know what they're doing on the payroll. There's a hell of
a lot of qualified people out there, people who're better
at this sort of thing than even the Feds. People who have
the same technology and training, but aren't beholden to
the same rules.'

'I don't know, Jon,' Abbey says, 'I get the feeling I'll
have a lot of latitude with the FBI's rules. I think they're
just happy to have me there, and I doubt they'll fire me
for not reading some supervillain his Miranda rights.'

'You might be right about that. But maybe not. If
you're in charge, it'll always be *your* game, and if it's *your*
game, it's *your* rules, and you can get things *done*, and
done *right*.'

She peers closely at his face. 'You're sweating, Jon.
You're getting pretty worked up about this.'

'I can't help it. This whole thing feels wrong, and I

want what's best for you. There are better ways to use your Weird Stuff. At least I think so.' Then, sarcastically, he adds, 'But hey, what do I know? I'm no Murphy Napier.'

'Hey, be nice. Murphy's okay.'

Jon says, 'Maybe he is, maybe he isn't.' Jon finishes loading the dishwasher, then, suddenly calm, he says, 'Okay, all clear in kitchen central. What say we move this to the boudoir?'

She checks her watch. 'It's only nine-thirty. Isn't that a little too early for bed?'

'It's a little too early for *sleep*. But not for *bed*.'

Abbey walks towards the bedroom, gives him a 'come hither' finger, then says, 'I should warn you that it's that time of the month.'

Jon grins – there's that full-blown Jon Carson smile we all know and love – and says, 'That's never stopped me before.'

She unbuttons her shirt slowly, noting how his eyes crawl all over her chest. 'No. It hasn't.'

Cheryl has slept with thirty-four men – compared to Abbey's eight – and she's said time and again that there's a significant difference between lovemaking and fucking. As Abbey and Jon go at it with a fervor and ardor she's never before experienced with him – or any other man, for that matter – she finally understands what it is her friend is talking about.

Abbey can't get enough of Jon's body. His arms are

like pythons, and his legs are like tree trunks. He
manscapes his entire body, and she adores licking his
smooth chest. After Jon's third orgasm – the most he's
ever had with Abbey; actually, that's the most *anybody's*
had with Abbey, although James Caraway came close
– she thinks, *Man, I wish I had more experience, so
I'd have something to compare it to. Was this plain
awesome, super-awesome, or super-mega-awesome?* She
rolls over to ask Jon what he thinks, but he's fast asleep,
with what appears to be a satisfied smile playing across
his lips.

Careful not to wake him, Abbey gives Jon a gentle
kiss on the cheek – he stirs, but stays asleep – then she
trudges to the bathroom, dreading the yucky process of
post-coital tampon insertion. 'Talk about a buzzkill,' she
mumbles aloud, then laughs. She sits on the toilet and
takes care of business, then, staring idly at the bathtub,
she feels a funny tickle in her ears. She blinks hard, and
three red balls of electricity shoot from each of her eyes.
They land on the tub, which promptly bursts into flames.

As is always the case when another piece of Weird
Stuff rears its head, Abbey knows that what just
happened actually happened, and it's pointless to dwell
on whether or not it's real. It's best to accept it, and, in
this case, put out the damn fire. In what she later thought
was one of the finest uses of Weird Stuff ever, she turns
on the bathroom sink, cups her hands under the running
water, and runs it over to the tub. She repeats this
process approximately two hundred times in a single

minute. The fire is out before the smoke even has a chance to drift into the bedroom.

Abbey goes into the living room and sits on the sofa. Part of her wants to wake up Jon and share with him the fact that she can now shoot bullets out of her eyes, and part of her wants to go home and curl up in her own bed, and part of her wants to call Paul and Murphy, then have them take her to a shooting range so she can see what the hell she can do with this, because it's not like she knows of any places where she can practice setting things on fire with her eyeballs.

But then her cellphone vibrates to life. After she reads Murphy's text message, she does none of the above.

21

This particular master goes by the ridiculous name of Godfather Neat-o Corleone, a moniker that's stupid enough in and of itself, but when you consider that Godfather Neat-o Corleone is Asian – not Italian, like most mafia dons – you're looking at a level of idiocy unprecedented among masters.

After the car that had been waiting in front of Jon's building drops Abbey at the FBI office, Murphy and Barb Jacobs start drilling it into her head that Corleone's silly name masks the fact that he's one of the five smartest masters in the United States. Murphy says, 'He is brilliant, but mentally unstable, and it is the FBI's opinion that if he were not such a megalomaniac – if he was not so in love with himself – he would be the first master to cause some serious damage.'

Shaken, Abbey trembles. 'What do you mean by serious damage?'

Jacobs says, 'We believe he has the capability to blow up the moon. And that's exactly what he's threatening to do.'

'That's not *all* he's threatening to do,' Abbey points out.

Murphy says, 'Yes, we realise that, which is why I will not waste our time discussing the ramifications of the moon's destruction.'

Abbey says, 'I don't give a damn about the moon. I want to go after Cheryl, and I want to fucking go *now*.'

(At this point, you should probably read the text message that Murphy sent to Abbey: *cheryl sheldon kidnapped by master . . . wants u in exchange . . . car will pick u up in front of trump hotel in 4 mins, and will take you to fbi hq . . . sincerely yours, murphy napier . . .*)

Jacobs says, 'We also want to fucking go now, too, but we need to set up a perimeter around his building, and get our electronics in place, and put extra fuel into the plane. That'll all take about thirty minutes.'

Murphy says, 'Besides, the Godfather will not do anything until you get there. Yes, time is of the essence, but if we arrive on schedule, he will keep his promise.'

Jacobs says, 'Oddly enough, for a dickhead supervillain, this guy is true to his word.'

Abbey asks Jacobs, 'Do you have something I can change into?' She points to her silky red shirt, short black skirt, and three-inch heels, and says, 'This isn't exactly crime-fighting gear.'

Barb says, 'Follow me', and leads Abbey to a room two floors below filled with a ton of FBI-brand clothes: hundreds of blue T-shirts, sweatpants, slacks, polo shirts, baseball caps and trainers all imprinted with a yellow

FBI logo. 'Your one-stop shop,' Barb says. 'Good thing you look nice in blue, right?'

Normally, Abbey would laugh. Right now, she can't even muster the tiniest of smiles.

After Abbey, Murphy and Jacobs board the airplane, they don't speak for several minutes. It's Abbey who breaks the silence: 'Okay. I think I've calmed down. I think I'm ready. Bring me up to speed.'

Murphy says, 'I wish this was not only your second outing. I wish you had more experience under your belt. And you need to realise that had the Godfather not asked for you specifically, you would not be here.'

Abbey nods. 'That's not exactly bringing me up to speed, Murphy. That's you complaining. Tell me who he is, tell me what he wants, and tell me how we can fix this.'

'Okay,' Murphy says. 'Be aware that what I am about to tell you is going to sound scary, but we will do everything in our power – and we will use every tactic or weapon at our disposal – to keep you safe.' He pulls a file from who-knows-where and opens it up, but, as he tells Abbey the backstory, he doesn't once refer to it. 'Godfather Neat-o Corleone's given name is Starling Park-Ho. He is a Korean-American from Coeur d'Alene, Idaho. Coeur d'Alene is a racially charged town, and he was bullied incessantly. He ran away from home at the age of sixteen, made his way to Boston, and stole classes at MIT and Harvard.'

Abbey asks, 'What do you mean, stole classes?'

'He attended school without paying. Whenever he got caught, he picked another class. Every month or three, it would get to the point that he was a recognised figure on both campuses, so he would have some minor plastic surgery, and continue his education. He stole both an undergraduate degree and a Master's Degree.'

Barb says, 'Master's Degree. Get it? *Masters?* Get it?'

Murphy snaps, 'Can it, Jacobs.' He says to Abbey, 'I apologise for Agent Jacobs, Ab. She sometimes lacks . . . decorum.'

Jacobs glares at Murphy, then says, 'I'll be in the bathroom.' Abbey wonders if they're sleeping together. For some reason, she hopes not.

Murphy continues, 'He set up shop in New York City two years ago, and started in on his lair.'

Abbey says, 'They *all* have lairs, don't they?'

'Yes. They all have lairs. His situation was particularly impressive, in that he managed to get it up and running on the Lower East Side of New York City without being detected by Homeland Security.' He scowls. 'Do *not* get me started about Homeland Security.'

'What's his lair like?' Abbey asks.

Murphy sighs. 'We do not know, and that is the problem. That is why I do not want to send you in there alone. But the Godfather wants to see you by himself, and I do not know what else to do, and we do not have the time to organise anything. We *are* comfortable with you going in there – we are fully confident you have the skills at your disposal to get out of there alive and well –

but we are *not* comfortable with being forced into this play. We could have used a week to prep.'

Abbey asks, 'Don't you have, like, a contingency plan in place?'

Jacobs comes out of the bathroom and says, 'We have about twenty contingency plans in place, but if we're going in blind, we won't know which one to use until we get there. What makes it more difficult is that the Godfather has high-intensity security cameras all over the area, so our perimeter won't be as tight as we'd like.' She shrugs. 'We can only do what we can do, you know?'

'I know,' Abbey says quietly.

Murphy says, 'We are landing at Teterboro airport in . . .' he checks his watch – 'twenty-eight minutes. There will be a car waiting for us on the runway. Once we are close to the Godfather's lair, the negotiations will begin.'

'And there's the big question, I guess,' Abbey says. 'What does he want?'

Murphy and Jacobs quickly glance at one another, then Murphy says, 'He wants two things: a billion dollars—'

'Right, the magic supervillain number.'

'. . . and you.'

Abbey Bynum had imagined that her first trip to New York City would be all about Michelin three-star restaurants, and off-Broadway shows, and dark jazz clubs, not kidnapping, hostage negotiation, and the possibility of some supervillain freak from Idaho killing her best friend.

Murphy spends the majority of the ride from the airport to Manhattan's Lower East Side apologising. 'I cannot tell you how sorry the Federal Bureau of Investigation is. If I may divulge something, we have eight paras working for us. Three of them have been doing so for over two years, and they have yet to be detected.'

'So why am I the lucky one? Why did he find me?' Abbey asks.

Jacobs says, 'Because you're the strongest. By far. But this is not a tragic turn of events. As a matter of fact, this might be a blessing in disguise. If the Godfather tracked you down, it was probably only a matter of time before an enemy regime did the same.'

Abbey asks Murphy, 'I guess that begs the question, what's worse, being imprisoned by another country, or by a master?'

Murphy says, 'Another country, without question. On US soil, we have the means to find you . . . not that you will need to be found, of course.'

'Right,' Abbey says drily. 'Of course.'

Jacobs raps her knuckles on the window. 'Okay. We're here. I'll get the dickhead on the phone.' She pulls out a fancy-looking cell, plugs it into a small laptop, and punches in a number. After a second, she says, 'Mr Park-Ho, this is Agent Barbara Jacobs of the Federal Bureau of Investigation . . . no, as I promised, I did not put you on speaker phone, but you should know that we are recording this conversation . . . okay, my badge number is zero four one dash one one four dash nine four one two dash two, and my middle name is Randi, and my mother's maiden name is Winchester . . . no, I will *not* call you Neat-o . . . because it's fucking ridiculous . . . Starling Park-Ho is a badass name . . . wait, you'd seriously harm a hostage because I won't call you Neat-o? Jesus Christ, fine, yes, Neat-o it is . . . yes, Abbey Bynum is here with us . . . okay, but I'd like to come in with her . . . can I at least escort her to the door? Well, I'll need to take Ms Sheldon with me for debriefing, so Agent Napier and I will remain in the area . . . yes, that's our Lincoln Town Car out front . . . yes, I agree, it was very nice of our bosses to send us such a nice vehicle. Bynum will be at your front door in sixty seconds . . . no, she will not be wearing a wire . . . um, sure, thanks, it was lovely talking to you too.' She hangs up the phone, turns to Murphy, and says, 'Send the sound file to Benderson in DC. I don't know if he'll be able to do anything with it, but it's worth a shot.' She says to Abbey, 'You ready?'

'Not even a little,' Abbey says. 'You guys haven't told me anything.'

Jacobs says, 'Trust me, Abbey, if we had something to tell you, we've told you. This is a clusterfuck, and you're trapped in the middle of it.'

Murphy says, 'Again, Ab, I apologise.' And then he

puts his hand gently on the back of her neck. It feels warm. It feels soothing. It feels nice.

'I appreciate the sentiment,' Abbey says, 'but it wasn't your fault, Murphy.' She then delivers one of Cheryl's favorite lines: 'Let's go start the first day of the rest of our lives.'

Godfather Neat-o Corleone is way less of a mutant than Baron von Stroheim, but he ain't exactly the kind of guy you'd bring to your Junior Prom.

The ill-named Godfather meets Abbey at the front door of his East Village brownstone. 'Ms Abbey Bynum,' he says in what he probably thinks is a suave voice, 'a pleasure to make your acquaintance. I understand your performance in Tennessee – your little skirmish with that misguided Baron – was a thing of beauty. At least that's what your friend Ms Sheldon claims.' He then cups his mouth and calls across the street, 'Close your car window, Agent Jacobs and Agent Napier, or Ms Sheldon dies.' He holds up a palm-sized metal cube and roars, 'Check it out!' Then he hits a button on the side of the box, and Abbey hears a yell from inside the building. The Godfather laughs. 'One of the delicious things about setting up shop in the East Village is that what with all the S and M places in the neighborhood, nobody bothers you if there's screaming coming from your apartment.' As if to prove his point, he again pushes the button, and again, Cheryl yells.

Jacobs says, 'Okay, okay, we get it, we get it. We'll

close the fucking window.'

'That's a wise decision,' the Godfather calls. 'I have cameras. Crack the window, and Ms Sheldon loses a body part. I think I'll start with her lips . . . but that wouldn't be nice, now would it? After all, no lips would make it hard for her to sing, correct? Oh, well, tra la la.' He turns to Abbey and offers his arm. 'Shall we, Ms Bynum?'

Abbey says, 'I can walk myself', and pushes past the Godfather – as much as she wants to send him flying into New Jersey, she manages to restrain herself, because she doesn't know where Cheryl is, and whether he has her surrounded with bombs or something – and heads into the building.

The Godfather's entryway is kind of a dump, not the kind of place you'd expect a supervillain with a stolen Master's Degree to be holed up in. His apartment, however, is a miracle of modern science, filled with giant computer screens, a laboratory replete with bubbling and boiling liquids, and what looks like a giant mixing board.

Pretty honking cool, Abbey thinks, despite herself.

'Do you like my lair, Ms Bynum?' he asks.

Affecting nonchalance, she says, 'Meh. Whatever.'

'That's all? Just *whatever*? You don't think it's *pretty honking cool*?'

Abbey gasps.

The Godfather smiles. 'Ah, the tables are turned, aren't they? The ESP-er becomes the ESP-ee. Pretty strange to have your mind read, isn't it? That's some weeeeeeeeeeeird stuff, isn't it? Tra la la.'

Abbey says, 'Great. You can read my mind. You're awesome. So what am I thinking now?'

He squints, then frowns. 'That I'm a rotting maggot who shouldn't be allowed to walk the earth? And that I smell like monkey farts? That's not nice, Ms Bynum. That's not nice at all.' He pauses. 'I showered before you came, and I know for a fact that I don't smell like monkey farts.'

She ignores him. 'I was told you're a man of your word.'

He smiles. 'That is correct. I am. I pride myself on it.'

'From what I understand, you agreed to trade me for Cheryl.'

'You understand correctly. Let me bring you your friend.'

'Wait, you don't have anybody to take care of that sort of thing for you? You have to get her yourself?'

The Godfather shrugs. 'I'm a solo act. Henchmen are unreliable. I can't be bothered.' He points to a ratty sofa in the far corner of the room. 'Have a seat.'

'I'll stand. Get Cheryl.'

Five minutes later, the Godfather leads a cursing, squirming Cheryl Sheldon towards the front door. 'I hope you enjoyed your stay at the Hotel Corleone, Ms Sheldon. I look forward to your next record.'

'Eat my ass, you piece of shit on a shoe scumbag fuck face!' Abbey notes that even though Cheryl doesn't look so hot, she sounds like her old self, at least vocabulary-wise. Then she sees Abbey and squeals, 'Oh my God oh my God oh my God, my superheroine's here to save me! How did you know?! How the fuck did you know where I was?! I love you so fucking much!'

The Godfather says, 'Ms Sheldon, you should know that Ms Bynum is trading herself for you. Quite the sacrifice.'

Cheryl pales. 'No. No way. No way, no how.' She looks at the Godfather. 'You're going to kill her, aren't you?'

The Godfather laughs. 'I don't even know if she *can* be killed, Ms Sheldon. But I intend to find out.'

Abbey says, 'Come again?'

'You are a mortal being, so you can die, Ms Bynum, but I'm certain your government isn't going to do what's necessary to find out what it will take to kill you. They probably should, for obvious reasons. If I were them, I certainly would.' As he unties Cheryl's wrists, he says, 'I'm going to study your friend, Ms Sheldon. I'm going to keep her here and learn everything I can about what makes this . . . this . . . this *paranormal* tick.' He shakes his head. 'They refer to you as a paranormal, and they say *my* name is stupid? Give me a break.'

Abbey says to Cheryl, 'It'll be okay. Just go. Please.'

Cheryl says, 'Don't do it. If you stay, I'll never see you again.'

Abbey says, 'But if *you* stay, you'll never see me again either. And I can take care of myself, really.' She points to the Godfather. 'If this guy was able to find me, I'm findable, and somebody else would've tracked me down eventually. I'm living on borrowed time, honey, and you aren't, which is why you need to go out that door and make a record that'll sell a zillion copies by tomorrow, then you could pay this chump his ransom, and I can go home.'

The Godfather says, 'Stop talking about me like I'm not here. It's not polite. Tra la la.'

Cheryl says, 'It's not polite to kidnap people either, dude.'

The Godfather nods. 'Point taken. Now get out of here before I put the shock collar back on.' He smiles at Abbey. 'I've invented a new shock collar. But it's not technically a collar, because it goes in between one's legs. I don't think Ms Sheldon appreciated it.'

'No,' Cheryl says, 'I fucking well didn't.'

'I didn't think so,' he says. 'Now vamoose before I shoot you with the garden variety handgun in the top drawer of my office desk.'

Abbey says, 'You heard the man. Vamoose.'

Cheryl says to the Godfather, 'Listen, buster, if you hurt one hair on my girl's head, I'm going to haunt you, and your dreams, and your family, and everything that you fucking care about.'

'I care about two things, Ms Sheldon.'

'Let me guess,' Abbey says, 'money and power.'

The Godfather blinks. 'Very good, Ms Bynum. How did you know?'

She turns to Cheryl, and says, 'These guys all think they're so original, but they all steal each other's material. They all want money, and they all want power, and they all want to blow up the moon, and they're all interchangeable.' She points at the Godfather. 'The only difference between this guy and Baron von Stroheim is twenty IQ points and nicer living quarters.'

Cheryl asks, 'Who has the higher IQ?'

'No comment.'

The Godfather's eyes flash, and he says, 'Ms Sheldon, please show yourself out. Ms Bynum and I have some business to conduct.'

As Cheryl trots to the door, she calls back, 'I'll get you out of here, Abbey. I promise.' And then she is gone.

'So,' the Godfather says, 'you think I'm unoriginal, do you? I bet your Baron von Stroheim didn't do this.'

They stand staring at one another for a few seconds, then Abbey says, 'Didn't do *what*?'

'Try flying, Ms Bynum. Go ahead and take off.'

'Gladly.' She jumps in the air . . . and comes right back down to earth. She looks at her feet and says, 'Hunh. That's strange.'

The Godfather nods happily. 'You like that? As long as you're in my lair, you will be unable to fly.'

Still staring at her feet, she repeats, 'Hunh. Why's that?'

'It's science. You wouldn't understand. They didn't teach those kinds of classes at Northwestern University, my dear.' Then he lets loose a cackle that could've come straight out of a Boris Karloff movie.

'Nice laugh, douchebag.' Abbey shakes her head. 'You know what? You're a cliché. A total cliché. You're less than a cliché. You're Supervillain Lite.'

He snarls, 'Oh, yeah? Would a cliché be able to do this?' Again, they stare at each other, and again Abbey asks, 'Do *what*?'

'Try using your telekinesis, Ms Bynum. Try moving something with your mind.' He points to his desk. 'Try that pen. That teeny, tiny little pen. It shouldn't be a problem for somebody with your strength, should it?'

It is.

'Okay, Starling, you've proven your point.'

'Don't call me Starling,' he says.

'Sorry, Starling.'

'Fuck you, Bynum.'

'Whatever. So what else can't I do while I'm in this dump?'

'Well, you can't read my mind, and you can't see through anything, and you can't run at super speed. I think that about covers the waterfront.'

'You think?'

'No. I don't think. I *know*.'

Abbey nods. 'Interesting. So it's science, you say? Wow, that's some pretty good science.'

The Godfather nods and smiles modestly. 'Oh, p'shaw, tra la la. I just soldered a few things together, snipped a wire here, squirted some glue there, and next thing you know, here we are. It's ironic that such a tiny machine can cause such a huge fundamental change in a person as powerful as yourself.'

Abbey perks up. 'It's tiny? Can I see?'

He stands straighter, bringing himself to his full height of five feet seven inches. (A large percentage of supervillains are of below-average height. Can you say Napoleon Complex?) 'Really? You want to see it? I never would've thought . . . I mean . . . *wow* . . . that's all I can say, is wow . . . you truly are one of a kind, Ms Bynum. The defeated warrior wishes to see the weapon with which she was defeated. Most paras would be begging for mercy.' He bows slightly towards Abbey. 'It would be my honor to show you my Para-lyser. Get it? Para-lyser?'

'Yeah. I get it. Hilarious.'

He reaches behind one of the computer monitors, and here it is, the device that turns paranormals into, well, *normals*. He says, 'It looks like an iPod, and it feels like an iPod . . . but it ain't an iPod.' Again, the cackle, and again, Abbey rolls her eyes. 'It's indestructible, you know,' he continues. 'You can drop it from the top of the Empire State Building, or have an elephant stomp on it, and it'll keep working. Tra la la.'

'Really?' Abbey asks.

'Really. Watch this.' He throws it across the room as hard as he can – which, Abbey notes, is pretty hard – and it falls to the ground unharmed.

'That's awesome, Godfather.'

'You think so?'

'I do.'

'Me too.'

'One thing: do you think it could survive being hit with . . . with . . . with . . .'

'With what?'

'Well, I haven't come up with a name for them. All I know is there're these weird red blobs that I can shoot from my eyes. Let me give that a shot.'

'Wait, what weird red blobs?'

Abbey shrugs. 'It's a new thing. The Weird Stuff hits just keep on coming.'

The Godfather screams, '*Noooooooooo!*'

Abbey melts Godfather Neat-o Corleone's fancy little superhero-stopper in two seconds flat, then says, 'Tra la la *that*, asshole.'

Twenty-six seconds later, the Godfather is in the backseat of the Lincoln Town Car, sandwiched in between Murphy Napier and Barb Jacobs, on his way to wherever it is the FBI takes these masters guys. As Abbey watches the car pull away, she thinks, *I can't believe that took twenty-six seconds. I can totally do better than that.*

I don't like it.'

So says Jon Carson.

'I know,' Abbey snaps. 'You've made that abundantly clear.'

'They sent you in there solo, Abbey. Again. There was no back-up. Again.'

'There was back-up.'

'Yeah, but it was four blocks away. That's not back-up. That's covering their asses. That's them making sure when you get killed, they'll be able to tell the Congressional Subcommittee, "We did everything we could" in good conscience. They may as well have sent you to the electric chair. I need you alive, Abbey.'

'It was my choice, Jon. I could've said no.'

He ignores her. 'This Godfather idiot wouldn't have killed Cheryl, because if she was dead, he'd have had no bargaining chip. And he knew that nobody in your position – with your predisposition for saving everybody around you – would've let her languish in his basement. He knew Napier would ask you to go after him. You're lucky he didn't know about the eye bullets. If he did, you'd either be dead now, or you'd be Neat-o Corleone's science experiment. Or both.'

It's almost midnight. Jon and Abbey have had a lovely night out – dinner at Blackbird, dessert at One Sixty Blue, a set of jazz at the Green Mill – and now they're back at Jon's apartment, going around and around in circles about this whole FBI thing.

Abbey walks over to Jon's window and takes in his remarkable view of the city. She thinks that right about now would be a perfect time to take off on one of her night-time flights – flying is still the best way for her to clear her head, even better than a hot bath, even better than great sex – but now that she knows her powers can be detected by a supervillain with the proper equipment, she's more inclined to stay on the ground unless it's absolutely necessary. She tells Jon, 'I understand what you're saying, and I respect it, and I respect *you*, but you have to respect me, too.'

Jon says, 'I do respect you. More than you know.' She feels his hands on her shoulders. As he kisses the nape of her neck, he repeats, 'More than you know.' He presses his body against hers and licks her ear. She can feel him getting hard, and she likes it.

Abbey lets out a tiny moan, then reminds him, 'I'm still on my period.'

'And I still don't care.'

'And I'm still glad to hear that.'

It's a repeat performance of the previous night: lots of

pushing, lots of pulling, lots of grunting, lots of groaning, lots of sweating, lots of swearing, and, best of all, lots of orgasms for everybody. Just like last night, after two-plus hours of fucking (not lovemaking, mind you, but fucking), Jon falls immediately asleep. And, just like last night, Abbey trudges to the bathroom for the inevitable post-coital tampon insertion.

And, just like last night, Abbey Bynum has grown another chunk of Weird Stuff, which she discovers when she blows the bathtub to bits with a single sneeze. Wiping her nose with a piece of toilet paper, she thinks, *I guess Jon won't be getting his security deposit back*.

As she stares at the pile of rubble, she hears a voice: 'Gesundheit, babe.'

Without taking her eyes from the wreckage, she says, 'Jon, I am *so* sorry. I'll pay for it. I don't know how – maybe I'll get money from my parents or something – but I'll fix it, I promise.'

He says, 'See, *this* is why you should freelance. It'd be nice to have a few hundred grand at your disposal right about now, wouldn't it? The FBI ain't paying you enough to remodel my john.'

'I can't lie. That's a legitimate point.' She flushes the toilet, pulls up her panties, turns to him, and says, 'But I still don't think—' And she stops.

Leaning against the bathroom doorjamb, Jon smiles – *A sadistic smile*, Abbey thinks – and says, 'Everything okay?'

She gawks at his face and says nothing.

'See something odd?' he asks.

Silence.

'Come on, Abbey. Look at my face. Tell me what you see.'

'I . . . I . . . I . . .'

'*You, you, you*. Speechless, eh? That's not a typical thing for you after sex, is it? You're usually a blabbermouth. That's always been the case. Even back in school.'

She points at his face and whispers a single word: 'James.'

Jon's smile doubles, no, *triples* in size. 'Aww, you remembered. I'm touched.'

'Who are you? *What* are you?'

'Right now? Well, right this second, James Caraway. Tomorrow morning? I have to be in court, so Jon Carson again. Next weekend? I'm going back to Nebraska to see my psycho wife and our mutual girlfriend, so I'll be good ol' James Caraway again. Then I'll be Jon, then James, then Jon. Oh, at some point, I should probably be Jerry Cranston.' He shakes his head ruefully. 'What with working on you, I haven't gotten to be Jerry in *months*. Check this out: Jerry's screwing a para in Paris – and I'm not making that up. A *para* in *Paris*! And her name is *Paulette. Paulette* the *para* in *Paris*. Lots of Ps. Love it!'

Abbey brushes past Jon and walks into the bedroom. *Stay cool*, she thinks. *Don't lose your shit*. She walks into the kitchen, opens the fridge, takes out a bottle of orange Vitamin Water, then says, 'You want one?'

Jon/James says, 'No, I'm good. Hey, don't you have any questions for me?'

Abbey says, 'Give me a second. I'm processing.'

'Oh. Well, process faster. I'd kind of like to explain this to you.'

Abbey downs half of the bottle in a single gulp. 'You guys like to explain things, don't you?'

He asks, 'What do you mean, *you guys*?'

'You know what I'm talking about.'

'Maybe. But I'd like to hear it from you.'

'You're a master, aren't you? You're a supervillain. That's why you keep trying to . . . to . . . to *recruit* me, isn't it?'

Jon/James wanders over to the living room, plops on to the sofa, and lays down. Gazing up at the ceiling, he says, 'Supervillain is such an ugly word, Abbey. I'm a businessman. I don't need to take over the world.' He pauses. 'Just Chicago. Maybe Illinois. Maybe the United States. Hmm, putting it that way, you might be right – I might be a supervillain. But when you think about it, being a supervillain is no worse than being a lawyer.' He sits up. 'I'll tell you this, Abbey: whatever I am, I'm damn good at it. And whatever *you* are, you're damn good at it, too. Put us together, and it's ours.'

'*What*'s ours?'

'*Everything.*'

She finishes her drink, then asks, 'I'm guessing it's time for your explanation?'

Jon/James stands up. 'Indeed. Any questions?'

'Yeah. Sure.' She points at his head. 'So what's the deal with the face thing?'

He smiles. 'You know, one of the things I was concerned about when we first started getting naked together was that you'd recognise my body. I mean, when we were at Northwestern, you went to town on it enough. I was kind of hurt you didn't remember.'

Abbey says, 'I wasn't asking about your body. I was asking about your face.'

'Ah, yes, that. A simple mask, provided for me by the lovely men of the lovely Inmann Technical College in the lovely city of Washington DC. Pretty impressive piece of work, I'd say. Easy on, easy off, impossible to tell it's not your own. I have six more at home.' He nods, then repeats, 'A pretty impressive piece of work.'

'What's Inmann Tech, really?'

'Oh, it's a school. But it's also a think-tank, and a home for wayward brainiacs. Some of the less serious students called it Supervillain University. Silly, but apt.'

'What do they teach you?'

'How to do supervillain stuff, of course. Mad Science one-oh-one. Muscles two-oh-two. Business three-oh-three. Weapons four-oh-four. The array of electives they offer is second-to-none. I'll show you the curriculum sometime.'

'Yeah, that'd be swell,' she mumbles.

'One other thing I learned,' he says, ignoring her, 'was how to help a female para realise her full potential.'

'What do you mean?'

'Remember when we were together in college?'

She nodded.

'Remember all the great sex we had?'

She nodded.

'Remember spending all those hours in bed?'

She nodded.

'Remember how, after a few weeks, you could read minds?'

She nodded.

'That was me. Purely accidental. I didn't learn how a guy can fuck a para into developing powers until I got to Inmann.' His chest swells. 'I got an "A" in that class. How cool is that?'

Abbey grumbles, 'Not very.'

'Oh, I disagree. It's *very* cool. Remember, if it weren't for me, you wouldn't have those eye bullets, and if you didn't have those eye bullets, you'd be a pile of ashes in Neat-o Corleone's basement. Also, if it weren't for me, you wouldn't be able to sneeze a city into submission . . .'

'Yeah, thanks for that.'

'My pleasure. If it weren't for me, all you'd be doing is flying, and running, and lifting, and that'd be it.' He pauses. 'You'll need to work on your superbreath, by the way. I know it was new to you, but that sneeze should've wrecked the whole bathroom. You'll get it down soon enough. You'll practice for a few days, and you'll be great. I have faith.'

'Wait, so you're saying you . . . you . . . you *used* me?'

'Abbey, I adore having sex with you. Our bodies fit

together wonderfully. And you're a great girl, and you're tons of fun, so being with you has been an absolute pleasure, both in and out of the sack. So I wasn't totally using you. Just partially.'

Stay cool, she thinks, *keep it together*. 'So what's the point? Why are we here? Why me?'

'I'm sure your pal Murphy has made it clear that you're one of the strongest paras out there, so if I'm going to get myself a partner, I'm going to get the best.'

Abbey blinks, then says, 'Partner?'

'Of course! Why do you think I spent all this time drawing out your full powers?'

She shrugs.

'So we can team up and take over the world!'

'I thought you said you didn't want to take over the world.'

'I lied.' Jon/James shrugs. 'It's a supervillain thing. And a lawyer thing. Another parallel.'

'Listen Jon, or James, or whoever you are – or whatever you are – I'm going to tell you something that's been said to me countless times throughout my life.'

He gives her an eager smile. 'What's that?'

'I just want to be friends.'

'Excuse me?'

'I don't want to be your partner. I have no interest in taking over the world. *None*. I think I'm even losing my taste for crime fighting. Now, if you'll excuse me, I'm going to put on my clothes, and head on home.' She has no intention of going home, and thinks it might be time to talk with Murphy about entering the Superhero Protection Program, Chicago Division.

Jon/James steps in front of her. 'I don't think so, Abbey. This isn't your decision to make.'

She says, 'Seriously? You're going there?'

'Going there? I'm already here.'

'And now you're going over there.' With one hand she shoves him, and he flies across the room and crashes into the flat-screen television. She then picks up an end table, hurls it out of Jon's window, then flies into the Chicago night.

Abbey needs to get away from her life. Quickly. But she has no place to go, or at least no place that makes sense.

She can't fly to see her parents, because she still hasn't had any navigation classes, and would probably get lost on her way east. Dave is probably recovering from a bender, and Cheryl's probably recovering from her *tête à tête* with Godfather Neat-o Corleone, so she doesn't want to call up either of them. She doesn't want to get Suzanne Addison involved any more than she already is, so that's out. She doesn't know where Murphy Napier, Paul Walton, or Barb Jacobs live, so after drifting over Lake Michigan in her underwear for three hours – and freezing her ass off – she only has one option.

Most of the daytime receptionists in the FBI building's lobby know Abbey and will wave her on through without putting her through the typical going-up-to-somebody's-office rigmarole, but the night-shifter on duty has never seen her before, so after she gets a gander of Abbey's panties, she has one of the agents escort Abbey to the intake room and bring her some clothes. She cools her jets until Murphy shows up an hour later.

Murphy takes Abbey to his office, where she promptly breaks into a crying jag that has her sobbing face down on his floor. She thanks God that Murphy knows enough not to open his mouth.

When Abbey regains control of herself, she sees Murphy kneeling over her, clearly wanting to give her some sort of comforting touch. She puts her hand on his knee and uses it as leverage to pull herself into a sitting position. Offering a weak smile, she says, 'Boy, do I have a story for you.'

'What is it about?'

'Jon Carson.'

'Ah. Jon Carson. Do tell.'

Abbey talks, and Murphy listens, and after she finishes, he helps her to her feet, guides her over to his couch, sits down, and drapes his arm over her shoulder. She rests her head on his chest, and begins crying again, this time silently. He caresses her neck, and they remain that way for a good long while.

Finally, he says, 'We have to get you out of sight.'

Abbey sniffles. 'That's exactly what I was thinking.'

'How do you feel about Phoenix?'

'Oh,' she says, 'I thought you meant out of sight like another place in Chicago.'

Murphy nods. 'Yes, you *could* stay in town, and I think you would be okay, but for my own sanity, I would prefer it if you disappeared for a few months. We could stash you away, and you could continue your training – Paul will gladly travel with you anywhere you want – and when you are ready, we can integrate you back into society.'

'What about my family? What about Cheryl? What about my job? What about my *life*?'

'Ab, it is time for you to accept the fact that your life, as you know it, is over. I am sorry it happened on my watch, and if I could change how it played out, I would. We did not expect you to be made for years. We did not know that anybody outside of The Company . . .'

'The Bureau.'

'. . . had the technology. That was our miscalculation, and for that, I am profoundly sorry, but this was inevitable. It would have been ideal if you had had more time to mentally prepare yourself, but life does not always work out the way one wants it to work out, does it?'

She searches Murphy's face, *really* searches it, and for the first time, she sees the sadness that's such an integral part of his psychological make-up. He was an outcast, and a nerd, and he'd had a lousy family life, and the one girl he ever had feelings for (that being Abbey, of course) wasn't interested in him in *that way*. If anybody knew about life not meeting expectations, it was FBI Agent Murphy Napier.

'You're right,' she says, then repeats, 'you're right.'

He stands up and paces the room. 'We can keep you safe here in town, so long as you do not tell a soul your location. That means your parents, and Cheryl, and everybody at your firm. We are cancelling your cellphone account immediately, and we will provide you with a secure phone you can use to stay in contact with your people, and those of us here at the home office.'

'Thank you, Murphy. I appreciate it.'

'It is the least I can do. I even have the perfect place for you to stay.'

'Fine. Please take me there. I need a long, hot shower to wash away any traces of Jon Carson, and then I need about twenty-nine hours of sleep.'

'I have one question: how do you feel about cats?'

The second she enters the apartment, two adorable kittens start batting at Abbey's ankles. 'I didn't know you liked cats.'

Murphy shrugs. 'I did not, but one of Jacobs's neighbors had a litter, and she threatened to do me bodily harm unless I took two of them.' He kneels down to scratch his new pets' ears. 'The white one is Kirk, and the gray one is Spock.'

Abbey laughs. 'Wow, Murphy, you are *owning* your nerdiness.'

He shrugs again. 'If the dweeb fits, then dweeb it.'

'I couldn't have said it better myself.'

She looks around Murphy's small, tidy place and

thinks, *This could use a woman's touch*. The furniture is all from IKEA, and save for a mounted fifty-two-inch television and a framed Mark Rothko print, the walls are unadorned. The only parts of the unit that have any personality – that reveal anything about Murphy's personality, for that matter – are the three bookcases next to the television, bookcases overflowing with sci-fi paperbacks and horror hardcovers. 'How long have you lived here?'

'Fifteen months.'

'Okay, I don't know how long I'll be staying here, but if it's for any significant amount of time, I'm giving this joint a makeover.'

'You do not have to do that.'

'Yeah, well, you didn't have to put me up. You could've sent me to Bumblefuck, Arizona.'

He says, 'I would not have done so without your approval.' They lock eyes for a minute, then Murphy smiles and says, 'Let me get you a towel. While you are in the shower, I will change the bedsheets. I will sleep on the sofa. No discussion.'

'But—'

'I said *no discussion*. I sleep out here two or three nights a week anyhow. It's quite comfortable.'

'But—'

'*No. Discussion. Period.*'

Abbey grins. 'I like it when you go into FBI tough-guy mode.'

Murphy blushes. 'You're probably the only one.' He

walks over to the linen closet and grabs a bath towel and a washcloth. 'One thing you should know: this apartment is as safe as any place in the city.'

'How so?' she asks.

'Security cameras as far as the eye can see, and a laser alarm system that's connected to HQ. If somebody trips it, there will be an agent here within three minutes.' He pauses. 'And, of course, there's Kirk and Spock.'

'Holy cow, Murphy Napier made a joke. And it's a pretty good one, yet.'

'I am full of surprises, Ab. Now go take your shower.'

Abbey tries to wash away every trace of Jon Carson – literally and figuratively – but she soon realises it isn't going to happen today. Or tomorrow. Or next week. Or next month. Bouncing back from this sort of betrayal will take a while. She thinks it might not be a bad idea to get the name of Murphy's shrink.

Murphy's gone when she gets out of the shower. She sees that he's left a handwritten note on the pillow of his bed:

Abbey,
There's some food in the refrigerator, and I left some money on the kitchen table if you wish to order out. I will be going grocery shopping tonight, so please start making a grocery list. I am afraid you will be stuck inside at Chez Napier for a while, so I would recommend having me get you foods that you love.

I will call you on my house phone at 5 p.m. If you need me, you may call my office from the same line. If Kelly takes the call, use the name Eve Adams. I will tell her I am expecting your call, and she will put you right through.

I am here for you, and I always will be. You will get through this, and come out the other end a better person.

Yours,

Murphy Napier

Abbey is asleep in five minutes. When she awakes eighteen hours later, she's shocked that she hasn't had a single nightmare.

It takes Jon eighteen days to track Abbey down. The voicemail he leaves on her supposedly secure cellphone is typical supervillain: Wordy and over-explanatory.

'Abbey Bynum, Jon Carson here. Hope you're doing well. Me, I'm kind of lonely. My bed's been cold and empty since you flew the coop, and this is greatly upsetting to me. But a woman wants what a woman wants, and if the woman doesn't want me, I'm not going to fight it. At least from a sexual standpoint.

'But I *will* fight to have you in my life. I still want us to work together, Abbey. We would make an unbeatable team. We could take over the world. I know I told you that I wasn't interested in that sort of thing, but, well, like I said, supervillain lawyers are super liars. I want it all. I want the money, and the influence, and the power, and the worship. I want the whole shebang.

'Don't get me wrong, Abbey: I can do this myself. It'll take a while longer, but I can do it. I'm missing a couple of Weird Stuff elements that you can bring to the table . . . but I'm not going to tell you which ones, because those're nuggets of knowledge that I'll need for our battle.

'A *battle?* you may be asking yourself right about now. *What kind of battle are you talking about, Jon?* Here's the deal: you and me fight, no holds barred. You can use all the dirty superhero bullshit you want, and I'll use every supervillain trick I can think of. We'll go at it until one of us submits. If you win, I walk away from the industry. If I win, I take you back to my lair, and cut you open, and figure out what makes you tick, so I can get a piece of it, and then, if I manage to put you back together again, we'll team up, and you'll like it.

'I'm confident I'll win, and when I *win* – and when I suck your body dry of Weird Stuff juices – I'll be *in*. Maybe I'll be in the Congress, maybe the White House. Heck, maybe I'll even take over the FBI and assign your pal Agent Murphy Napier to Antarctica, or Mars. That could be fun. He strikes me as annoying.

'In any event, I know where you are right now – I won't bother you with details of how I found you; suffice it to say that Eve Adams is a crappy *nom de plume* for a variety of reasons – so you have two choices: either I launch a surprise attack on you where you're at right now, which would most certainly fuck up an entire neighborhood, and which would leave you and Napier with a whole lot of explaining to do . . . if you survive the attack, that is. Or we can go at it over by Lake Michigan tomorrow at midnight. We'll start at Oak Street Beach and work our way north. Or south. Or east. Or west. Whichever way our muses take us.

'You might want to have a big dinner, because this isn't going to be some in-and-out deal like Baron von Stroheim or Neat-o Corleone. I'm not quite as strong as you – not yet, anyhow – but I know your weak spots, and you don't know *any* of my spots, so I think it'll be a fair fight. Ugly, but fair. So, you know, load up on those carbs.

'Also, it goes without saying that you shouldn't bring any back-up. I won't, because, frankly, I won't need it.

'Okay, that's that. I look forward to seeing you again. Oh, I suppose I should mention that I have your parents locked in a shed in, well, I'm not going to tell you where they are . . . but I will tell you that if you find them, you probably shouldn't touch them, because they're booby-trapped like you wouldn't believe. They will be with me at the lake. If you arrive on time, they're free to go. If you don't show, they're dead. Ta ta.'

A shell-shocked Murphy Napier listens to the message four times, and each time it finishes, he says some variation of, 'How in God's name did he find you?'

After the last time, Abbey tells him, 'I don't know, and I don't care, but I'm doing this.'

Murphy says, 'Absolutely not. There is no way I will let you be involved in an engagement with this man. We do not know what kind of electronic capabilities he has. We do not know anything about his arsenal. We do not know if he has enhanced strength, or has developed the ability to fly.'

'People can do that now?' Abbey asks. 'People can get off the ground?'

'The technology is in its infancy. It is available, but it is also questionable and dangerous. Carson may be ahead of the curve, though, which is why I am not allowing you to engage.'

'Murphy, he has my parents booby-trapped, and you have no clue where they are.'

'We can find them and rescue them unharmed. I guarantee it.'

'No, Murphy. No you can't. You guaranteed Jon wouldn't find me, and he did. I'm doing it. I'm in.'

Murphy paces his apartment. 'You could die, Ab. Or he could capture you and cut you open. I forbid you to engage. *I. Forbid. It.*'

Abbey stands up, stops him in mid-pace, and puts her palm on his cheek. 'This has to happen, Murphy. I need to do this. This is going to be resolved. By me. I'm going to rescue my parents. I'm going to be a superheroine. It's my job. It's me.'

She's shocked to see tears in his eyes; as long as she's known him, Murphy was never one to show any deep emotion. 'Ab,' he says, 'you do not have to rescue anybody to be a superheroine.'

Without taking her hand from his face, she kisses him. She can't help it. And it's a *real* kiss, a kiss unlike any they'd ever previously shared – and don't forget, they've shared a *lot* of smooches. When Abbey feels his tears on her cheek, she pulls away, and says, 'Thank you for your concern.'

Murphy says, 'Thank you for . . . for being you.'

She shrugs. 'Being me is all I can be.' She claps her hands. 'Now that I can leave the apartment, we're going out for Italian food.'

'Why Italian?'

'Pasta, my man. I need to do some carbo loading.'

Abbey arrives at the Oak Street Beach at 11.58 p.m., wearing her lucky Chicago Bears sweatpants and her beloved Black Flag T-shirt. She wears no make-up, and her hair is tied up in not one, not two, but *three* scrunchies. She's prepared.

A voice cuts through the night: '*Sweet Pea!*'

She looks in the direction of the scream, and sees Gary and Carin running towards her at full-speed. Abbey flies at them, and the three crash into a group hug. None of them can speak through their respective tears.

A minute later: 'Okay, Bynums, enough with the waterworks. Parents, take a hike. I want you out of my sight in sixty seconds. Go, go, go! One . . . two . . . three . . . four . . . Jesus Christ, get out of here, you idiots . . . I can still see you.'

In unison, Gary and Carin tell Abbey they love her, and she answers in kind. As she watches her parents run towards Michigan Avenue, she's overcome with a sense of resolve and strength that she's never felt before. She didn't even know she had it in her.

Abbey Bynum spins around, and there's Jon Carson, wearing a skintight black Under Armour bodysuit. 'Nice outfit,' she says.

'Yeah, you too. Really classy, showing up at an epic battle in sweats. So how do you want to start this?'

'This was your idea. You tell me.'

He gives her a cheesy grin. 'Ladies first, Abbey, because—'

Before he can finish the sentence, Abbey lands a fist to his stomach. As he doubles over, she throws a knee towards his face, and hits . . . nothing.

Because Jon Carson is gone.

She mumbles, 'Where the hell is . . . ?'

Before she can finish the sentence, something smacks her in her stomach. As she doubles over, Jon says, 'Surprise!' He kneels down on the sand and looks up at Abbey so she can see his face. 'What has two thumbs and can run as fast as Abbey Bynum?' He cocks his thumbs at his face. 'That's right, baby, *moi*.' He throws a right cross towards her cheek, which lands with a sickening thump.

Abbey's head is spinning, and her gut is on fire, but she manages to launch herself straight up into the air; she can't get to full speed, but even at half-power, she climbs a hundred yards in thirty seconds. As she hovers over the lake for a minute, she regains her wind, and the pain in her face subsides.

Jon calls to her, 'You can fly, Abbey, but you can't hide.' And then he leaps into the air, and keeps climbing, and climbing, and climbing.

Abbey is too shocked to move.

Jon doesn't fly as fast as Abbey at full power, but he still has a whole lot of giddy-up, plus the added advantage of surprise, so when he hurls himself fist-first towards her stomach again, she's almost as unprepared as she was on the beach.

Almost.

Abbey neatly ducks Jon's punch, then clocks him on the back of his head with a closed fist. She isn't able to get her whole body into it, so Jon tumbles straight down, and falls harmlessly into the water. Had she nailed him with all her might, he'd be at the bottom of the lake, sleeping with the fishes.

He calls up to her, 'Nice one! Why don't you come down here and fight like a man?'

'Why don't you come up here and fight like a girl?'

'If you insist.' And then he's out of the water, moving twice as fast as before.

Abbey says, 'Oh, *shit*!' then darts to the left, then to the right, then she does a couple of the loop-de-loops she'd worked on so hard with Paul. She climbs up again, peeking over her shoulder to see where Jon is. Nothing. He's either gone, or camouflaged in the night sky. (Right then, Abbey thinks, *This was a dumb outfit. I totally should've worn black*.) She hears a scream, then feels a kick to the side of her knee. Again, she cries, 'Oh, *shit*!'

She sees Jon ten feet below her; he's breathing heavily, so she heads down feet-first and nails him in his left temple. He falls towards the water, screaming the entire way, but a few feet before splashdown, he rights himself, and zooms up towards Abbey.

Flying straight towards the heavens, Abbey thinks, *This isn't working. It's time to take this back to earth*, so, angling down, she zooms towards the mainland, with Jon only ten yards behind. They land at the same time, but before Jon can get his footing, Abbey takes a deep breath and blows about three hundred pounds of sand into his face. As he tries to rub it away, Abbey shoots ten red laser bullets from her eyes . . . all of which bounce harmlessly off his chest.

Coughing, he says, 'I can't shoot weird bullet things from my face, but I don't think those sweatpants of yours are bulletproof, so I guess we're kind of even on that front.'

Abbey lets out another deep breath, but before the sand flies, Jon's gone. She thinks, *I wish there was a way I could trade my eye bullets for night vision. Eye bullets suck.*

And then a wooden lifeguard chair crashes down on her head.

For the first time in her short superheroine life, Abbey Bynum is seriously hurt. There are three horrible cuts on her head, her neck is jacked up, and her left arm is hanging at a strange angle from the elbow. On the plus side, her legs are fine, so when Jon jumps towards her, she kicks him so hard that he lands on the Michigan Avenue sidewalk, some seventy-five feet away.

Right now, Abbey's primary objective is to hide so she can assess the damage to her body in peace. She scans the area, and decides to fly to the top of the Drake Hotel, an ancient building overlooking the lake. Once on the roof, she lays on her back, and would have liked nothing better than to close her eyes and fall into unconsciousness. Indeed, she closes her eyes, not to rest, but rather to picture her loved ones: Mom, Dad, Cheryl, Dave, and, oddly enough, Murphy. *This is who I'm fighting for*, she thinks. *These people want me back. And for them, I will come back.*

Eyes open again, she gingerly touches her left arm. All her medical training came from watching *ER* when she was a kid, which amounts to a whole lot of nothing. But after giving her arm a gentle examination, she guesses nothing's broken, just dislocated. So she takes a deep breath, bites down on her shoulder, then, with her right hand, she pulls on her left arm as hard as she can.

The pain is unbearable. She sees stars, and planets, and comets, and spaceships.

And then it's gone.

Abbey gingerly lifts her arm above her head: no problem. She stands up and moves it around in a backstroking motion: again, no problem. She grins and says, 'Oh my God, I fixed me!' She wipes some blood from her forehead, but after the mess with the elbow, a few cuts are nothing.

Now the question is, of course, *Where's Jon?* The last thing she wants to do is play Hide and Seek with him; she wants to put an end to this mess, and fast. But Jon, being a supervillain, probably wants to milk this for all it's worth, so Hide and Seek it shall be.

Before she jumps off the roof, she tries to formulate a plan. *Where the hell would he go?* she wonders. *If I'm him – if I'm an arrogant fuck who wants to mess with a para whom I'd dated – where would I go?*

And then a possibility dawns on her: *Maybe he's at the Chipotle where we had our first date.* That was as good a place as any to start, so she leaps into the air and flies towards the south-west part of the Chicago Loop. Moving at near-full-speed, she's floating over the restaurant in under a minute.

Jon is nowhere to be seen, and she's again concerned with tonight's choice of clothing: *I'm wearing white, and he's wearing black. What with all these streetlights around, I'm screwed. Advantage: Carson.*

Sure enough, she hears a metallic scrape, and feels a whoosh, but sees nothing; purely on instinct, she darts to the left. That's a good, almost miraculous choice, because had she ducked right, she would've been flattened by a steel girder. She hears Jon grumble, 'Shit.'

'Nice aim, Jonny Boy,' she taunts. 'Looks like all that time on the FBI target range really paid off for you. Oh . . . wait . . . you never went to the FBI target range. That was me.' And then she spots him crouching in the doorway of a restaurant, with his back turned to her. She thinks he's lost sight of her, so, as quietly as possible, she touches down on the sidewalk and looks for something she can throw at him: a street sign would been good, but the closest one is half-a-block away, and by the time she gets there and back with the sign, he might well be gone.

Abbey looks on to the sidewalk: *That manhole cover would work. So would that newspaper box.* But then her eyes fall onto a fire hydrant.

Perfect.

She rips the hydrant from the ground, hurls it at Jon, and it hits the mark. Listening to Jon moan in pain is one of the most satisfying sounds Abbey has heard in her entire adult life.

Carefully, she tiptoes towards the doorway, figuring out the best, most apt way to put an end to this. She remembers the pain from her elbow dislocation, and decides that busting any of Jon's hinges will be poetic justice at its finest. While she's deciding whether to go after his knees, his elbows, or his shoulders first, Jon leaps out of the doorway like a rabid cat and conks Abbey in the noggin. She falls backwards and her head hits the concrete hard. She doesn't lose consciousness, but it's damn close.

Jon laughs. 'Goodness, gracious me, that was so simple. Couldn't have been easier.' He kneels down and clamps his right hand around Abbey's neck. 'So here's how it's going to play out, Abbey.' When she doesn't respond, he gives her a little backhand on her cheek. 'Yoo hoo! Abbeeeeeey! Anybody home?'

Abbey moans.

'Close enough. Like I was saying, here's how it's going to play out. I'm going to strangle you a little bit, just enough so you'll be conscious, without dying. I'd hit your head again, but a hard blow might kill you, and, well, I don't know my own strength.' He laughs. 'Ah, I crack myself up. Anyhow, once you're in la-la land, I'm going to grab . . .' he looks around – '*that*.'

Again, Abbey moans.

'I'm sorry? Did you ask me what that is? You can't see it?'

Again, Abbey moans.

'Oh, right, no wonder you can't see it. I'm holding your head against the sidewalk. That would make sense, then. So what we're looking at here is a Toyota Prius – at least I *think* it's a Prius; it's kind of dark out here. Doesn't matter, I suppose. Anyhow, I'm going to pick up the car and use it to crush your legs. At that point, I'd like to think it'll be difficult for you to fly, and impossible for you to run. And if you only have two working limbs, I think I could take you in a fight.' He laughs. 'Yeah, I know you're practically unconscious, which means technically I've already *won* the fight, but why take chances? After that's all done, I'll carry you back to my lair, and then I'm going to cut you open, and examine each of your organs, and your brain, and maybe I'll figure out how the hell you became you. Maybe I won't figure it out. Who knows? Regardless, it'll be fun.' He takes a deep breath. 'Okay, let's let the choking begin!'

Jon closes his hand around Abbey's neck. She tries to fight back, but her world is turning white, and her limbs are becoming weaker with each passing second. Finally, as Jon predicted, she blacks out.

Jon clears his throat, stretches, and mumbles, 'Man, this ain't as easy as it looks', then he crosses the street and – using his legs just like he was taught in elementary school gym class – lifts up the Prius. *Thank God this is almost over*, he thinks, *because I'm ex-fucking-hausted.* He carries the car the twenty yards, takes a deep breath, lifts it as high above his head as he possibly can, and, utilising the remaining bit of his dwindling strength, hurls it at Abbey Bynum's legs.

Nobody filmed the end of the Bynum/Carson clash, but if they had, what happened during the endgame would've looked unreal . . . that is, unless you played the movie in super-super-super-slow-motion, and saw what really happened.

What happened was, the Prius fell towards Abbey, and then, when it was three-inches away from crushing her legs into dust, a hand flew out of the night and caught the car.

That hand was attached to an arm.

That arm was attached to a torso.

That torso was part of a body.

And that body belonged to FBI Agent Murphy Napier.

The Prius flies straight into the air, and Jon Carson yells, 'What the *fuck*?!'

Murphy Napier roars back, '*This* the fuck.'

And then Murphy Napier punches Jon Carson into kingdom come.

Epilogue

Abbey Bynum's eyes open.

It's dark. Pitch black. She can't see a thing. She wonders if there's even anything to see.

She tries to move. Nothing. She can't wiggle her fingers or her toes. Her arms and legs, same deal.

What's scariest is that she can't feel *anything*.

Total oblivion is calling. Abbey answers.

Abbey Bynum's eyes open.

It's light. Blinding light, so bright she can't see a thing.

She speaks: *'Ow.'*

She hears voices: *She's back . . . She talked . . . Did she move? . . . Is she breathing okay? . . . What did she say? . . .*

Okay, Abbey thinks, at least I'm alive. At least I think so.

More oblivion.

Abbey Bynum's eyes open.

It's not too dark. It's not too bright. It's just right.

She focuses on the punchboard ceiling, then says aloud, 'Looks like a hospital.'

Somebody says, 'You're awake!'

She looks for the source of the voice, but she still can't move. 'Where are you?' she asks.

A smiling young man appears at the side of her bed. 'I'm over here. I'm Sam Bell. I'm your doctor.'

'So I'm alive?'

'Yes, Abbey. You are very much alive.'

I'm not going to lose my shit, I'm not going to lose my shit, I'm not going to lose my shit. She asks, 'Am I paralysed?'

Dr Bell laughs. 'Not even a little bit.' He raps his knuckles on the full body cast. 'You're pretty broken up inside, but you're going to be okay in a few months. Rehab is going to be less than fun, but it's better than any of the alternatives.'

'So you're saying I can move?'

'Wiggle your toes.'

She wiggles. Nothing.

Dr Bell says, 'Excellent. Now do your fingers.'

'Wait, I didn't move the toes yet.'

'Yeah you did.'

'It didn't feel like it.'

'I suspect you have a massive case of foot-falling-asleep. Let's see those fingers.' She wiggles, and he smiles. 'Did you feel that?'

She meets his smile. 'A little.'

'And tomorrow, it'll be a lot. You hungry?'

'Now that you mention it, I am.'

'You're a few days away from solids, so I'll have a nurse bring you a smoothie. I'll call your parents and your friends, let them know you're okay.' As he heads to the door, he says, 'Pretty cool that you're pals with Cheryl Sheldon. Her new album is epic. She's one of my faves.'

Abbey says, 'Yeah. Mine too.'

Abbey's initial reunion with Gary, Carin, Dave, and Cheryl is kind of useless because, what with all the joyous tears, nobody can spit out a single coherent word. By the time everybody gets themselves under control, visiting hours are over.

The next day is better.

Patting the cast on his daughter's leg, Gary says, 'Sweet Pea, I am *so* proud of you.'

She gives her father a cockeyed smile. 'For what? For getting my ass kicked up and down the Chicago Loop?'

'For doing the best you could do.'

Cheryl rolls her eyes. 'That's what you're proud of? That's the best you can come up with?'

'It's true.'

Carin says, 'I just want you to be happy.'

Dave says, 'You're being cheesy, guys.'

Cheryl flicks Dave on his cheek and says, 'Stop it. They're being sweet.'

Dave flicks her back. 'And you're being a bitch.'

'David,' Carin says, '*please*. Language. We're in a public place.'

Dave says, 'Fuck that noise.'

Abbey says, 'Now *this* is what family's all about. If I was dead, this is what I'd have missed the most: bickering. I'm *so* glad I survived the beating of all beatings. So very, very, *very* glad.'

Cheryl says, 'We are too.'

'I'm only sort of glad,' Dave says. Again, Cheryl flicks him, this time, in a place where boys don't like being flicked. Hunched over and moaning, Dave says, 'I hate you.'

Riding the wave of her second dose of opiates today, Abbey closes her eyes, then repeats, 'So very, very, *very* glad.'

Abbey wakes up after midnight, and there's Murphy Napier.

She yawns. 'Didn't visiting hours end, like, four hours ago?'

He opens the jacket of his bland, government-centric suit, pats the badge in his breast pocket, and says, 'Being an FBI agent has its privileges. Not many, mind you. But some.'

'Cool. Hey, do you want to sign my cast?'

Murphy gives Abbey's plaster a once-over. 'It does not look like there will be room.'

'Yeah,' Abbey nods, 'apparently Cheryl and Dave went a little nuts one day when I was still fast asleep.'

'Can you see what is written on the cast?'

Abbey says, 'Nope. They did a great job of immobilising my neck. Clue me in.'

'Well, it looks like somebody drew a comic strip—'

'That would be my brother.'

'. . . of you flying around Chicago, randomly beating up people. There are a lot of stick figures involved. And it appears that Cheryl wrote out the lyrics for, maybe, four-dozen songs. And your parents wrote . . . well, it is not right for me to read that. You should read that on your own.'

'Thanks, Murphy. And thanks for wielding your power to stay here after hours. That's pretty cool.'

He straightens his tie. 'I am a pretty cool guy, Abbey.'

'No. No, you're not.'

'You are correct,' Murphy says. 'I am a nerd.'

Abbey says, 'Way to own it. And don't forget, my level of nerd-ocity pings in the red zone.'

'Yes, but nerdiness *looks* better on you.'

'Oh, stop. Despite that boring old suit of yours, you're looking pretty good yourself.'

Murphy blushes. 'Thank you. That's kind of you to say.'

'You're welcome.' They sit in companionable silence for a bit, then Abbey says, 'So. Murphy.'

'So. Abbey.'

'Care to tell me about it?'

'About what?'

'About that whole saving my life thing.'

'Oh. That.'

'Yeah. That.'

'It was not really that big a deal, to be honest,' Murphy says. 'Dr Walton and I figured a few things out, and here we are.'

'No, no, no, no, no. You're not getting off that easy. What was the deal?'

'Really, Ab, the *deal* is not that big.'

'I don't care how big it was or wasn't. *Tell me, tell me, tell me!*'

'There is not much to tell. The process started out slow. We worked on it for eighteen months, and didn't hit on anything useful until two weeks ago. Then it all came together fast. Shockingly so.'

'What came together?'

'The formula. Dr Walton figured out how to replicate your strength.'

Abbey blinks. 'Wow! That's pretty awesome.' An idea dawns on her. 'Hey, since anybody can be strong now, does that mean I can quit the superhero business?'

'Well, at this point, the effects of the drug are temporary.'

'Oh. Bummer. How long does it work for?'

'Your friend Jon Carson's version of it lasted about forty-five minutes. Ours lasted about forty-five seconds.'

'Whoa. So you have forty-five seconds from the time you take the formula to the time it wears out?'

'Not quite. It takes two minutes to kick it. We had to time it perfectly.'

'Interesting. Here's a question for you: how did you find me during the fight?'

'I never lost you.'

'What do you mean?'

'I followed you.'

'How? How did you do it without Jon seeing you? For that matter, how did you do it without *me* seeing you?'

'I happen to be pretty good at my job, Ab. And when I am on a mission that I care about *very* deeply, I am *very* good at my job.' He gets up off his chair and kneels beside Abbey's bed. 'And I care about you very deeply.'

Looking at Murphy's smiling, uptight, nerdy, handsome face, Abbey wishes she was ambulatory. 'Hey, Murphy. Do me a favor.'

'Anything, Ab.'

'I don't know if you noticed, but I've got all this dry plaster wrapped around me.'

Murphy nods. 'I actually did notice that.'

'And it makes it really difficult for me to move. Impossible, even.'

'I can imagine.'

'So here's the thing: I want to kiss the man who saved my life. And this cast deal is making it tough.'

Again, Murphy nods. 'Yes, I can see how that might be a problem. I guess the man who saved your life will have to go ahead and kiss you.'

'I guess he will.'

After what could be described as the least sexy make-out session in modern history – turns out body casts aren't good for setting a mood – Abbey says, 'So what's next?'

'You get healthy. You enjoy the bonus you will be receiving shortly from my boss's boss's boss. Your job at the law firm is waiting for you, should you choose to return to it. And I intend to take you on a date when you are ambulatory.'

'And I will accept that date. And I promise you a kiss goodnight. And I look forward to it.'

'The date or the kiss?'

'Both.' They stare into one another's eyes as if they're seeing each other for the first time. And, in a way, they are.

After Murphy gives Abbey a lingering farewell kiss, she asks him, 'Hey, one more question.'

'Yes?'

'The Weird Stuff.'

'What about it?'

'Is it still there?'

Murphy shrugs. 'No idea. Do you think it is?'

'No idea either. Do *you* think it is?'

'I do not know, and I do not care. You don't need it. You are lovely the way you are, with or without it.'

'That's sweet. But I'd kind of like to keep kicking some supervillain ass.'

'When it gets to be that time – when we find out your, um, *status* – we will all make a decision. But I believe I am speaking for the entire Company when I say that we

would be thrilled to have you aboard.'
    'You mean The Bureau.'
    'I mean The Company.'
    'The Bureau.'
    'The Company . . .'

Pick up a *little black dress* – it's a girl thing.

THE TRUE NAOMI STORY
A.M. Goldsher
PB £5.99

Naomi Braver is catapulted from waiting tables to being the new rock sensation overnight. But stardom isn't all it's cracked up to be . . . Can Naomi master the game of fame before it's too late?

978 0 7553 3992 1

A rock'n'roll romance about one girl's journey to stardom

FORGET ABOUT IT
Caprice Crane
PB £5.99

When Jordan Landeua is hit by a car, she seizes the opportunity to start over and fakes amnesia. But just as she's said goodbye to Jordan the pushover, the unthinkable happens and she has to start over for real. Will she remember in time what truly makes her happy?

978 0 7553 4204 4

Pick up a *little black dress* – it's a girl thing.

THE FARMER NEEDS A WIFE
Janet Gover
PBO £5.99

Rural romances become all the rage when editor Helen Woodley starts a new magazine column profiling Australia's lovelorn farmers. But a lot of people (and Helen herself) are about to find out that the course of true love ain't ever smooth . . .

It's not all haystacks and pitchforks, ladies – get ready for a scorching outback read!

978 0 7553 4715 5

HIDE YOUR EYES
Alison Gaylin
PBO £5.99

Samantha Leiffer's in big trouble: the chest she saw a sinister man dumping into the Hudson river contained a dead body, meaning she's now a witness in a murder case. It's just as well hot, hard-line detective John Krull is by her side . . .

'Alison Gaylin is my new must-read' Harlen Coben

978 0 7553 4802 2

You can buy any of these other
Little Black Dress titles from your
bookshop or *direct from the publisher*.

FREE P&P AND UK DELIVERY
(Overseas and Ireland £3.50 per book)

TO ORDER SIMPLY CALL THIS NUMBER

01235 400 414

or visit our website: www.headline.co.uk

Prices and availability subject to change without notice.